Marek Halter speaks ten languages, and is fluent in French, English, German, Russian and Yiddish. He is the author of several internationally acclaimed novels, and is a regular contributor to *Die Welt* and *La Republica*.

ZIPPORAH

Zipporah was a black child who was found on the shores of the Red Sea. But, because of the colour of her skin, no man wanted her as his wife. Then she met a stranger. An outcast like herself, he was a fugitive. His name was Moses. A beautiful woman and a generous lover, Zipporah was to share Moses' destiny. Together they set out on an epic journey across the desert to Egypt, where they would confront the Pharaoh and beg him to set their people free. But Zipporah's love for Moses condemned her too: for among the Hebrews of the Exodus her status as a black woman was to have catastrophic consequences . . .

Books by Marek Halter
Published by The House of Ulverscroft:

SARAH

MAREK HALTER

ZIPPORAH

Translated from the French by
Howard Curtis

Complete and Unabridged

CHARNWOOD
Leicester

First published in Great Britain in 2005 by
Bantam Press, a division of
Transworld Publishers, London

First Charnwood Edition
published 2006
by arrangement with
Transworld Publishers, a division of
The Random House Group Ltd, London

British Library CIP Data

Halter, Marek
  Zipporah.—Large print ed.—
  Charnwood library series
  1. Zipporah—Fiction 2. Moses (Biblical leader)—
  Fiction 3. Outcasts—Fiction 4. Jews—History—
  Fiction 5. Historical fiction 6. Large type books
  I. Title
  843.9′14 [F]

  ISBN 1–84617–119–9

Published by
F. A. Thorpe (Publishing)
Anstey, Leicestershire

Set by Words & Graphics Ltd.
Anstey, Leicestershire
Printed and bound in Great Britain by
T. J. International Ltd., Padstow, Cornwall

This book is printed on acid-free paper

If a stranger lives with you in your land, do not ill-treat him. Treat him as you would your native-born, and love him as you love yourselves, for you were strangers in the land of Egypt.

Leviticus XIX: 33–4

Moses failed to enter Canaan, not because his life was too short, but because it was a human life.

The Diaries of Franz Kafka,
19 October 1921

Are you not for me like the children of Cush, children of Israel? says the Lord. Did I not bring Israel up from Egypt, just as I brought the Philistines from Caphtor and the Arameans from Kir?

Amos IX: 7

I am dark but beautiful,
Daughters of Jerusalem,
Dark as the tents of Kedar,
As the tent curtains of Solomon.
Do not stare at me because I am dark,
It is the sun that made me so.

                    Song of Songs I: 5–6

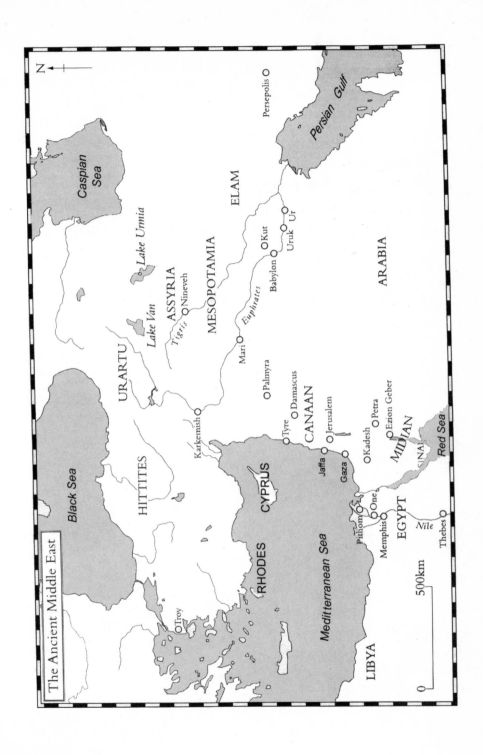

The Ancient Middle East

N

Black Sea

Caspian Sea

HITTITES

URARTU

Lake Van

Lake Urmia

ASSYRIA
Nineveh

Tigris

Euphrates

MESOPOTAMIA

ELAM

Persepolis

Persian Gulf

Karkemish

Mari

Palmyra

Tyre
Damascus

CANAAN

Jerusalem

Babylon
Kut

Uruk
Ur

ARABIA

Kadesh
Petra
Ezion Geber

MIDIAN

SINAI

Red Sea

CYPRUS

Jaffa

Gaza

RHODES

Troy

Pithom
On

Memphis

EGYPT

Nile

Thebes

Mediterranean Sea

LIBYA

0   500km

Prologue

Horeb, god of my father Jethro, accept my offerings.

At the north corner, I place the barley cakes I have baked. At the south corner, I pour the wine made from grapes I picked.

Horeb, god of glory, you who make the thunder rumble, hear me! I am Zipporah the Black, the Cushite, who came here from beyond the Sea of Reeds, and I have had a dream.

In the night, a bird appeared to me, a bird with pale plumage flying high in the sky. I laughed as I watched it. It circled above me and cried out as if it was calling me. I understood then that this bird was myself. My skin is as black as burnt wood, but in my dream I was a white bird.

I flew over my father's domain. I saw his houses of whitewashed brick, his tall fig trees, his flowering tamarisks and the canopy of vines beneath which he gives his judgements. Towards the gardens, I saw the servants' tents in the shade of the terebinths, the palm trees, the flocks, the paths of red dust and the great sycamore on the road to Epha. On the path that leads to your mountain, O Horeb, I saw the village of the armourers, with its circle of rough brick houses, its furnaces and its pits of fire. I flew far enough to see the well of Irmna and the roads that lead to the five kingdoms of Midian.

And I flew towards the sea.

Its surface was like a sheet of gold, so bright I found it impossible to rest my gaze on it. Everything was blinding: the sky, the water and the sand. The air through which I flew had lost its coolness, and I wanted to cease being a bird and become myself again. I touched the ground with my feet and my shadow was restored to me. I shaded my eyes with my shawl, and it was then that I saw it.

A canoe was swaying on the water among the rushes. A beautiful, solidly built canoe. It was the canoe that had carried my mother and me from the land of Cush to the land of Midian, from one shore to another, keeping us alive despite the sun, despite our thirst and fear. And there, in my dream, it was waiting to take us back to the land where I was born.

I called to my mother to hurry.

She was nowhere to be seen, either on the beach or on the cliff.

I waded into the water. The sharp rushes cut my arms and hands. I lay down in the canoe. It was exactly the right size for me. It set off, the rushes parted, and the sea opened before me. The canoe advanced between two huge walls of hard green water, so close I could have touched them with my fingertips.

My stomach was tight with fear. I huddled in the canoe. Terror made me cry out.

Soon, I knew, the cliffs of water above me would come together like the edges of a wound and swallow me.

I was screaming, but I couldn't hear my voice,

only the lament of the sea, like something broken and suffering.

I closed my eyes, sure I was about to drown. Just as the canoe was about to crash against the seabed, there, on the seaweed, wearing the pleated loincloth of the princes of Egypt, his arms laden with gold bracelets from wrist to elbow, a man stood waiting. His skin was white and his brow was covered with brown curls. With one hand, he stopped the canoe. Then, lifting me in his arms, he walked across the Sea of Reeds. On the opposite shore, he clasped me to him and put his mouth on mine, giving me the breath the sea had tried to take from me.

I opened my eyes. It was night.

True night, the night of the earth.

I was in my bed. I had been dreaming.

'O, Horeb,' I asked, 'why send me this dream?'

Was it a dream of death or of life?

Is my place here, beside my father Jethro, the high priest of Midian, or is it in the land of Cush where I was born? Is my place among my white-skinned sisters, who love me, or there, beyond the sea, among the Nehesyou, who are under the yoke of Pharaoh?

O Horeb, listen to me! In your hands I place my breath. I will dance with joy if you answer me, you who know my distress.

Why was the Egyptian waiting for me at the bottom of the sea?

Why erase my mother's name, and even her face, from my memory?

What path did the dream you interrupted indicate to me?

3

O Horeb, may my call to you be answered. Why are you silent?

What is to become of me, Zipporah the stranger?

No man here will take me as his wife because my skin is black. But my father loves me. In his eyes I am a woman worthy of respect. Among the peoples of Cush, what would I be? I do not speak their language, do not eat their food. How would I live there? Only the colour of my skin would make me similar to my countrymen.

O Horeb! You are the god of my father Jethro. Who will be my god if not you?

Part One
Jethro's Daughters

The Fugitive

That day, and all the days that followed, Horeb was silent.

The dream lingered in Zipporah's body, like poison left by an illness. For several moons, she dreaded night. She lay on her bed without moving, without closing her eyes, without even daring to touch her lips with her tongue for fear of finding the taste of the stranger's mouth on them.

She thought of confiding in her father Jethro. Who better to counsel her than the sage of the kings of Midian? Who loved her more than he did? Who better understood her torments?

But she said nothing. She did not want to seem weak, childish, too much like other women, who were always ready to believe their hearts rather than their eyes. He was so proud of her, and she wanted to show him that she was strong and held firm to all the things he had taught her.

With time, the images of the dream faded. The Egyptian's face became blurred. A season went by without her thinking of it. Then, one morning, Jethro announced to his daughters that the next day young Reba, the son of the King of Sheba, one of the five kings of Midian, would be their guest. 'He has come to ask counsel of me. He will be here before the end of the day. We shall welcome him as he deserves.'

The news provoked much mirth among the

women of the house. All of them — Jethro's daughters, the handmaids — knew what was going on. For more than a year, barely a moon had passed without Reba coming to seek Jethro's counsel.

While everyone bustled to make ready for the next day's banquet, some preparing the food, others the reception tent, the carpets and cushions that had to be laid out in the courtyard, it was Sefoba, the eldest of Jethro's daughters still living in their father's house, who, with her usual directness, said aloud what everyone was thinking: 'Reba has had more counsel by now than anyone needs in a lifetime — unless, behind his handsome face, he's the stupidest man Horeb ever created. What he really wants to know is if he still appeals to our dear Orma. He's hoping Father will think his patience a sign of wisdom and make him his son-in-law.'

Orma shrugged. 'We all know why he's coming,' she agreed. 'But his visits bore me. They're always the same. Reba sits down with our father, spends half the night chatting and drinking wine, then goes home, without speaking up.'

'I wonder why,' Sefoba said, and pretended to think hard. Then, 'Perhaps he doesn't find you beautiful enough.'

Orma glared at her sister, unsure whether she was joking. Sefoba laughed, pleased with her teasing. Zipporah sensed they might be building up to one of their customary quarrels. She stroked the back of Orma's neck to calm her,

8

and received a slap on the hand by way of thanks.

Although Sefoba and Orma had the same mother, they could not have been more dissimilar. Sefoba was short and round, sensual and kind, with nothing dazzling about her. Her smile revealed her lack of guile, the honesty of her thoughts and feelings. She was completely trustworthy and Zipporah had confided to her more than once what she could not tell anyone else. Orma, on the other hand, was like a star that keeps its brilliance even when the sky is flooded with sunlight. There was no woman more beautiful in Jethro's house, perhaps in all Midian. And certainly no woman prouder of this gift of Horeb.

Suitors had written long poems about the splendour of her eyes, the grace of her mouth, the elegance of her neck. In their songs the shepherds, although they did not dare mention her name, praised her breasts and her hips, comparing them to fabulous fruits, strange animals, and spells cast by goddesses. Orma savoured her fame, never tired of it. But she seemed content to inflame others while remaining aloof. No man had yet aroused in her an interest greater than her fascination with herself. She was the despair of Jethro, who saw her fuss over her robes, her cosmetics and her jewels as if they were the most precious things in the world. Although she was the youngest daughter of his blood and he loved her dearly, there were times when even he, who rarely lost his composure, could not restrain himself.

'Orma is like the desert wind,' he would rage, in Zipporah's presence. 'She blows first one way then another. She's like a bladder that fills with air, then bursts. Her mind is an empty chest. Even the dust of memory won't settle in it! She's a jewel, of course, and she grows more beautiful every day, but I wonder sometimes if Horeb is angry with me and using her to test me.'

'You're too hard on her,' Zipporah would protest gently. 'Orma knows what she wants and has a strong will, but she's young.'

'She's three years older than you,' Jethro would reply. 'It's high time she thought less about making hay and more about making babies!'

In fact, there had been no lack of suitors. But Jethro had promised Orma that he would not choose a husband for her without her consent so he was still waiting, just like the suitors. Now new songs were being sung across the land of Midian, saying that the beautiful Orma, daughter of Jethro the sage, had been born to break the hardest of hearts and that Horeb would soon transform her, as virgin as the day she was born, into a rock on his mountain, caressed only by the wind. But now Reba had taken up the challenge, and came endlessly to pay his respects to Jethro with the impatience of a warlord before a battle. Nobody doubted that his persistence deserved its reward.

'This time, little sister,' Sefoba resumed, 'you must make up your mind.'

'Why should I?'

'Because Reba deserves it.'

'No more than anyone else.'

'Oh, come!' Sefoba said, warming to the argument. 'Which other man would you prefer? Everything about him is pleasing.'

'To an ordinary woman.'

'To you, Princess. Do you want a man worthy of your beauty? Ask any of the women here, young or old. Reba is the handsomest of men — tall and slim, skin the colour of fresh dates, firm buttocks! Who wouldn't want to take him in her arms?'

'That's true.' Orma chuckled.

'Do you want a rich man, a man of power?' Sefoba went on. 'He'll soon be succeeding his father as king, and then he'll own the most fertile pastureland and caravans so richly laden they'll stretch from sunrise to sunset. You'll have gold and fabrics from the East, and as many handmaids as there are days in the year.'

'What do you take me for? Would I become a man's wife because his caravans are impressive? How dull.'

'They say Reba can sit on a camel's hump for a week without tiring. Do you know what that means?'

'I'm not a camel so I don't need to be straddled every night — unlike you, who squeal loudly enough to keep the rest of us awake!'

Sefoba's cheeks turned crimson. 'How do you know that?' she cried, as the other women laughed. 'Well, perhaps it's true,' she admitted. 'When my husband isn't with his flocks, he comes to me every night! My heart isn't starved like Orma's — I enjoy nourishing it. And doing

11

so every night,' she concluded, joining in with the laughter, 'isn't as easy as lighting a fire to bake cakes!'

'But the seasons are passing,' Zipporah said softly, when calm had returned. 'You've already rejected every other suitor, my dear Orma. If you send Reba away, who else will dare want you?'

Orma looked at her with surprise, and wrinkled her pretty nose. 'If Reba is only coming here to talk to Father, without declaring himself, then I shall stay in my room tomorrow. He won't see me.'

'You know perfectly well why Reba doesn't ask Father for your hand. He's afraid you'll refuse him. He has his pride. Your silence has become an affront. This may be the last time — '

'Tell them I'm ill,' Orma interrupted. 'Just look sad and worried, and they'll believe you.'

'I shan't say anything!' Zipporah protested. 'I certainly shan't lie.'

'It won't be a lie! I will be ill. You'll see.'

'Nonsense!' Sefoba exclaimed. 'We know exactly what we'll see. You'll paint your face until you glow and, as usual, you'll be more beautiful than a goddess. Reba will have eyes only for you. He won't touch the delicious food we serve him. That's the saddest thing about being your sister. The proudest, most handsome men come here and leave looking foolish!'

The handmaids, who had been all ears, burst out laughing, and Orma laughed with them.

Zipporah got to her feet. 'Let's take the sheep to the well,' she said decisively. 'We're late

12

already. Forget about husbands for the moment — real or imagined.'

★ ★ ★

The well of Irmna was a good hour's walk from Jethro's domain. In the distance rose the great mountain of the god Horeb, its covering of petrified lava sparkling in the evening sun. Below it, between the folds of red rock, plains of short grass, which were sometimes green in winter, stretched to the sea. Such was the land of Midian, vast, harsh and tender, a land of burning sand and volcanic dust where scattered oases shimmered like oil in the desert heat. The wells at the oases were both a source of life and a gathering-place.

Every seven days, those who had pitched their tents less than two or three hours away by road, or who, like Jethro, owned gardens, flocks and brick houses were entitled to fill their goatskins at the well of Irmna. They were also allowed to let their flocks drink there, provided they finished in the time it took the shadow of the sun to move six cubits.

It was late summer, and the men had already left Jethro's domain with livestock to sell in the markets of the land of Moab, along with the iron weapons produced by the armourers. They would not return until dead of winter. In the meantime, the women led the remaining animals to the well. This was where Zipporah and her sisters were taking their sheep. As they tramped along in their clogs, the dust rose

13

off the road like flour.

The tall shaft of the *shadoof* was already in sight when Jethro's daughters noticed a herd of long-horned cows pressing round the adjoining troughs.

Sefoba frowned. 'Look, they're drinking our water. Whose animals are those?'

Four men appeared, pushing aside the cows with their staffs. They all had thick beards, and were dressed in patched old tunics white with dust. They positioned themselves at the top of the track, and planted their staffs in the ground.

Orma and Sefoba came to a standstill, but their sheep went on. Zipporah, who had been walking behind, now joined them and shaded her eyes from the sun. 'They're Houssenek's sons,' she said. 'I recognize the eldest, the one with the leather necklace.'

'Well, this isn't their day,' Orma said, and set off again. 'They'll have to leave.'

'They don't look as if they'll want to,' Sefoba observed.

'Whether they want to or not, this isn't their day, and they must go!' Orma retorted, angry now.

The sheep had sensed water. It was too late to stop them. They trotted towards the troughs, jostling each other and bleating.

Zipporah caught hold of Sefoba's arm. 'Less than a moon ago our father passed an unfavourable judgement on Houssenek. He and his sons are still angry.'

Eyebrows raised, Sefoba asked her to explain

14

what she meant. But they were both interrupted by Orma shouting, 'What are you doing? Have you gone mad?'

Houssenek's sons were running towards the sheep, yelling raucously. Within a few seconds, the animals had scattered in all directions. Zipporah and Sefoba tried in vain to stop them. Some ran down the slope, risking breaking their necks on the rocks. Houssenek's sons laughed and swung their staffs.

Sefoba stopped running. Out of breath, eyes dark with rage, she gasped, 'If a single sheep is hurt, you'll regret it. We are Jethro's daughters, and this is his flock.'

The four men stopped laughing.

'We know who you are,' muttered the one Zipporah had pointed out as the eldest.

'Then you also know it isn't your turn to be at the well,' Orma snapped. 'Go away and leave us in peace. You stink of oxen!' She pulled a face to underline her disgust, adjusted her tunic, which had slipped from her shoulder, and walked towards Zipporah. Heedless of her insults, the men watched her, fascinated. 'It's our day today,' one said. 'And tomorrow, and the day after tomorrow, too, if we feel like it.'

'You know very well that isn't true,' Orma hissed.

Zipporah laid a hand on her arm to silence her.

The one who had spoken before was laughing again. 'It's our day whenever we like. We've decided this well belongs to us.'

Sefoba gave a cry of rage.

15

Zipporah stepped forward. 'I know you, son of Houssenek. My father passed judgement on you and your brothers for stealing a she-camel. If keeping us from the well is your revenge, you are foolish. This time your punishment will be worse.'

'We didn't steal any she-camel!' one of the brothers exclaimed. 'She was ours.'

'Who are you, black woman, to tell me what I can and can't do?' the eldest jeered.

'I am Jethro's daughter, and you are lying.'

'Zipporah!' Sefoba murmured.

It was too late. Brandishing their staffs, the men stepped between Zipporah and her sisters.

The eldest of Houssenek's sons jabbed a finger at her. 'Your father is only your father because he kissed the arse of a black ox.'

Zipporah slapped his cheek with such force that he staggered back. His brothers were no longer laughing. Zipporah took advantage of their surprise to run away. But one man was too quick for her: he threw his staff, aiming it at her legs, and she fell headlong.

Before she could get up, a heavy body, stinking of sweat and grunting, fell on top of her. She cried out, in fear as much as in pain. Rough fingers clutched at her, then tore the fabric of her tunic. A knee was shoved between her thighs. Her head throbbing, she could hear Sefoba and Orma screaming. Her gorge rose, and her arms felt weak. The man seemed to have a thousand hands, as he scratched her thighs, mouth and stomach, crushing her wrists and breasts.

Then Zipporah, eyes closed, heard a sound

16

like a water-melon bursting. The man groaned and rolled on to his side. She did not dare move, but she could hear heavy breathing, a struggle and pounding feet.

Sefoba cried out and Zipporah opened her eyes. Sefoba was dragging Orma towards the well. Close to her, Houssenek's eldest son seemed to be asleep, his cheek squashed against a rock, his mouth bloodied and his arm strangely twisted.

Zipporah leaped to her feet, ready to run. Then she saw him.

He was facing the three men who were still on their feet, holding his staff at shoulder height. It was no ordinary shepherd's staff but a weapon with a heavy bronze tip. He was dressed in a pleated loincloth, and his feet were as bare as his chest. His skin was very pale, his hair long and curly.

Suddenly he swung his staff in a perfect curve. With a dull thud, it struck the legs of Houssenek's youngest son, who toppled over with a cry of pain. The other two leaped back, but not fast enough to escape the weapon, which came down on their necks, forcing them to their knees.

The stranger pointed at the eldest, who still lay motionless. 'Take him away,' he said.

His voice was sharp, and his accent unfamiliar; it made the words sound odd. He's from Egypt, Zipporah thought.

As Houssenek's sons were lifting their injured brother, the stranger prodded them with the tip of his staff. 'Now go or I'll kill you,' he said, in the same tone, stumbling over the words.

Zipporah heard her sisters' cries of joy. She heard them calling her name. But she was incapable of turning to them and replying. The stranger was looking at her with eyes that seemed familiar. There was something about his expression, about his mouth — self-confidence, perhaps. His arms were reaching out to encircle her waist and lift her, and she knew them, too, even though they were not covered with gold.

For the first time in many moons, the dream that had so troubled her came alive in her.

★　★　★

With the shepherds gone, there was a moment of awkwardness. Sefoba ran to clasp Zipporah to her, then set about repairing her torn tunic, trying to hold it together with her silver brooch.

'Are you all right?' she asked. 'They didn't hurt you? Oh, may Horeb strike them dead!'

Zipporah did not reply. She could not take her eyes off the stranger with his pale skin, burning eyes and wide mouth. The one thing that distinguished him from the Egyptian in her dream was that he had the beginnings of a beard. It was reddish and sparse, leaving his cheeks visible, the kind of beard that looked as if it was often shaved, unlike the beards of the men of Midian.

He was looking at her, too, still clutching the staff as if he feared he might have to fight again. It struck Zipporah that he must have seen black women before because there was no surprise in his expression — rather, she saw admiration.

18

Nobody had ever looked at her so intently, and she found it unsettling.

Orma broke the tension. 'Well, whoever you are, we are in your debt!'

The stranger turned. It was as if he were seeing Orma for the first time. His lips quivered and his smile widened. Finally he released his grip on his staff and straightened his shoulders. His chest swelled. He was reacting like any other man when faced with a beautiful woman.

'Who are you?' Orma asked, in a voice as sweet as her gaze.

He frowned, turned his eyes from her and looked towards the shimmering hills, the flock climbing noisily up the slope to the well. He raised his staff and pointed towards the sea. 'I'm from the other side of the sea.' The words came with difficulty, one by one, as if he were lifting stones.

Orma laughed. The sound was both seductive and ironic. 'You crossed the sea?'

'Yes.'

'You're from Egypt, then.'

He's a fugitive! Zipporah thought.

Sefoba put her hands together in a respectful greeting. 'I thank you with all my heart, stranger. Without you, those shepherds would have taken my sister's honour. They might even have assaulted all three of us.'

'And then they would have killed us,' Orma said.

The stranger glanced at Zipporah, who stood rigidly, like a statue. With a modest gesture, he pointed to the coping of the trough, where he

19

had left a water-skin of fine hide, which was flat. 'I came here by chance. I was looking for a well.'

'Are you travelling alone?' Orma asked. 'With no escort and no flock? Drinking water wherever you find it?'

The stranger looked embarrassed.

'Orma!' Sefoba said, coming to his rescue. 'Don't ask so many questions.'

Orma dismissed her sister's reproach with her loveliest smile. She stepped away from him, went to the well and observed that the water level was low. Zipporah was in no doubt that her sister was moving about to make sure that the stranger kept watching her, like a bee unable to extricate itself from a fig that has burst open in the sun.

Orma was now casting into the well the rope at whose end hung a little leather pouch. 'Zipporah!' she cried. 'Come and drink some water. You're so quiet — are you sure you're all right?'

The stranger looked at Zipporah again, and suddenly she became aware of the pain in her thighs and belly where Houssenek's son had scratched them. She went to the well and took the water-skin that Orma had brought up.

'We are Jethro's daughters,' she heard Sefoba say, behind her. 'My name is Sefoba. My sisters are Orma and Zipporah. Our father is the sage and judge of Midian . . . '

The stranger nodded.

'Did you know you are on the lands of the kings of Midian?' Orma asked, curling her lip.

The stranger did not seem to notice the irony in her voice. 'No, I didn't. Midian? I don't know

20

your language well but I learned a little of it in Egypt.'

Orma was about to say more, but he raised his hand. It wasn't a shepherd's hand, any more than it was a fisherman's hand, or the hand of a man who works the land or kneads clay to make bricks. It was a hand that could hold weapons but also make the simple gestures of those accustomed to power who give orders, call for silence and attention.

'My name is Moses,' he said. 'In Egypt it means 'pulled from the waters'.'

He laughed, which made him seem curiously older. He glanced again at Zipporah, as if hoping she would speak, noted her waist, the slender thighs beneath the tunic, the firm breasts, but did not dare look into the luminous black eyes that stared at him. He pointed to the sheep. 'The animals are thirsty. I'll help you.'

⋆　⋆　⋆

They watched him in silence, sure that he was a prince. A fugitive prince. Everything about him indicated a mighty lord: his clumsiness as well as his strength, his fine hands and the quality of his belt. It was obvious he was not used to drawing water from a *shadoof*. He caught the cedar pole too high, then slid too close to the pivot. When the water-skins came up, dripping with water and as heavy as a dead mule, he had to hang on to the pole with all his weight to turn it above the trough where the sheep were waiting, bleating impatiently. Beneath the folds of the loincloth,

21

his thighs swelled, powerful and hard, while the muscles of his shoulders and lower back rippled and his skin glistened with sweat.

Despite his lack of skill, or because of it, he persevered, and watered the animals without the help of Zipporah and her sisters. When he had finished, he took his weight too quickly off the pole and almost lost his balance. Orma giggled. Zipporah had the presence of mind to catch the empty water-skin as it slapped the air. When she turned, she saw Orma's slender hand resting on the pole, close to the stranger's.

'The sheep have enough water now, and thank you for your help. But I can see that, in your country, you aren't used to working a *shadoof*.'

Moses let go of the pole. 'That's true,' was all he said. He went round to the other side of the well, picked up his own water-skin and dipped it.

'There is a feast in our father's enclosure tonight,' Orma said. 'He's receiving the son of the King of Sheba, who's coming to ask his counsel. He would be pleased to have the opportunity to thank you for saving us from the shepherds. Come with us and share our meal.'

'Oh, yes!' Sefoba cried. 'What a good idea! Of course Father must thank you.'

'Our beer and wine are the best in Midian.' Orma's laugh was like a flight of birds.

The Egyptian raised his eyes and studied her in silence.

'You have nothing to fear,' Sefoba insisted. 'Nobody is gentler than our father Jethro.'

'Thank you, but I must refuse,' he said.

'But you must come!' Orma cried. 'I'm sure

22

you have nowhere to sleep, perhaps not even a tent.'

Moses laughed, and the hair at the back of his neck glistened. It would have been nice to stroke his cheeks and smooth the rough bristle of his beard. He pointed to the sea again with his staff. 'I don't need a tent. Over there, I had no tent.'

He slipped his water-skin over his shoulder, turned and started to walk away, his staff held out in front of him.

'Wait!' Orma cried. 'Moses! You can't leave like this!'

He turned back, as if uncertain that he had understood, or as if there were some threat in Orma's protest. But then he smiled again, revealing even white teeth. 'Thank you for the water. And you're beautiful, all three of you.'

When she heard him say, 'all three', Zipporah regained her composure and raised her arm in farewell.

★   ★   ★

'So!' Orma cried to Zipporah, pouting. 'Is that how you thank him? He saves you and you don't say a word?' She watched Moses walking away fast in the ochre dust until he was swallowed up in the shadows. 'You could have called him back — said something! You aren't usually lost for words.'

Zipporah did not answer.

Sefoba sighed and took her by the arm. 'How handsome he is! He's a prince.'

'A prince of Egypt,' Orma said approvingly.

'Did you notice his hands?' She turned to Zipporah. 'Well? Did Houssenek's son cut out your tongue?'

'No.'

'At last! Why didn't you say anything to him?'

'You said enough for both of us,' Zipporah said hoarsely.

Sefoba chuckled.

Orma gave a grudging smile and adjusted Zipporah's brooch in order to hold together her torn tunic. 'And his clothes! Did you see his belt?'

'Yes.'

'His loincloth is worn and dirty because he has nobody to take care of him. But I've never seen a belt like that before.'

'No woman of Midian could weave such fine linen or dye it so well,' Sefoba admitted.

They strained to see Moses through the grey foliage of the olive trees, but he was out of sight.

Sefoba frowned. 'Perhaps he isn't a prince.'

'He is, I'm sure of it,' Orma said.

'Perhaps. But, prince or not, what was he doing here?'

'Well . . . ' Orma began.

'He's a fugitive,' Zipporah said in a neutral voice. 'He's in hiding.'

Her sisters looked at her, intrigued, but Zipporah said no more.

'Do you know something you aren't telling us?' Orma asked, suddenly suspicious. 'Perhaps he's on a journey.'

'An Egyptian, a prince, if that is what he is, doesn't travel to the land of Midian with no one to carry his chests or water jars, no woman, no tent.'

'Perhaps he's with a caravan.'

'Then where is it? No caravan leader has come to pay Father his respects recently. He's in hiding.'

'From what?' Sefoba asked.

'I don't know.'

'A man like him is afraid of nothing!' Orma said angrily.

'I think he's in hiding,' Zipporah said. 'I don't know if he's afraid.'

'Are you forgetting how easily he broke the bones of Houssenek's son? Without him . . . ' Orma made a threatening little gesture with her chin.

Zipporah did not reply. At the foot of the slope that led to the well, there was nothing to be seen now but the gold and white earth, the path that disappeared among the silvery olive trees and the mass of dark, chaotic rocks on the cliffs overlooking the glittering blue sea.

'Zipporah's right,' Sefoba said thoughtfully. 'He's a fugitive. Why else would he have refused to pay his respects to Father tonight?'

Orma shrugged and turned away. Sefoba and Zipporah followed her back to the sheep and took turns in lifting the pole to fill the trough one last time. Each time they did so, they raised half as much water as the Egyptian had, but with much less effort. They went about their task in silence, thinking of him, his strangeness, his beauty, his strength, his hands on the hoist, his smile — and the way he had suddenly lowered his eyes and looked sideways at them.

It was as if their thoughts were a gulf between them. Even Sefoba, who was married, could not help thinking about him as any woman might.

Zipporah was on the point of confessing: 'I dreamed about Moses more than a moon ago. He's saved my life once before. He took me in his arms and carried me away from the seabed when I was about to drown.'

But who would understand? It was only a dream.

On the other side of the trough, Orma was gathering the sheep together with sharp little cries, hurrying them needlessly. It was clear from her determined expression and burning eyes that she intended to conquer the Egyptian. What she said on the way back came as no surprise to her sisters: 'We're going to tell Father what happened at the well. He's sure to want to see the Egyptian. When he sends for him, Moses won't be able to refuse.'

'No!' Zipporah's tone was so peremptory that her sisters were startled. They stopped in their tracks, letting the sheep go on alone. 'We mustn't say anything.'

'Why not?' Sefoba asked softly.

'Father will want to punish Houssenek's sons.'

Orma burst out laughing. 'They should be beaten, left to fry in the sun without water!'

'They deserve it,' Sefoba agreed.

'They've had their lesson,' Zipporah insisted. 'The eldest may already be dead. They wanted to show off how strong they are, but they met someone stronger. What's the point in making

26

them angrier and letting their plans for revenge poison our lives?'

'Zipporah's thinking she's Father again!' Orma threw her veil back over her shoulder and set off, hips swinging. 'I don't care about Houssenek and his sons. It's the Egyptian who interests me. I'm going to tell Father about him as soon as we get home.'

'Are you so stupid?' Zipporah's voice snapped in the heat.

Sefoba looked at her, startled by her tone.

Zipporah strode up to Orma. 'He said no! You heard him as well as I did. Can't you respect his wishes?'

'His wishes?' Orma repeated, glancing at Sefoba for help. 'What do you know of his wishes? He felt awkward, that's all, because he can't speak our language properly.'

'He knows the difference between yes and no.'

'You didn't thank him. Not a word!'

'What of it?'

'You should have done. Now we owe him — '

'I know what I owe him. It was I whom Houssenek's son attacked.'

'Father must thank him.'

'He will, I assure you.'

'He . . . Oh, Sefoba, you tell her!'

'What can I say?' Sefoba sighed. 'Zipporah's right — he said no!'

'His eyes told me the opposite — I can read a man's eyes better than you two.'

'Orma, listen to me!'

'I've heard you. And I will speak to Father. Nobody can stop me, not even you.'

27

Zipporah gripped Orma's wrists and squeezed them hard, forcing her sister to look her in the eye. 'Yes, the man saved my honour. He may even have saved my life. I know what I owe him. But I also know that he doesn't want anyone making a fuss. He wants to stay in the shadows. Didn't you see the way he rushed off? There's only one way to thank him for his help and that is to respect his wishes and leave him alone. Why don't you understand that?'

As always when Zipporah lost her temper she sounded like Jethro. Orma pursed her lips.

'Why don't we give him time to change his mind?' Zipporah went on, calmly now, as if she was speaking to a stubborn child. 'Orma, please give him time. He won't forget your beauty. What man could?'

The flattery made Orma curl her lips. 'You always think you know everything.'

Sefoba put her arms round her sister. 'Let's not quarrel. Your prince won't fly away. We'll see tomorrow.'

Orma pushed her away. 'You always think Zipporah's right.'

'In any case,' Sefoba added, 'what would you do with him tonight? You're going to be busy. Reba will be there.'

'Oh, him . . . '

' 'Oh, him'! Yes, him. He's just crossed the desert and he thirsts for your beauty.'

'I'm already bored with him.'

'We'll see.'

The Gold Bracelets

Jethro's domain resembled a small fortress. It was an enclosure a thousand cubits long containing some twenty flat-roofed houses of clay bricks, the backs of which formed the outer wall. There was only one opening: a heavy acacia-wood door, with bronze fittings, that was kept open from dawn to dusk so that approaching travellers could be seen in the distance.

The doors and windows of the houses, painted blue, yellow and red, looked out on a courtyard of beaten earth, where the servants would bustle about among the camels, mules and asses on which Jethro's visitors arrived, depending on their wealth and rank. Whether men of power or of lowly status, they came from far and wide, from all of the five kingdoms of Midian, to ask counsel and justice of the sage. Jethro would receive them on a platform at the end of the courtyard, just in front of his room, beneath a canopy of sycamore beams over which grew the shady foliage of a precious vine.

In honour of young Reba, the platform had been covered with magnificent purple rugs, brought at great expense from Canaan. Gold-embroidered cushions had been placed beside enormous brass-covered olivewood platters of grilled mutton stuffed with aubergines, marrows

29

and leeks, and decorated with terebinth flowers. The jars were full of wine and beer, and azurite-studded bronze bowls overflowed with fruit.

Musicians and dancers in multicoloured tunics were waiting impatiently on a dais that had been built for the occasion. The intermittent crash of cymbals and jingling of bells increased tenfold the excitement in the house.

So far, the evening had gone as Sefoba had predicted. But Zipporah remained on the alert: Orma might show herself incapable of holding her tongue. Fortunately, the King of Sheba's son, and the opulence with which he was surrounded, captured her attention.

Reba arrived on a white she-camel, followed by a troop of servants, who unrolled a magnificent Damascus carpet, purchased from an Akkadian caravan. After the customary greetings, and thanks to Horeb for a journey that had passed without incident, he presented the old sage with a gift: cages of pigeons and doves. Then a cedar chest, inlaid with bronze, was placed before Orma and opened to reveal a fabulous bolt of fabric, which the handmaids unfolded. It seemed to float in the air like smoke, displaying all the colours of the universe. Then it was passed from hand to hand so that everyone could feel how extraordinarily fine it was. At last, it reached Zipporah, who marvelled at its lightness on her palm.

'Is it from Egypt?' Orma asked.

Zipporah held her breath. Reba, pleased with the response to his gift, paused to drink some wine. No, he replied. It had been woven somewhere far to the east — not by women, so they said, but by men.

Egypt was forgotten. The lump in Zipporah's throat vanished.

Reba's gift was so dazzling, had cost so much — perhaps an entire herd of beautiful white she-camels? — and had required such effort to bring here that, for once, Orma's resolve seemed shaken. She did what her father and sisters had hoped for so long: she knelt before Reba. Her hands crossed over her chest, which was rising and falling with her excitement, she bowed. 'Welcome to my father's house, Reba. I am glad you have come. May Horeb watch over you and keep his wrath from you.'

Reba's face was radiant. Jethro, uncharacteristically, flushed with emotion. Zipporah looked at Sefoba, who winked. Was this evening to be blessed above all others? Tomorrow, at last, Reba could ask for the hand of Jethro's most beautiful daughter without fearing ridicule.

But, to the anxiety of his hosts, when the feast began Reba paid little attention to Orma, seeming far more interested in the music and his conversation with Jethro. Everyone wondered if he was playing a game or still cautious.

As the jars of beer emptied, the feast became noisier and merrier. The naphtha torches were sputtering when Sefoba began to dance before the women, who, like her, had waited many moons for their husbands to return. It was a signal. Orma summoned a group of young handmaids, who now came and danced before

31

Reba. Jethro stopped talking and watched, smiling.

When Reba's attention had been captured by the dancers, Orma joined them.

In the light of the torches everyone could see that she was no longer wearing her tunic but had wrapped herself in the magnificent fabric Reba had given her. Held together with brooches, it covered her from her breasts to her feet, leaving only her shoulders, neck and arms bare. It clung to her body and surrounded her with a moving aura. As she danced, her necklaces and bracelets jangled in time to the music.

Jethro raised his hand, as if he were about to reprimand her and order her to withdraw. But then he put his hand on his knee and turned away, with a wicked gleam in his eyes. Like the others, he had seen Reba's mouth open — and stay open.

Zipporah had been waiting impatiently for this moment. Nobody was paying her any heed. A shadow among the shadows, she moved away from the circle around the dance and crept into the kitchen. Apart from two little girls sleeping beside a basket of figs, it was deserted: the handmaids had joined the celebrations. She unearthed one of the pack-saddles, used for carrying provisions on the backs of asses and mules. It was a large sack of thickly woven unbleached linen with two pockets. In the darkness, occasionally lit by the flames from the ovens, she filled it with all the food she could find: cooked meat, cornmeal, loaves of barley bread, watermelons, dates, figs, almonds, medlars — as much as the saddle could take and her shoulders could carry.

Bent under its weight, she left the kitchen and went to hide it near the door of the domain, which had been closed for the night.

There, she crouched and rested. From the courtyard came the trilling of flutes, the roll of drums and the tinkle of the dancers' ankle bells. From time to time, laughter pierced the air. Clearly nobody cared that she had left. Zipporah plunged into the darkness and crept to Jethro's storeroom. Carefully, she pulled out the heavy bar blocking the door. Groping her way, she found a jar of beer, carried it outside and hid it with the saddle.

By the time she returned to the party, Orma had stopped dancing and now sat facing Reba on a pile of cushions, leaning forward, listening, as he whispered to her. A few steps away, two old nurses, the chaperones, were sleeping in each other's arms. Sefoba had disappeared. To the delight of Reba's men, only the youngest of the handmaids were still dancing. Jethro's noble head was nodding — clearly the effect of the wine he had drunk. Zipporah slipped her arm under her father's shoulders, kissed his cheek and helped him to his feet. 'It's time for bed, Father. Lean on me.'

'My little girl!' Jethro murmured in gratitude. He let himself be led to his bed. As Zipporah was pulling the blanket over his chest, he caught her hand. 'It's not the wine,' he muttered.

'Not the wine?' Zipporah repeated, not understanding.

'No, no . . . '

'I think it is. You've had a lot . . . '

'No, no!' He grimaced. 'Are they still talking?'

This time, Zipporah had no difficulty in understanding. 'Reba seems to have become a bottomless pit of words. And, for once, Orma seems content to listen to him.'

Jethro closed his eyes and laughed softly, his old face as relaxed as a child's. 'All this effort to persuade a silly, beautiful girl to marry a rich, powerful, handsome man.'

Zipporah laughed, too. 'And he's clever! The fabric from the East was a brilliant idea! This time, my sister isn't finding it so easy to resist. How could she? Has anyone ever seen such splendour?'

Jethro muttered inaudibly and groped for her hand. 'May Horeb hear you, my child.'

Zipporah bent to kiss his forehead.

When she straightened, he sat up abruptly. 'Zipporah.'

'Father?'

'The hour will come when you, too, will learn what awaits you in the future. I know it. You will be happy, daughter, I promise.'

Zipporah's lips trembled. Jethro collapsed on to his cushions and began to snore. Zipporah stroked his brow. 'Perhaps,' she murmured.

As she crossed the courtyard, thoughts and images danced in her mind, even more wildly than the young handmaids. She still had to endure the torture of waiting.

34

Zipporah decided not to sleep in the room she shared with Orma: her sister would talk endlessly about what Reba had said to her. She took one of her blankets and went to lie on the straw next to the hidden pack-saddle.

The musicians were still playing. She looked up at the stars, and searched for those areas of complete darkness from where, it was said, Horeb might be watching.

*　*　*

She was up before dawn. She crept silently to the pen and untethered a mule.

Some young boys, servants of Jethro and Reba, were sleeping on some straw baskets not far from the animals. They, too, had been at the celebration, and were snoring peacefully. The mule snorted when Zipporah slipped the pack-saddle on to its back, but even that did not wake the boys. She tied on the beer jar with a leather strap. Then she closed the door behind her, and set off on the road to the sea.

At the well of Irmna, when Moses had pointed to the seashore and said that he did not need a tent, Zipporah had guessed where he might have taken refuge. Wind and time — men, too — had hollowed many caves in the cliffs overlooking the beach. They were used occasionally by fishermen, who rested there before they set out to sea. Zipporah herself, when she was a child, had hidden there after a scolding from Jethro. She had no doubt that this was where she would find the stranger.

But once she reached the escarpment overlooking the sea, she realised it would be harder to find him than she had thought. The cliff stretched further than the eye could see and, in places, there were dozens of caves. Also, from where she was standing, they were not easy to locate, and she could not venture with the mule along the narrow paths that led down the side of the cliff.

She tied the animal to a bush, then ran up the first path she came to. What had seemed so easy earlier now proved almost impossible.

The sun was rising. The shadows were retreating. Zipporah thought of her father and Orma. She had supposed she would be back by mid-morning, without anyone having noticed her absence: after the night's feasting, everyone would get up late. But time was passing rapidly. Should she turn back?

She should. She knew it. But to have come so far for nothing!

Suddenly she remembered another path, wider and less steep — the fishermen used it when they carried down wood for building their boats. Once she got down to the beach with the mule, she would have a view of all of the cave entrances. Moses might see her too . . . To herself that was what she called him now: Moses! Since she had left Jethro's house, she no longer thought of him as a stranger. He was Moses.

She had never behaved so recklessly before, she thought. It was as if she was no longer responsible for her own actions, as if something was impelling her onwards. She hurried on, lashing the mule's back with a rope.

Then, abruptly, she came to a standstill. Down below, about ten cubits from the shore, a man was standing up to his waist in the water.

He was only a silhouette, too far away for her to make out his face. But she could see his hair glinting in the sun.

After a little while, he cast a net. From the way he swung his arms, she was certain it was Moses. He was fishing. He pulled in the net, folded it, hung it over his arm and stood motionless, then cast it again, with a quick, broad gesture. Suddenly Zipporah saw a fish flash silver in the dark net. Moses emerged from the water and threw his catch on to the shingle where the waves could not reach it. At this point, the beach was a narrow strip of pink and ochre pebbles set against the vivid blue of the sea, which glowed like a vast jewel.

The heat was becoming intense and stifling. Zipporah took some deep breaths. An image from her dream came into her mind: the boat moving away from the shore when she had felt the cool sea spray on her brow and cheeks.

For a moment, she wanted desperately to be in the water, by Moses' side, while he sought another spot from which to fish.

Apparently he was capable of feeding himself. He would not need the food she had brought. Would he mock her?

During the night, Zipporah had decided what she would say to him. Now, she had lost the desire to speak.

She would take the food to whichever cave he

had chosen and leave before he got back with his catch. He would guess who had brought it. Or, more likely, he would think it was Orma's doing. Well, that couldn't be helped.

★   ★   ★

Carrying the jar of beer on her shoulder, she reached a point half-way down the cliff where the path widened to form a sizeable terrace under a rocky overhang in front of the dark, gaping mouth of a cave. She had found it.

A stone oven stood against one wall, and several old mats with fringed edges, covered with a big blue and white canvas sack and a tunic, served as a bed. It was the perfect place, protected from the sun and from the gusts of wind that brought sand and dust from the mountain.

White embers in the oven smouldered under a broad flat stone, giving off the peppery odour of terebinth. Moses knew not only how to fish but how to make a fire. And he had settled in a cave where he could live comfortably for some time.

She imagined him — a prince, accustomed to luxury — sleeping on that pallet. But he wasn't a prince here, only a fugitive. The simple bed was proof of that.

Why had he fled? What crime could a lord of Egypt have committed to be forced to live so roughly?

Zipporah was about to put the jar on the terrace when she decided it would be better to leave it inside the cave where it was cool. She crossed the threshold, and was surprised not only by the darkness but by how long and narrow it was. The bronze-tipped staff with which Moses had fought off the shepherds was leaning against the wall. His water-skin was there, too. She placed the jar beside it, a gift.

Below, Moses was still fishing, with the same slow, measured gestures, never once raising his eyes to the cliff. She ran back along the path, the sun burning her brow and lips.

When she returned, bent beneath the weight of the pack-saddle, Moses was no longer casting his net. He was walking back and forth between the sea and the shingle, washing and gutting the fish.

Breathing hard under the weight of the pack-saddle, Zipporah carried it along the track as quickly as she could.

When she reached the cave, she could not help stealing another glance at the beach. It was then that she became aware of an intense shimmering on the sea, as if the wind were spreading light to the shore.

For an instant, Moses seemed suspended there, as if the sky and the earth had united beneath his feet. The beach, the water, the air had disappeared, leaving only a dazzling light in which his calves and arms, hips and torso floated.

Zipporah was rooted to the spot, fascinated yet terrified, heedless of her burden, overwhelmed by an unknown sensation that spread through her and made her quiver.

The shimmering ceased.

Once again the sea was a soft, transparent blue, pricked with needles of light. Moses gathered together the fish he had caught and pushed a cane stalk through their cheeks.

At last, Zipporah dropped the pack-saddle at her feet. She could barely believe what she had just seen. Perhaps her eyes had been playing tricks on her. But she knew it was more than that. The sensation was still there, in the dryness of her mouth and the quivering of her flesh.

She could not take her eyes off Moses. He placed the fish in a water-filled hollow in the rocks and covered them with a few stones. Then he walked out again into the water, and dived. He swam with ease away from the shore, and put his head below the surface.

Looking down on him like a bird, Zipporah watched his body in the transparent sea. Waves that sparkled like eyes glided over his back, buttocks and thighs, which were white where the loincloth had protected them from the sun.

Suddenly she felt dizzy. Her stomach and chest felt tight, her back and shoulders heavy. Her knees started to give way, and she pressed her hands on her thighs to steady herself. She should have turned away — a step or two back would have been enough — or lowered her eyes, but she couldn't. Her dizziness had nothing to do with the void beyond the cliff.

She had never watched a man like this. And it was not only because he was naked.

Moses' head emerged. He shook the water from his hair, passed his hand over his face, turned on to his back and swam slowly in a wide

40

circle, surrounded by glittering reflections, until he reached the beach.

What she could not see — his eyes, his mouth, the water streaming over his temples — Zipporah tried to imagine. She was suddenly filled with a desire to go into the sea and swim to him, to see the creases round his eyes, touch his shoulders. Her skin felt as sensitive as if she had been rubbed with nettles. She was afraid.

At last she turned away. For a few seconds, she bent double, as if at a blow from a stick. She waited, mouth open, eyes tight shut, until she had caught her breath. Her heart was pounding.

She cursed herself and straightened with a kind of rage.

She took the pack-saddle in both hands, and pulled it towards the mouth of the cave. All she had to do was leave it in the shade, then run away. The thought of finding herself face to face with Moses filled her with terror now. He would see the jar, the food, and guess. He would think: The girls from the well. Or perhaps he would think of her, the black girl. The girl the shepherds had wanted to violate. The girl for whom he had fought.

Perhaps he wouldn't think any of those things. She would soon find out.

But, unlike Orma, she would be patient. The prince of Egypt would hide here for some time, there was no doubt of that.

Having reached the cave, Zipporah stopped, taken aback again by the darkness. Inside, the cool chilled the sweat on her brow and neck. She hit the wall with her shoulder, moaned with pain and almost fell. Then she stumbled into something hard, which overturned with a dull thud.

She crouched and felt the ground with her fingertips. Her heart was beating fast, and her throat was dry: she felt as if she was sinning.

'Horeb,' she murmured, 'don't abandon me!'

She touched something wooden and angular, a long, narrow casket. She pulled it to her. In the light coming from the mouth of the cave, she made out the blue and ochre paint on its sides. On the lid, there were columns of small figures, silhouettes of birds and plants, simple lines and strokes, all meticulously drawn. Egyptian writing.

She knew something of it from Jethro. He had traced a few symbols for her in the sand and, on another occasion, had written some in octopus ink on a sheet of crushed cane. She had thought his efforts clumsy, but these were light, pure and exquisite.

She remembered the noise the casket had made when she overturned it. It was not empty. The fear that Moses would return took hold of her again. She listened, ready to run, but all she could hear was the surf against the cliff. She had time to put everything back in its place.

She got down on all fours and groped about feverishly, grazing her knees on sharp rocks. Something glinted in the darkness, a long, cylindrical object, then another, identical, beside it. They were heavy. They were ... Zipporah gave a cry of surprise. She could not believe her eyes. She stood up and went to the cave mouth to see better.

Gold! Two thick bracelets of polished gold, at least as long as her own forearms. A snake was carved in relief on each. Between its coils, there were signs, strange crosses, tiny silhouettes, half men, half beasts.

Somewhere a stone was dislodged, and the sound it made echoed against the cliff.

Moses was coming.

Zipporah thought of the golden arms of the man who had embraced her at the bottom of the sea.

Quickly she put back the bracelets, and rushed out of the cave, her mind racing.

The beach and the sea were deserted. Moses was about fifteen paces from her, his fish swinging from the reed he had placed over his shoulder. When he saw her, he stopped in surprise, perhaps even fear.

She hesitated. She could run, she told herself. He would see the food and understand. Then he raised a hand to shield his eyes from the sun so that he could see her better.

She was ashamed of wanting to flee. Wasn't she always telling her sisters that you had to confront your destiny? But, in truth, she had no choice. Her feet refused to move.

He took his hand away from his brow in a little gesture of greeting, smiled, and approached.

★　★　★

In the days, weeks and years that followed, Zipporah was often to remember that moment, which she was sure had been neither as brief nor as supernatural as it had seemed to her at the time.

Moses was in front of her, and she was terrified that, as on the previous day, she would be incapable of uttering a word. She looked at his lips as if she might be able to find there the words she wanted to speak. Instead, she realized that when she had seen him at the well of Irmna she had not noticed his ear-lobes, or how his mouth stood out from his sparse beard, or that one of his eyelids was lower than the other. She remembered his nose and his high cheekbones. And, of course, she said nothing.

He was looking at her candidly, eyebrows raised, waiting for her to explain why she was there.

She had forgotten the casket and the gold bracelets, but the thought of the dizziness she had experienced when she had watched him swimming made her chest tight again, like a threat. Her feelings must be written on her face, she thought, and clearly visible to Moses. It was an image Zipporah did not like: a woman dazzled by the presence of a man, the sight of his body. An image he must know well. How many women had displayed to him the same open-mouthed amazement? Egyptian beauties, queens, handmaids . . . She was furious with herself. But she could not pretend she was unmoved by him.

Moses seemed to approve of her silence. He

44

nodded and went to put down his catch by the stove. He lifted the stone that covered the fire, removed the cane from the cheeks of the fish, broke it into several pieces of equal length, arranged them on the stones of the oven and laid the fish on them. Then he bent to stoke the embers which began to smoke gently.

Although Zipporah was relieved, she was also offended that he was attending to his fish while she was there. But Moses stood up and smiled at her. 'They'll cook slowly,' he said.

He might have been talking about the fish, but the look he gave Zipporah quivered like a harp.

She straightened, trying to hold her head high, and spoke slowly so that he understood: 'I was afraid you didn't have enough food. You have no flock. Nor anyone to . . . But you know how to fish . . . I didn't think about your bed. You need a cloth and some new matting . . . I didn't think of that . . . But it wasn't only the food — I wanted to thank you . . . for yesterday. I owe you . . . '
She stopped, unable to find the right words.

Moses was following her gestures, and gazing at her curly hair, spread over her shoulders like black feathers. He glanced at the pack-saddle and the jar, then at Zipporah's lips. He was waiting for her to finish the sentence, but she said no more. They heard the surf and breathed in the scent of the terebinth embers, now mixed with the aroma of fish.

Moses moved towards Zipporah. They were on the border between sun and shade, two cubits from the void.

She took a deep breath: Moses smelt of sea

salt. He folded his arms, as Jethro sometimes did, and she thought of the gold bracelets and her dream.

'I'm pleased,' Moses said, 'that I hear your voice. Yesterday you said nothing. Not a word. I thought, Can't she speak? Is she a stranger here?' His speech was slow, hesitant, his accent heavy.

She laughed. 'Did you think that because my skin is black?' she asked.

'No. Only because you said nothing.'

She believed him.

'You said nothing,' he went on, 'but you listened. And you knew where I was. There are many caves here.'

And I would have walked the length of the beach until the sun went down to find you, Zipporah thought.

'There is something you should know,' Moses said. 'I am not an Egyptian. I may look like one, but I'm a Hebrew.'

'A Hebrew?'

'A son of Abraham and Joseph.'

She remembered the casket and the bracelets. He stole them, she thought, chest tight again. That's why he's a fugitive. He's a thief! Blood pounded in her temples. 'Like my father,' she replied mechanically. 'My father Jethro, the sage of the kings of Midian, is also a son of Abraham.'

If he was wondering how a son of Abraham could have a daughter with black skin, he did not show it. 'In Egypt,' he said, 'the Hebrews are not kings or sages. They are slaves.'

'You don't look like a slave.'

He turned his eyes away from her and said

46

something curious: 'I'm not from Egypt any more either.'

Both fell silent. Moses' words could have meant so many different things that Zipporah found it impossible to make sense of them. Perhaps he wasn't a thief. Perhaps he wasn't a prince either. Perhaps he was simply the man in her dream. The thought frightened her. As he watched, she took a step away from him. 'I must go back,' she said.

He nodded, gestured to the cave and thanked her.

'You will always be welcome in my father's house,' she said, still trying to read his face. 'He will be pleased to see you.' She turned away from him and walked out of the shade and into the heat of the cliff.

'Stop!' Moses called. 'You can't leave without a drink.' Without waiting for a reply, he went to the mouth of the cave and picked up his water-skin. He came back, took the wooden stopper from the neck, and offered it to her. 'It's still cool.'

Zipporah was quite used to drinking from a water-skin, but she felt incapable of lifting it, so Moses held it for her. The water gushed out, spattering her chin and cheek. They laughed.

Zipporah did not know how to seduce a man, even though she had watched Orma. She did not know what love was, even though she had watched Sefoba. But what she felt rising within her now was love and the desire to seduce. She defended herself against both. 'I'm wasting your water,' she said.

Moses put his fingers to Zipporah's cheek and gently wiped away the water from her dark skin. Then his fingers brushed past her lips and slid to the hollow of her chin. Zipporah gripped his wrist.

How long did they stay like that?

Probably no longer than it takes a swallow to pass overhead, but long enough for Zipporah to feel Moses' caress, for that was what it was, all through her body, as if he were enveloping her, lifting her, as the man in her dream had done. Long enough for her to lose consciousness of what was really happening.

When she opened her eyes she saw the same desire on Moses' face. She saw the gestures he was about to make, even thought of the bed awaiting them, so close. She still had the strength to smile, let go of his wrist and run into the furnace of the day.

* * *

The sun had long since passed its zenith when Zipporah returned to Jethro's domain. Silence reigned, and not only because of the afternoon heat. Reba's tents, servants and she-camels were gone.

She pushed the mule back into the pen. The men took care to look away, while the handmaids threw her worried glances and ran into the shade of the house. Clearly, her absence had not gone unnoticed.

She had been dreaming of her cool room and the jug of water she would pour over her body

48

before she put on a fresh tunic; the one she was wearing was sticky with sweat. But, afraid she would find Orma in her room, she headed for the big one used by all the women. She had almost reached it, and could hear the cries of the children playing there, when her name rang out. Sefoba was crossing the courtyard to meet her, looking distraught. She threw herself into Zipporah's arms, and hugged her. 'Where were you?' She gave Zipporah no chance to reply: without pausing for breath, she told her that everyone had feared for her safety, thinking of Houssenek's sons and the horrors they were capable of inflicting in revenge for the punishment meted out to them by the stranger — may the wrath of Horeb be assuaged!

'Oh, my Zipporah, I imagined you in their hands — I saw them doing to you what they couldn't do yesterday!'

Zipporah stroked her sister's brow and neck, kissed her damp cheeks, and assured her that nothing terrible had happened to her.

Sefoba did not have time to question her further, because just then a mocking laugh rang out behind them.

'Of course nothing terrible happened! Don't worry, Zipporah, Sefoba was the only one of us who imagined any such thing.' Orma, looking all the more beautiful in her fury, took Zipporah's arm and pulled her away from Sefoba.

'Where you were, you weren't in any danger, were you? Certainly not from the vengeance of Houssenek's sons.'

She had guessed where Zipporah had been

— and envied her. Orma might be a foolish girl, but she was wise in some things.

Zipporah remained calm. 'Has Reba left already?' she asked.

Disconcerted, Orma screwed up her eyes. She waved her hands in the air. 'Why should I care about Reba?'

'She gave him back the fabric he brought her.' Sefoba sighed.

'You gave it back to him?' Zipporah was astonished.

'That's all you can think about! Do I have to marry for a length of cloth?'

'You seemed proud enough to wear it last night.'

'It suited me — so I put it on and danced. What of it? In the torchlight it looked beautiful. This morning, in the light of day, I didn't like it any more — I didn't like it at all — so I gave it back to Reba, and that was that. Of course, if you'd been here, you'd have stopped me.' Orma was proud of how annoying she could be.

Sefoba dried her tears with the back of her wrist. 'Reba was so humiliated,' she said, 'that he took out his knife and cut that beautiful fabric into little pieces. Then he called for his she-camels and bade our father farewell. Poor Father was ill from drinking too much last night so you can imagine how he felt about it. And, of course, you weren't there — ' She broke off, and smiled to soften her words. 'I picked up the pieces and put them under my bed.'

'I don't care a fig for Reba,' Orma muttered. 'Let's not talk about him. Besides, all this is your fault, Zipporah.'

'My fault?'

'Don't pull that face. You found out where the Egyptian is hiding, didn't you?'

Zipporah's silence betrayed her.

'I was sure of it,' Orma said triumphantly. 'So that's where you've been!'

'Is it true? Did you go to see him?'

Sefoba's surprise, with its hint of reproach, upset Zipporah more than all of Orma's nagging. 'Yes,' she admitted at last.

Orma seemed to find this hard to swallow.

'You found him?' Sefoba said, wide-eyed and open-mouthed. 'You saw him?'

'I saw him.'

'Of course!' Orma said. 'What a hypocrite you are, Zipporah! Yesterday you told us to say nothing to Father, to leave the Egyptian alone. Oh, the poor man, we must let him keep his secrets! But today you didn't even wait until daylight to run after him!'

'I took him something to eat and drink, that was all.'

'Oh! How kind!'

'I thanked him for what he did yesterday.'

Orma laughed. 'Where is he?'

'He is where he is.'

'Oh, all right,' Orma hissed. 'Don't tell me. But Father wants to thank the stranger — he's been waiting for you to come back and tell him where he is.'

'What did you say to him?'

51

'I told him the truth. I'm not like you. I don't try to hide it.'

★ ★ ★

Jethro was lying on his bed where Zipporah had left him the previous night. Someone had arranged a few extra cushions around him. It was dark in the room, and his white hair shone like limestone. His eyes were still shut and his hands crossed high on his chest. With rapid fingers, a young handmaid was massaging his stomach through the thin linen of his tunic, while another, so old that her face was a mass of lines, stood near the doorway, preparing an infusion.

Occasionally, a little murmur escaped Jethro's lips, although it was hard to say whether it was an expression of suffering or relief. The young handmaid would relax the pressure of her hands and peer into her master's face, but all it showed was the pallor of a sick old man.

When Zipporah appeared neither woman interrupted her work. She stood waiting in the doorway, watching, with revulsion, as a brown liquid oozed from a distended cloth the older handmaid held. When she stood aside for Zipporah to enter, Jethro opened his eyes. His lips drew back in a smile of contentment. 'Daughter, you've come home.'

'Good day, Father.'

'Let him drink his infusion,' the old handmaid interrupted. 'You can talk afterwards. It mustn't wait, or it'll lose potency.'

She pushed aside her young companion unceremoniously and placed the wooden bowl in Jethro's hands with an authoritative gesture. He sat up, grumbling, and barely looked at the mixture before he gulped it down. Then he held out the empty bowl. 'Bah!' he said scornfully.

The old woman clucked. 'What were you thinking? That Horeb would make your stomach young again?' She gathered her things together in a basket. 'You'll feel better in a moment,' she went on, in a tone that brooked no argument, 'and by tonight you'll be completely restored. Next time speak to me before you try something you aren't accustomed to.'

Jethro said nothing in reply. He touched the young handmaid's thigh with his wrinkled fingers. 'You can go, too, my dear. Your hands are blessed by Horeb.'

The two women went out into the dazzling light of the courtyard. Jethro's eyelids closed again, like rumpled curtains. He groped along the side of the bed until he found Zipporah's hand and clasped it firmly.

'Reba gave me an eastern concoction. A kind of tar. You heat it on the embers and breathe in the smoke. Apparently, if you go about it the right way, it puts all kinds of images into your mind, and everything seems different — tastes, smells, objects. Perhaps I'm too old, or it wasn't properly prepared . . . ' He laughed into his silky white beard, then sighed and grimaced. 'I feel as if I've drunk all the wine and beer in the house and Horeb is punishing

53

me by patting me on the head with rocks from his mountain.'

'Do you want some water? More cushions?'

'Your presence is enough.' He opened his eyes again, and his pupils gleamed in the darkness. 'Reba's a good boy, worthy of the duties awaiting him. He's curious about the world, and he has a sense of justice. He knows the difference between truth and illusion. I felt ashamed when he left this morning. For the first time in a long time, I, Jethro, was ashamed. Of myself and my daughters!'

'Father! I didn't — '

He squeezed Zipporah's hand tighter. 'Not so loud. Words become stones if you utter them too forcefully.'

'Please don't think I could have prevented Orma giving back the fabric to Reba. There's no one she hates more than me at the moment.'

Jethro groaned. 'The stranger.' He sighed. 'Is it true there's a stranger among us? A stranger who rescued you from the hands of Houssenek's sons?'

'Yes.'

'Yesterday?'

'At the well of Irmna.'

'And you said nothing to me about it.'

'We were safe. And Reba was here last night. I would have told you today.'

Jethro shook with laughter. 'After your long walk?'

The old handmaid had told the truth. The infusion was taking effect. Colour was returning to the sage's cheeks, his voice was regaining its

54

clarity, and he was capable of mockery. Zipporah set her lips and said nothing. She did not feel guilty, but she was hurt.

Jethro patted her hand. 'According to Orma, the stranger is a prince of Egypt. What is a prince of Egypt doing in the land of Midian?'

'He may be a prince, but he isn't Egyptian.'

'Oh?'

He waited for her to continue, but she paused, remembering Moses' fingers on her face. 'He told me this morning,' she said shyly.

'That's good news. So Orma's talking nonsense.'

'I took him some food and beer.'

'Why doesn't he come here so that I can thank him for what he did for my daughters?'

'I don't know.'

Jethro gave her a sharp look.

'I don't know,' she repeated. On the way home, she had decided to confide in her father, to tell him everything — she had never before tried to conceal anything from him — yet now she could not bring herself to speak. The words she had planned to use, all the things she had wanted to confess, including her fears — almost none of it would cross her lips. There was only one thing she felt able to reveal: 'The reason I didn't say where I was going this morning was to stop Orma going with me.'

Jethro shook his head cautiously. 'My daughters!'

'Orma is Orma. I'm not like her.'

'As far as pride is concerned, anyone would think you had the same father and mother!'

Zipporah shrugged her shoulders, and her tunic rippled.

'What is he, then, your stranger, if he isn't Egyptian?' Jethro persisted.

'A Hebrew.'

'Oh!'

'That's what he says.'

Surprise had jolted Jethro out of his stupor. 'A son of Abraham?' he asked.

'Of Abraham and Joseph,' he says.

Jethro nodded. 'Of course. A Hebrew of Egypt.' He stared up into the darkness at the beams and palm leaves above his bed, where flies were buzzing. Then he leaned down, picked up the goblet of water left by the handmaid and sipped. 'That may be so. Those who trade with Pharaoh say that in Egypt the Hebrews are slaves. If this Moses is a slave from Egypt, Orma is even more foolish than I thought to take him for a prince.'

'I don't think he *is* a slave,' Zipporah said gently.

'Oh?'

'Sefoba and I also took him for a prince. He has the bearing. He doesn't fight like a slave either.'

'You talked to him. What did he say?' Now Jethro's gaze was calm but penetrating.

'He said: 'I'm not from Egypt any more.''

'And then?'

'That's all.'

'Just one sentence? You went to see him and he spoke only one sentence?'

Zipporah laughed, but it sounded false. 'He

isn't at ease with our language.'

'But you are,' Jethro said, with a smile.

Not with him, Zipporah thought. Not with Moses.

'Orma says you forbade her to tell me about him.'

'You can't forbid Orma anything.' Zipporah sighed.

Jethro waited.

'If you saw him . . . His manners . . . Orma and Sefoba said to him straight away, 'Come and see our father.' He refused. He didn't hesitate. I thought, He's a fugitive. He wants to stay in the shadows. He's a man in hiding. And I owe it to him to respect his wishes and not force him to talk about things he'd prefer to keep to himself.'

Jethro studied her for a moment and nodded. 'You did right. But I'm your father, and he's on my land . . . I'm curious. I want you to send two boys to him, with a camel and a sheep. The sheep is for milk and the camel so that he can come to see me. He's to be told that I would go to him if I could to express my gratitude, but I'm too old and frail. He's also to be told that he would do me the greatest honour if he came to sit with me under the canopy.'

Zipporah sat in silence, eyes lowered, fingers fidgeting with the folds of her tunic.

'Well? Aren't I polite enough for a prince of Egypt? Have I forgotten something?'

'What if he still refuses?'

'Let's wait until he does.'

'I'm sure he's done nothing wrong.'

57

'You're making me even more curious.'

'Orma will want to go with the boys.'

Jethro wagged a finger, a gleam in his eyes. 'Oh, no! Not you, not Orma. I said two boys, and two boys it will be.'

Orma's Anger

The stranger Moses did not come back with the boys. 'He thanked you for the animals, and asked to be shown how to milk a ewe. That was all.'

Jethro looked pensive, but made no comment.

A day passed, and there was no sign of a prince of Egypt coming along the road from the west on a camel. The hours passed with a slowness Zipporah had never known. The more time elapsed, the more anxious she became. The fear never left her: that Moses would come and that he would not. Fear, too, of her memory of their last moment in the cave.

It was difficult to sleep. She had to endure Orma's sighs as she tossed and turned on her bed. 'Zipporah, are you awake?' Orma would whisper from time to time, half sitting up.

Zipporah did not move.

'I know you're not asleep. You're thinking of him.'

Zipporah still did not move.

'I am, too,' Orma would moan.

When Orma had dozed off, Zipporah was left with her own confused thoughts, and beneath her closed eyelids she would see again the moments she had shared with Moses, in dream and in reality.

On the second morning, she lost patience. She rose at dawn and rushed to the door of the domain to look along the west road. It was as pale as milk — and empty. She waited for the rocks and bushes to regain their dusty colours, then for shadows to form. But the road remained empty.

Wearily, quelling the desire to jump on to the back of a mule and trot to Moses' cave, she went to the women's room. Faces turned to her, all bearing the same question: 'Isn't the Egyptian coming?'

Orma appeared. 'What's happening?'

There was a silence, then a voice replied, 'Zipporah went to wait for him at dawn at the door of the courtyard. And still he didn't come.'

Chuckles broke out. Orma's face, previously taut with anger, was now mocking, which merely enhanced her beauty. Zipporah left the room, her back rigid with determination. She promised herself she would not show any more signs of impatience.

On the evening of the third day, when the sky was aflame but still no man or camel had appeared, Orma asked Jethro if she might go to see Moses the next day.

'To do what?' Jethro asked, feigning surprise.

'To persuade him to come here, as you asked.'

'I asked no such thing! I invited him to sit beside me, which would have given me pleasure and honoured me. But I respect his refusal as much as I would his acceptance. He can keep the camel and sheep I sent him, and then I won't feel indebted to him.'

His answer disconcerted Orma, but did not convince her. 'You're wrong, Father,' she said, knitting her brows. 'He won't come. And I know why.'

'Oh?'

'He's a prince of Egypt.'

'So it would seem.'

'A man accustomed to being shown great respect.'

'You mean a camel and a sheep are not enough to express my gratitude?'

'No, I mean that sending two boys to tell him you want to see him isn't enough to overcome his wounded pride.'

'Is his pride wounded?'

'If it weren't, he would have come by now.'

'Do you think so?'

'He fights for us, your daughters, and saves us. One against four. He could have been killed. And then he runs away! It makes no sense, Father. Have we ever before known a stranger refuse to sit with you? Something has been said or done to displease him.'

'By whom?'

'Zipporah. You know how she speaks sometimes — as if she were you! Or she says nothing when she should speak. Did you know that when we were at the well she didn't utter a word, didn't even thank him?'

'She went to see him afterwards to apologize. She took him food and beer. The only thing she didn't do was pass on my invitation.'

'But was she able to forget her pride and be less stiff in the way she spoke to him?'

'She had no reason to be stiff towards him. Didn't you ask her what they said to each other?'

61

Orma laughed scornfully. 'You don't ask Zipporah such things! All I know is what I saw. When she came back, she looked like someone with something to hide.'

Jethro sighed. 'So if you'd gone to the cave it would have been different, would it?'

'He'd have been here by now.' At that moment, Orma's smile was irresistible.

Jethro pulled at invisible knots in his beard, surprised by how perceptive she could be. He considered telling her that the prince of Egypt was merely a Hebrew, perhaps even a runaway slave, which would curb her enthusiasm, but he said nothing, fearing the scene his daughter would make. In truth, he was a little annoyed to be kept waiting for so long. Orma was right: no stranger had refused before to sit with him. But why did the man not come? And what made him so extraordinary? It might be quite normal for Orma to think nothing of seducing a stranger, but the same could not be said of Zipporah, the most sensible of all of them. At least until now!

'No,' he said, abruptly. 'You will stay here. Jethro welcomes anyone who wishes to enter his house in friendship, but that is all. As for your prince of Egypt, I've done as I should, and that's enough.'

★   ★   ★

Several more days passed. Twilight followed twilight.

The endless waiting should have worn down Jethro's daughters, but the opposite happened.

62

Their impatience spread to all the women of the household, like a disease. The few men — husbands, brothers and uncles — who had not left with the flocks wondered if they would ever meet the stranger who occupied so much of the women's chatter.

Now no one went to work, either within the domain or outside, or even took a nap beneath the terebinths or tamarisks, without turning their eyes automatically towards the west road. But there was nothing to be seen except the changing blue sky, a flight of curlews or cormorants or, sometimes, a runaway ass.

Until, at long last, it happened.

One afternoon, when the heat was like a furnace, Moses was at the door of the domain without anyone having seen him come.

There was a shout from a young girl or a child, and everyone emerged hurriedly from the shade and ran to the door. Yes, there he was.

Nobody dared say a word.

He was not wearing a tunic, only a pleated loincloth, held in at the waist by the magnificent belt that had so impressed Jethro's daughters at the well of Irmna. On his head was a hat with purple stripes. Although he was naked above the waist, and his chest was hairless, he did not seem to mind the sun. His beard, now as thick as a Midianite's, did not conceal the beauty of his mouth. The expression in his eyes was hard to describe, at once shy and powerful.

The women understood immediately why Zipporah and Orma had not been the same since their encounter with the stranger, although the

63

men were irritated by the stiffness of his manner.

He asked, in an accent that gave the words a new sonority, if this was the house of Jethro, the sage of the kings of Midian. Before anyone could reply, he saw Zipporah's face among those looking up at him and smiled at her. Then he struck the camel's neck with his long bronze-tipped staff. The beast stretched out its neck, bent its forelegs and knelt down so that Moses could get off. Now that he was standing before them, everyone became aware that he was taller than the men of Midian, even though his feet were bare.

Orma's voice rang out: 'Moses!'

The silence was broken, and everyone joined in the welcome.

★　★　★

'Forgive me, wise Jethro, that I have not come sooner to see you. Do not think me rude. I had never ridden a camel before and had to learn before I could come,' he said, without taking a breath between the sentences. It was evident that he had been repeating them to himself.

Jethro, who was about to eat a fig, stopped, open-mouthed. 'You had to learn to ride a camel?'

Moses bowed solemnly. 'I did. You gave me an animal so that I could come here.'

There was general laughter, but Jethro remained silent.

They were in the shade of the canopy, reclining comfortably on cushions, with pitchers of beer and bowls of fruit within arm's reach. Sefoba, Orma and Zipporah stood nervously behind their father, holding baskets of cakes. At a distance, in the baking sun, the handmaids and children formed a large circle. They were laughing so much they had to wipe their eyes, but they did not miss any of what was said.

Jethro raised his hand to silence them, and threatened to send them all back to their duties if they did not show the stranger more respect.

Moses smiled modestly. 'They're right to laugh. Everyone here knows how to ride a camel. It's stupid not to.'

'Now you know — and you learned quickly,' Jethro replied.

Moses sipped his beer.

He had received the compliment with as much humility as he had accepted the laughter. If anything, Jethro's curiosity about the stranger was even greater now than it had been before. 'But perhaps you can ride a horse?' he said. 'They say there are many horses in Egypt.'

'Indeed there are.'

Moses fell silent. Jethro waited. 'Pharaoh has them, and they're used in war.'

'Does Pharaoh ride a horse?'

'He stands.'

'He stands?'

'In a chariot pulled by four horses. The generals and the great warriors who accompany him ride horses. Others walk — or run when they have to. There are boats, too, on the Great River, Iterou, many boats. Sometimes, also, horses.'

With each sentence, Moses' voice became more muted, as if he were less and less sure of his ability to express what he wanted to say. His accent obscured his words, which made him seem less confident too.

The children and the younger handmaids were unable to hold back their laughter. The stranger was even less familiar with their language than he was with sheep and camels! He was different, and there was something appealing about that, but perhaps he should have remained silent.

Jethro tried to ignore his guest's shortcomings — first for the sake of courtesy but also because he was eager to learn everything he could about how people lived far from the desert where he held sway. As he was about to ask another question, a swishing sound made him look up. Zipporah was kneeling between him and Moses. Unasked, she filled their goblets, even though they were not yet empty. As she held out Jethro's, she gave him a firm look of command. It said, 'Stop asking questions. Just thank him — that was why he came.'

Jethro had no time to ponder what to do next. Orma pushed Zipporah aside and knelt before Moses to offer him a basket of honey cakes — and herself in all her splendour.

Everyone heard the most beautiful of Jethro's daughters declare, with unusual humility, how happy she was to offer these gifts, which were paltry in comparison with what Moses had done for her and her sisters, and the luxury to which a lord of Egypt must be accustomed.

Jethro saw Zipporah's fists clench while Moses

seemed embarrassed. For a moment, he feared that a quarrel might ensue between his daughters. But then, unexpectedly, Moses got to his feet, gripping his staff. A strange silence fell on the courtyard. Orma retreated, and the women put their arms round the children's shoulders.

Moses bowed, as if he was about to take his leave. 'You're wrong, daughter of Jethro,' he said clearly.

Taken aback, Orma giggled.

'Don't laugh! What you said is not true.' Moses' voice was harsh, like pebbles rubbing together. Orma looked about her for support, but everyone was watching Moses, anxious not to miss a word he said. 'I'm not a lord of Egypt, daughter of Jethro. You believe I'm from Egypt and a prince, but I'm not.'

Was he angry or did his accent make him seem so? It was impossible to say.

Orma got to her feet, cheeks flushed, lips quivering. She took a step back and found herself beside Zipporah. Moses' golden eyes swept over them and Jethro. Then he turned to face the people standing in the courtyard. He opened his arms, but not very wide. 'It's the truth,' he said, his voice no longer menacing. 'I'm not an Egyptian. I'm a Hebrew, the child of a slave, a son of Abraham and Joseph.'

Jethro had stood up, his tunic flowing around his thin body. He caught Moses' elbow, seized his hands and forced him to sit down again. 'I know. Sit, Moses, please. Zipporah told me.'

Orma looked at Zipporah in astonishment, but

67

Zipporah ignored her. Moses and their father sank down on the cushions. Jethro patted Moses' knee. 'What you say is good news for me, Moses, and I am all the happier to welcome you. We Midianites are the sons of Abraham and his second wife Ketourah.'

'Oh?'

'You should think of this as your home, and stay for as long as you wish. I owe you everything that my daughters owe you.'

'All I did was fight, and the shepherds weren't strong.'

'But you didn't know that before you put them to flight. From today, the names of Moses and Jethro are joined in friendship.'

'You are a good man. But you don't yet know what led me to the land of Midian.'

Moses smiled sadly, apparently determined to continue being humble, even though it was no longer necessary.

Jethro launched into a long tirade: 'No, I don't, any more than I know how you came here. You will tell me if you wish to. I love to hear men's stories. But that doesn't matter. You are alone here. You have no companion, no flock, not even a tent to shelter you from the heat of the day and the cold of the night. It seems you have no handmaids, no wife, no one who knows how to bake your bread, brew your beer or weave your garments. Let me welcome you to my domain as if you were one of my people. It is the least I can do, after what you have done for me. My daughters and I thank Horeb that you have come. Choose twenty of my sheep to start your flock and take the canvas you need to erect a tent in the shade of one of the great trees beyond these walls. It would make me happy. As you will have noticed, and for a reason that I will explain to you later, I have only women around me — daughters, nieces or handmaids. Among them, you will find hands to care for you. And I dare say I shall have someone to talk to in the evenings.'

Zipporah expected to see a smile of relief on Moses' face. Instead, his whole body grew rigid.

'I came to Midian because I killed a man,' he said.

A murmur went through the courtyard. Abruptly the laughter ceased. Zipporah held her breath. On either side of her, Sefoba and Orma gripped her wrists, as if to stop themselves collapsing. The only person who remained impassive, without even a glint of surprise in his eyes, was Jethro.

Moses placed his staff across his knees, and took a deep breath. 'I killed a man. Not a shepherd, one of Pharaoh's lords, a highly placed architect. I am wearing noble garments, but they are not mine. I stole them in order to flee. This staff, too, I stole from Pharaoh's court. That is what you must know before you welcome me among you.'

'If you killed a man,' Jethro said, in a voice of unruffled calm, 'you must have had reason to do so. Will you tell us about it?'

★   ★   ★

Moses was not a man to take a long time in telling his story. In any case, his lack of fluency in the language of Midian forced him to be brief. But to everyone, including the children — those who had been in the courtyard had drawn closer — his story was all the more terrible for that. They filled his silences with their imagination, seeing in their minds the teeming world beyond the Red Sea. Thinis, Waset, Djeser-Djeserou, Amon, Osiris — names they had heard from passing traders assumed a new reality as Moses spoke.

They saw the splendour of the cities, the roads and the temples, the fabulous palaces, the huge stone sculptures of animals asserting the power of men who were no longer entirely men. Then Moses turned, in his staccato phrases, to the *nekhakha*, Pharaoh's whip, which he held tight to his chest in statues found everywhere in the country, in temples and on tombs. A whip that cracked ceaselessly, raining blows on countless Hebrew slaves: it was with their blood, their screams and their deaths that extraordinary buildings were erected to the living god, the Life of Life, the ever-reborn power that reigned over the vast land of the Great River. 'Where the slaves work, anyone who protests will die,' Moses said. 'On a building site, the death of a Hebrew counts for less than a broken plank.' From dawn to night, the slaves endured insults, injury and humiliation. As punishment, the weakest made bricks, stamping mud into straw until they could no longer lift their feet. 'Those too exhausted to continue are beaten until they fall in the mud. If their companions try to help, they too are beaten.'

Now, in the heat of Midian, everyone heard the crack of Pharaoh's whip. Even the flies had stopped buzzing.

'Anyone unable to pull the sledges that bear the stones is beaten,' Moses resumed. 'Anyone who is thirsty, anyone who makes a mistake, anyone who tries to bandage his wound is beaten. Young and old, men and women.'

At times, Moses fell silent, and his eyes wandered over the baskets of fruit before him. Jethro and his family respected his silence, trying to imagine what he was seeing with his inner eye: the long chains of men tied together with rope, the thousands of arms beating the stone, cutting it, polishing it, lifting it; the endless days spent in carving rock from the cliffs, transporting it from one end of Egypt to the other, and finally piling it high in dizzying constructions. 'It wasn't always thus,' Moses murmured. 'But today Pharaoh's whip is greedier for their blood than the mosquitoes.'

His eyes met Jethro's, then Zipporah's. There was no pain on his face, or anger but, rather, incomprehension.

'I stood next to a man who enjoyed the suffering of the slaves and took pride in inflicting harm on them. His name was Mem P'ta. I felt soiled by him. I was ashamed of what he was doing and ashamed that I did not stop him. One morning, it happened. I hadn't planned it. Mem P'ta went alone to the river, and I followed him. I waited in the reeds while he did his business.

71

Then I killed him. It wasn't difficult, and I was relieved that he'd never again raise his whip. I wanted to kill him.' Moses gave a half-smile. 'But I was afraid they would soon discover his body if the river swept it away, so I pulled it over to a strip of sand and buried it. I think that was where I was seen.'

Again, he fell silent. It was not difficult to imagine what he left unsaid.

He rolled his staff between his hands and looked at the faces around him. Curiously, he seemed more at ease now, more sure of himself. He shrugged his shoulders.

'I killed the Egyptian,' he said, 'but it didn't lessen the suffering of a single Hebrew. Instead Pharaoh's wrath grew. To strike one of Pharaoh's architects or overseers is to strike Pharaoh. And who would dare do that?'

Jethro remained silent, unmoving. Moses' smile grew wider, although his eyes were bleak.

'I stole clothing, and the boat that brought me here. Until your daughters said to me, 'You are in the land of Midian, on the property of Jethro, the sage of the kings of Midian,' I had no idea where I was.'

Jethro nodded. 'You are indeed in the land of Midian, on the property of Jethro. Nothing you have told us makes me want to retract anything I've said. I stand by my word: this is your home. If such is your wish, and a modest life suits you, tomorrow you will pitch your tent and choose the first animals for your flock.'

★ ★ ★

72

The sky had turned a deeper blue. The constant plume of clouds and smoke that wreathed the summit of Horeb's mountain was tinged with an almost liquid pink. It was a long time since Moses, sitting upright on his camel, had ridden off into the west.

As soon as he had left, everyone spoke at once, but Orma's voice stood out from the rest. Zipporah had kept her distance. She had only to close her eyes to see the muscles rippling on the stranger's back as the camel swayed from side to side. She relived each moment of their encounter. Everything was inside her: Moses' voice, his expressions, his awkwardness . . . and all he had left unsaid.

'What a strange man,' her father said, as she and her sisters set the evening meal before him. 'Did you notice how he answers questions without answering them? I'm sure he knows how to ride a horse and that he was once at Pharaoh's side. A man like him should be more confident. His eyes glow with pride, yet he's humble. I can't believe he was a slave, although he holds the slaves in higher esteem than he grants himself. Moses seems to be one thing but also its opposite. He's caught between light and darkness. I like him.'

His words inflamed Orma, like fire touching dry grass. 'But he killed a man!'

'You heard why he did it.'

'How do you know he was speaking the truth?'

'Yes, Father.' Anxiety clouded Sefoba's brow. 'How do we know Moses wasn't lying?' She glanced at Zipporah, whose face was impassive.

'A man who killed another man can easily lie,' Orma asserted.

'I'm pleased we're helping him,' Sefoba said, 'but must he pitch his tent so close to us?'

Jethro smiled and shook his head. 'A man who has killed another man can lie to conceal his sin. But a man who confesses it unasked — why would he lie? His confession proves he has a strong sense of justice that won't allow him to lie.'

'He lies in his appearance,' Orma replied implacably. 'As you said, Father, he pretends to be something he is not.'

'That's not what our father said,' Zipporah intervened, unable to conceal her irritation. 'Moses is honest, but he has the manners of a stranger. And it is not for us to judge what he did in Egypt.'

'Oh, you!' Orma said. 'Of course you take his side — especially if it means saying the opposite of what I say.'

'Orma, my daughter — '

'You, too, Father! You knew he was neither Egyptian nor a prince and you let me debase myself, kneeling before him and speaking to him as I did!'

The tears Orma had held back now poured down her cheeks. Her lips quivered and her temples throbbed. Jethro looked at her tenderly. Then, because she was angry and ashamed of her tears, Orma mimicked Moses: 'Don't laugh! What you said is not true! I'm not a lord of Egypt, daughter of Jethro.' She was so accurate that Jethro could not help laughing, any more than could Sefoba and Zipporah.

'Go on!' Orma exploded, gesticulating at her father and Zipporah. 'Laugh at me! That's what you like to do, isn't it?' She was beside herself with rage, shouting at the top of her voice. Handmaids appeared in the doorways. The whole courtyard vibrated with Orma's words. 'You don't love me! I know, Father, that for you, only Zipporah counts. And it doesn't surprise me that you like the stranger. He's deceitful — he plays at being a slave. He and Zipporah should understand each other! He's just like the woman you've forced us to accept as our sister — but who's never been *my* sister!'

Sefoba gasped. Orma ran to the other end of the courtyard and vanished into the women's room. There was a stunned silence.

Jethro sighed. 'Daughter, daughter!'

Sefoba slipped her hand into Zipporah's. 'She didn't mean it.'

Zipporah nodded, her eyes a little too bright.

'She didn't mean it,' Sefoba repeated. 'She's disappointed. Today she lost a prince.'

'She meant it,' Jethro said sadly. 'At least a little. And perhaps I don't love her enough.'

Sefoba and Zipporah lowered their eyes.

Jethro touched his eldest daughter's shoulder. 'Go to her. She needs comfort.'

★   ★   ★

After Sefoba had gone, Zipporah and Jethro remained silent for a long time. Orma's harsh words had brought them closer, but also

75

frightened them. They had heard the pain beneath her fury, and felt guilty rather than offended. They felt themselves truly father and daughter, sharing a joy and strength that went beyond the tie of blood or the colour of their skin. But who would understand that? No one in the land of Midian — not even Sefoba.

The summit of Horeb's mountain had turned grey. The evening breeze was blowing in little gusts, carrying with it the scents of the garden and the cries of children reluctant to sleep. The handmaids lit the lamps, and the moths began their nightly dance.

Zipporah's thoughts had drifted away from Orma's outburst. Now she was pondering the gold bracelets she had discovered in Moses' cave. She had not yet mentioned them to Jethro, and could not bring herself to do so, even now when they were united in the heat of the evening. What she had seen in the cave was Moses' secret, which she must not reveal.

'Of course he didn't tell us everything!' Jethro said, in a low voice, as if he had read her thoughts. 'He spoke of Pharaoh's slaves like a man who has only recently seen the truth, not one who was born into such suffering and has known it all his life.'

'He didn't lie, though.'

'No, he didn't.'

'He's a Hebrew, not an Egyptian.'

Jethro's voice became pensive again. 'He's a son of Abraham, I believe that. But apparently the Hebrews of Egypt know nothing about the people of Midian.'

76

'*Moses* didn't know about us,' Zipporah corrected him. 'Just as he doesn't know our language.'

Jethro smiled. 'You're right.'

'You didn't ask him who his god is. Usually, Father, it's the first question you ask strangers.'

'He has no god. Neither the gods of Egypt, nor the god of the Hebrews. That's why he doesn't yet know what he must do with his life.'

Zipporah wondered how Jethro could be so sure of what he was saying, but she did not ask. By now, darkness had fallen. The handmaids glided past the walls like shadows. Jethro batted away a moth that fluttered about his beard.

'When he said he'd killed a man,' Zipporah said, 'you didn't seem surprised.'

'There was no reason to be. What else would force a man to cross the sea without knowing where he's going and with no company but his own fear?'

So Jethro, too, had sensed Moses' fear. Zipporah was glad that it had not made him mistrustful. She thought of the expression on Moses' face as he had climbed onto his camel to leave them. He had said nothing to her, had not bidden her farewell, had not said he would see her tomorrow. He had simply looked at her with the mixture of determination and awkwardness that she had come to know. A look that said: 'You understand the kind of man I am.'

'Almost a moon ago, I had a dream,' she murmured suddenly, as if the words had come of their own volition. 'A dream that frightened me yet drew me. I asked Horeb to help me understand it, but he was silent. I didn't dare tell you about it. I was afraid I would seem ridiculous and lose my dignity, as Orma did.'

Zipporah described the dream, and her struggle to make sense of it. Did it mean she must take a boat across the sea and go to live in the land of Cush? Must she lose everything she had, everything Jethro had given her — especially a father's love? She could not imagine that. 'But we know what awaits me here. Sefoba has found a husband, as have our elder sisters. Soon Orma will accept Reba, or someone else. It will all be over. You will have no more daughters to marry off. No man in Midian, not even a shepherd, will come to ask for my hand. I will give you no grandchild.'

She had uttered these words as lightly as she could, but they fell from her mouth like stones.

Jethro let the note of sadness fade in the silence. 'Nobody knows for certain what dreams tell us. They come to us at night and there is something dark about them. But they may be as blinding as the brightest sunlight. Wise men say, 'Live your dream in sleep, but do not let your life become a sleep.''

Zipporah, too, let a moment pass before she spoke. 'Do you think he will come and pitch his tent here tomorrow?' There was no need to say Moses' name.

'I'm sure he will,' Jethro replied. He paused to reflect. 'We must be patient. He bears a heavy burden. He cannot relieve himself of it so soon.'

'May Horeb come to his aid.'

'What makes Horeb all-powerful is that he

78

does not do what we expect of him. He surprises us, and thereby corrects us, encourages us and shows us the path to follow. Let him surprise you. Have patience. There are many days before you.'

The Handmaid

What Jethro had said came to pass.

The next day, Moses arrived early, riding on his camel, with the sheep on a lead behind him, his few possessions in the pack-saddle Zipporah had taken him. He pitched his tent beneath the big sycamore that marked the beginning of the road to Epha. It was a good choice, far enough from Jethro's domain to preserve the solitude that Moses liked, and near enough not to give the impression that he was keeping his distance.

Moses had learned quickly to ride the camel. With the same ease, he learned to live in a tent and to tend a flock of sheep. In less than a moon, he was able to gather the animals, pen them in, and distinguish those that needed attention. He was shown how to make the tools for cutting flints so that they were as sharp as metal blades. He was taught how to cut and sew leather, how to make a comfortable saddle, how to dry meat, and how to recognize from a distance the cool, shady spots where scorpions and snakes might lurk.

Day by day, his presence and manner became more natural. He even abandoned his habit of walking barefoot on the burning stones and started to wear sandals as everyone else did.

Imperceptibly, Jethro's household, too, began to change.

At first, a new face and the strangeness of his

accent made him congenial company for the young handmaids. Moses did not hesitate to laugh at himself, to mock his own clumsiness, and they laughed with him. But what, above all, made the days different from how they had been before his arrival was all that he told them about Egypt.

The children of the household — first, small groups of the eldest, then the younger ones — began to join him outside his tent at twilight. They asked a thousand questions and Moses answered patiently, his voice increasingly confident. He would tell them, in words and gestures, how the quarrymen cut the blocks of stone from the mountains, and how they were transported on the Great River, Iterou. How, sometimes, the needles of rock were so huge that it took more than a hundred boats and thousands of men to bring them to the temples, a ten-day journey from the mountains. In the sand he traced the outlines of the cities and palaces. He drew gardens, and sometimes flowers that did not have names in the language of Midian.

The children's eyes grew large at the scale of the marvels they heard about. Their nights were filled with fabulous dreams, their thoughts no longer of the slaves or Pharaoh's whip but of those incredible cities, those paradise gardens, those stone animals drawn from the heart of the mountains, so enormous that one of their claws stood higher than a man.

Soon, the children were joined by the young handmaids. Once twilight had come, Jethro's domain was filled, as if by magic, with a new

81

kind of silence, until the sky above Horeb's mountain was swallowed by the darkness.

For a whole moon, applying to himself the same counsel of patience he had given Zipporah, Jethro was careful not to share his meal too frequently with Moses. It was just as well, since, whenever he did so, they sat for the most part in gloomy silence, Moses seemingly weighed down by respect and gratitude, Jethro by caution.

It was quite otherwise when Moses sat outside his tent with the children and the handmaids, and it was not long before Jethro heard of the pleasure he gave them. One evening, he asked for his meal to be taken to Moses' tent, with a great jar of honey wine.

As soon as he was seated, he poured the wine into olivewood goblets and asked the children to come closer, practically pushing them into Moses' arms. Although he did not let it show, he was surprised to discover the ease with words that Moses had acquired. His accent no longer hampered understanding, but made the language of Midian newly seductive. Jethro listened, enthralled, to Moses' account of how the priests of Egypt transformed the bodies of the dead kings and princes into sculptures of flesh, empty of their entrails, to face eternity. He laughed with the children when Moses imitated the cries of the monkeys that the Egyptians kept as pets, prizing them for their playfulness.

At dawn the following day, when Zipporah brought him his morning meal of cakes and cold milk, Jethro seized her hand and squeezed it with unusual emotion. 'I listened to Moses last night,' he said, 'and discovered a new man. He knows more than I do. He has seen more things in heaven and earth with his own eyes than I have. I'm sure now that he was never one of Pharaoh's slaves. I'm even certain that, until he fled the land of the Great River, Iterou, he was happy and proud to be Pharaoh's subject.'

Zipporah said nothing. Jethro's eyes took on a wicked gleam, and he asked if Moses had told her anything about his past since he had pitched his tent here.

'No, of course not! Why should he? And, besides, he's very busy with the children.' There was a trace of bitterness in her voice. Jethro was still looking at her intently. To evade the questions she feared to hear, she added, with a laugh: 'If he continues to please everyone so much, people will start forgetting that Jethro is master here. The whole household is at Moses' beck and call. He has only to raise an eyebrow and the handmaids come running!'

'The whole household, except your sister.' Jethro dipped his fingers in the bowl of cold water that Zipporah was holding out to him.

It was true. Orma was the only one to keep her distance. Her anger had not abated since Moses' first visit. She never went near the tent beneath the sycamore. When Moses' name was mentioned, she grimaced scornfully. Whenever he entered Jethro's domain, which rarely happened, she was careful not to look at him. And if ever their paths crossed outside, she immediately turned away her head.

Watching her, Sefoba and Zipporah laughed

like the handmaids, who nudged each other with their elbows and winked. But Zipporah's laughter was less an expression of gaiety than of her own dismay and sorrow. Now that Moses was here, so close to her, and pampered by the household, it was she, suddenly, who felt a stranger, forgotten and ignored. In the two moons since Moses had pitched his tent, none of the things she had hoped for deep in her heart had come to pass. In fact, quite the contrary.

At first, fearful of appearing impatient, perhaps even impertinent, she had obeyed Jethro's words. 'Be patient. You have many days before you.' With all the willpower of which she was capable, she had resisted the desire to make any move that might recall their brief intimacy in the cave. She had deliberately refrained from taking him his morning meal, had left to others the pleasure of initiating him into his new life and receiving a grateful smile in return. The pleasure of being there, as if by magic, when he needed help.

She had succeeded so well that her contacts with Moses became rare and superficial. As time went by, Moses busied himself with his various tasks, and gave most of his attention to the handmaids or the children. The pair hardly met. And when they did meet, instead of the joy Zipporah had imagined she would feel at seeing him so close and, perhaps, loving him, she felt only emptiness and disappointment. Moses paid her no greater heed than he did anyone else in the household.

She began to doubt that she had ever been

overwhelmed by the sight of him fishing. To doubt that he had once touched her lips with his fingers. Even to doubt that the stranger was what he said and what he seemed.

She would go to sleep remembering Moses' body naked in the sea, and the gold bracelets in the painted casket covered with writing. Did any of it truly exist? Had she forgotten the difference between dreams and reality?

Her longing for a moment alone with Moses turned to pain: the pain of jealousy. It made her awkward. Never before had a man so occupied her thoughts. She felt frustrated and ashamed, but dared not show it, let alone talk about it, even to Sefoba.

At last, one morning she rose, determined to have done with her torment. It was time she became herself again. She had been patient for too long.

The sun was just touching the sycamore on the road to Epha when she came within sight of the tent. She stopped dead because at that moment the flap was raised and a handmaid appeared. Zipporah recognized her and whispered her name: 'Murti!'

She was a pretty girl, a little younger than Orma, with a slender figure. She looked graceful as she leaned against the trunk of the sycamore.

Zipporah felt as though her blood were turning to sand. How stupid she had been not to think of it! She had seen the way the young handmaids stared at Moses. There was no shortage of attractive women in Jethro's domain. What had happened was inevitable. There was

85

no point in being angry with Moses.

Murti was on all fours outside the tent now. She seemed on the verge of collapse. But she got up and began to run like a madwoman, mouth wide open and cheeks streaked with tears.

As she came closer, Zipporah stepped out into the middle of the path and caught her arm. Murti had been running so fast that both women staggered. 'Murti! What's the matter? Where are you running to?'

Murti was sobbing. Zipporah repeated her name softly. The handmaid's weeping grew more intense, and her chest heaved. Zipporah pulled Murti to her, and put her arms round her. Beneath the sycamore, the flap of the tent did not move.

'Murti, what happened?'

The handmaid shook her head, and pushed at Zipporah's shoulders, trying to break free.

'Don't run away!' Zipporah said, holding her tightly. 'You can talk to me, and what you say will remain between ourselves.'

Murti knew this, but she needed time. She laid her head on Zipporah's shoulder, her body shaken with spasms, until she regained her breath. 'You won't tell anybody?' she asked, voice barely audible.

'I promise before Horeb I won't.'

Murti put her hands over her face. 'I'd been wanting to do it for days. I couldn't help it. I thought about it as soon as I woke up.'

It was not difficult for Zipporah to believe her and understand her. There was no doubting Murti's sincerity, no doubting she had been

86

powerless to resist the force that had impelled her towards the stranger.

She had slipped into the tent while Moses was still asleep, and had woken him with the caresses that, night after night, she had lavished on him in dreams. She had not doubted that he would welcome them with joy. But when he opened his eyes, he had seemed more surprised than pleased. He had taken hold of Murti's hand. But she had persisted, had taken off her tunic and placed Moses' palm on her bare skin.

What happened next was so terrible that Murti found it hard to express: the way Moses had looked at her, the tunic she fumbled to put back on, the noise of her weeping, which filled her with shame.

Zipporah stroked her neck and shoulders. 'What did he say?' she asked.

Murti shrugged.

'Did he push you out of his tent without a word?' Zipporah persisted.

Murti sniffed and dried her cheeks. She glanced anxiously at the tent. 'I don't know, I wasn't listening. We mustn't stay here.'

'Try to remember.'

Without answering, Murti began to walk towards Jethro's domain. Zipporah followed her. She felt no anger towards her, only a kind of tender complicity, mixed with fear and sadness. And a curious sense of relief.

What would have happened if she herself had woken Moses?

As they were nearing the enclosure where the mules were kept, Zipporah stopped Murti again.

The handmaid was no longer crying and her face had grown curiously ugly. Without waiting for Zipporah's question, she pointed to the west, which was still milky with dawn. 'He told me I was beautiful,' she said, in a voice swollen with rage, 'and that I shouldn't be angry with him. But he couldn't. That's what he said: 'I can't!' Not because he wasn't a man, but because something was stopping him. I tried to mock him. 'What?' I asked. 'What can stop a man taking a woman?'' She broke off, and gripped Zipporah's wrists. 'Do you promise you won't tell anyone — even your sisters?'

'Have no fear,' Zipporah assured her. 'And he will say nothing. I know.'

Murti sighed. 'I was struggling to get dressed again. I felt like scratching his face. He helped me to fasten my tunic by putting the brooch in place on my shoulder. That was when he said: 'Memories stop a man taking a woman.' I didn't know what he was talking about.'

Part Two
The Call of Yahweh

News from Egypt

Winter had come, and with it the rains that each year made the plains green between Horeb's mountain and the sea. Moses now had his flock. It was small, one of those reserved for a younger son to teach him about breeding and migration.

Jethro sent for Moses and told him it was time to leave for his first pasture. 'My son Hobab, my sons-in-law and my nephews have gone to Moab to sell our biggest animals. On the way back, they'll take advantage of the rains to put the lambs and calves out to pasture on the hills of Epha and Sheba, which are infinitely greener and better for the young animals than ours. That's how the rulers of those territories repay me for the counsel I give them and the offerings I make to Horeb in their names. Go to them. Tell them Jethro sent you.' From his tunic, Jethro took a thick metal disc with a hole pierced in it, through which a length of thin woollen cord was threaded. 'Show them this, and they'll know you're telling the truth. They'll welcome you and teach you what you don't yet know.'

Moses was so moved that his fingers shook as he touched the metal coin. 'How will I find them? I know none of the roads in Midian.'

Jethro could not help laughing. 'You won't be alone, Moses. I'll send handmaids and shepherds with you to show you the way.'

Moses was about to put the medallion round

his neck when he hesitated. 'You have long since paid your debt to me, Jethro. What I did for your daughters, you have repaid me a hundredfold. Why are you still so good to me?'

Jethro screwed up his eyes, and gave an ironic growl. 'I cannot answer that question yet, my boy.' Moses was disconcerted by his answer and Jethro laughed. He covered the other man's hand with his own. 'Go in peace. You need know only that I like you and that I'm weary of being surrounded by so many women.'

★ ★ ★

Of course, all the children wanted to go with Moses. Jethro had to lose his temper and make the selection himself, much to the delight of those chosen. The little caravan, consisting of the flock, and some mules and camels, set out under a sky full of low cloud. The sun did not appear all day. At twilight, the winter wind swept over Jethro's domain, bringing with it a kind of languor.

The next day, a fine rain fell, and the surface of the courtyard and the paths around the domain turned to mud.

'Let's weave a woollen tunic for Moses. You can give it to him when he gets back,' Sefoba said to Zipporah.

Zipporah claimed that she had other tasks to attend to.

'Come on!' Sefoba teased. 'Don't think you can hide anything from me!'

Zipporah's lips set in stubborn pride, so

Sefoba pointed out that now was the time for weaving and that Zipporah had to join in. Besides, nothing could be more pleasant than to work by the fire while outside the palms swayed in the icy wind.

They set to work, and for several days nobody spoke Moses' name. On the other hand, there was much talk of the latest gift Reba had sent Orma: a belt made from stones, feathers and pieces of silver. 'This time, Reba didn't risk coming to give it to her himself. But how constant he is! Has anyone ever known such perseverance? And the belt is so beautiful!' Like the fabric Orma had disdained, it had come from somewhere far away in the east. Sefoba and the others chuckled, and wondered how long it would be before Reba declared himself.

'Who knows?' Sefoba said. 'The belt may end up in little pieces under my bed with the fabric.'

The other women giggled.

Later the same day, when she and Zipporah were alone, Sefoba cried suddenly, 'I'm so happy for you!'

Surprised, Zipporah stared at her.

'For a long time,' Sefoba went on, 'I thought, like the rest of the women, that you would never find a husband. And now look!'

'Look at what?'

'The men of Midian are stupid. It took a man from Egypt to see the daughter of Cush for what she is — a precious jewel!'

'What are you talking about?'

'Zipporah! Don't pretend with me — or I'll think you don't love me any more.'

Zipporah returned to her work.

'I have eyes in my head,' Sefoba went on. 'Orma isn't the only one who can read a man's face. Or a woman's.'

Zipporah's hands were shaking, and she gripped the weaving frame to steady them. 'And what do you read in my face?'

'That you love Moses.'

'Is it so obvious?'

Sefoba laughed. 'As plain as the nose on your face. On his, too, I promise.'

'You're wrong.'

Sefoba protested with another laugh.

'You're making a mistake, Sefoba, because you love me.'

'Am I? Are you telling me you're not in love with him? Are you telling me you don't fall asleep every night thinking about him, that you don't wake up in the night hoping he's beside you in the darkness? Are you telling me it isn't true?'

'It *was* true, but not any more.'

'What do you mean? May Horeb protect us! Are you going as mad as Orma?'

Zipporah tried to laugh with her, but she could not stop the tears, long suppressed, that welled in her eyes. Sefoba's laughter vanished as quickly as a flame is extinguished. 'What's the matter? Zipporah, my darling!' Sefoba knelt by her sister and lifted her face. 'I wasn't mocking you. I've seen the two of you and . . . Not often, perhaps, but I know what I see.'

Zipporah pushed away Sefoba's hands, and wiped her eyes on her sleeve. 'You're mistaken.'

'Perhaps I am. Explain it to me, then.'

'Leave it be. It doesn't matter.'

'Come now.'

Zipporah hesitated. She had given her word to Murti, but Sefoba was like a part of herself. 'You must promise to say nothing. Not to Father, not to anyone!'

'I promise before Horeb,' Sefoba said, raising her hands.

So Zipporah told her of her days and nights of torment since Moses had pitched his tent nearby, and how, one morning, she had found herself beneath the sycamore on the road to Epha just as Murti fled from him.

'Poor Murti,' Sefoba said, 'but what a silly girl. You can do that to a shepherd but not to a man like Moses.' She touched Zipporah's face with her fingertips and wiped away the last tears. 'What a relief she didn't tell you it was because of Orma.'

'Yes, it was,' Zipporah admitted. 'I was afraid Murti would say, "Moses wants your sister, and nobody but her."'

'He's too clever for that.' Sefoba chuckled. 'Only Reba wants Orma and no one but her.'

'I was relieved at first. Then I realized what a fool I am. Of course he had a life before he came here. A wife even, perhaps children. And if not a wife, then a woman. Many women. They say Egyptian women are beautiful. I'm sure he's just waiting for the moment when he can go back to Egypt. What am I to him? Jethro's black daughter.'

Sefoba had been listening in silence, but now

95

her anger burst out: 'Listen to you! 'Not a wife, but a woman! Many women! They say Egyptian women are beautiful . . . ' Why not goddesses with the heads of cats or birds? Or Pharaoh's own daughters! May Horeb and my father forgive me, but this is the first time you've been in love and it's made you stupid. Moses turned away a handmaid. So what? Moses thinks about his past! He has memories! Does that stop him taking a woman into his bed? I don't believe a word of it. I've also looked at him long and hard. I'm a married woman — perhaps that's what gives me a clearer view of things. All I've seen is a man like any other man. From head to foot, and even in the middle.'

'Sefoba — '

'Let me speak! Moses is like any other man. Of course he thinks about his past. But he's here now, and his past is vanishing like water from a gourd in the desert! And soon, when his gourd is empty, Moses will want a woman, like any other man. Or, rather, not like any other man, but like a lord. He certainly behaves like one, and he doesn't want to be caressed by a handmaid. Jethro's daughter, though, the finest, the most intelligent, her father's favourite, now that's another matter — No! Don't protest! It's time you faced the truth. You haven't seen the way Moses looks at you. You're in love, which is more painful than shedding blood every moon. You don't know day from night. But, as Horeb is my witness, I tell you this: Moses hasn't only been taking an interest in the children. He's been studying you, your skin, your breasts, your waist, your back. He's been hanging on your words and your silences, your knowledge and your pride. He, too, has pride, so he has the measure of yours. And he likes it all. When he sees you, I'd swear he isn't thinking about his memories then. Wait till he gets back — then you'll see for yourself.'

But twenty days later, when the caravan of Jethro's sons, sons-in-law and nephews returned, Zipporah was unable to confirm that what Sefoba had said was true, because Moses was not with them. One morning at dawn, a few days from home, he had disappeared.

★ ★ ★

That day Jethro arrived back, dusty, from a visit to the palace of King Hour, whom he had advised not to launch a punitive expedition against some lords of Moab who had stolen a flock and killed three shepherds. It was in the evening that he heard the news. 'Disappeared? Moses?'

Hobab nodded and drank a long draught of beer. Like his companions, Jethro's son seemed as thirsty as if he had crossed the desert without a gourd of water within arm's reach. 'One morning I went to his tent,' he said, giving his goblet to a handmaid. 'I was thinking of going hunting with him — we'd seen a small herd of gazelles on the previous days — but his tent was empty. We waited two whole days before we set off again. Everyone was impatient to get home.'

He fell silent and watched, with a smile, as

more beer was poured into his goblet.

Softened by his son's smile, Jethro waited until he had taken another long drink. Zipporah was biting her lips to hold back the cry of impatience rising in her throat.

It was already night, and she had had to wait all day. Several times she had broken off from her work with tears in her eyes, barely able to breathe. Since she had learned of Moses' absence, she had been tormented by wild thoughts, like a knife twisting in her guts. The handmaids glanced at her anxiously and spoke quietly when she came near, as if she were a woman in mourning. Two or three times Sefoba had put her arms round her trembling shoulders and hugged her, trying to console her. But they would know no more until Jethro asked questions so they had to wait, as if for deliverance. And Jethro, drunk with joy at seeing his beloved son again, seemed to have forgotten Moses.

Hobab and he had been inseparable all day, sitting side by side under the canopy to receive the greetings of other members of the household and caravan. Jethro asked the same questions of those returning from the long journey: how had the journey been? Whom had they met? How well had they traded? How had the women and children fared? Who had been born and who had died? Hobab called his companions one by one, and each time the greetings began again.

Jethro and Hobab had the same thin face, the same incisive eyes. The long road from the land of Moab, the dust and heat of the desert had

98

furrowed deep lines in Hobab's face, making him look older than his years. He and his father might easily have been mistaken for each other, were it not for their hair and beards — Jethro's thick and white, Hobab's short and black. Like Jethro, Hobab was scrawny, but everyone in Midian knew he was capable of enduring a long trek across the desert. No one had a better sense of direction amid the deadly valleys of sand and stone in Ecyon or the Negev, or in the sun-baked folds of Horeb's mountain. Admittedly, he possessed neither Jethro's wisdom nor his sharp intelligence, but his father was proud of him. 'Hobab,' he would say, 'knows the strength of the desert and the power of Horeb's mountain. That's just as important as wisdom.'

Now, as he warmed his hands over the fire, Jethro frowned. 'There must be a reason. A man doesn't disappear for no reason. Especially that man.'

A half-smile on his lips, Hobab looked at his father, then at his sisters. Of the three Orma seemed the least concerned, but it was evident to him that her indifference was pretence.

'A man unlike other men,' Hobab said at last. 'And a man who seems to have worried you and my sisters.'

'Speak for them, not for me,' Orma protested. 'I've long held my own opinions about him — the Egyptian slave! I'm not surprised he vanished without warning. He came to us out of the desert like a mad dog. He would have stayed there if Zipporah and our father hadn't become besotted with him.'

Sefoba sighed. Jethro, as if he had heard nothing, took a piece of meat from the platter of roast lamb before him and chewed it.

Zipporah found it impossible to be so casual. 'Did you welcome him, you and your families?' she asked, with a throb in her voice.

'We gave him all the consideration he was due because Father had recommended him to us.'

'Did he tell you who he was?' Orma mocked.

Hobab took another gulp of beer. 'Orma, beauty of the age,' he replied tenderly, 'don't pull that face. I know as much about him as you do. I also know he thinks you're beautiful and that he's sorry he disappointed you by not being a prince of Egypt.'

'He disappointed me? Well, really!'

Hobab ignored her. 'I was with him in the desert. I hunted with him, I sat with him and the armourers in the evening,' he went on. 'He didn't need any prompting to tell us about Egypt and the reason he fled. I liked his honesty. I'm pleased you gave him your trust, Father. It didn't take me long to know that I wanted him as my friend. But he still left without a word.'

'Perhaps he didn't plan to be gone long,' Zipporah suggested.

'I doubt it, sister.'

'Why?'

'The day before yesterday, we were joined by a group of armourers returning from the quarries on the mountain. They said they'd seen a man on a camel riding away from the road to Yz-Alcyon.'

'Going west,' Jethro muttered.

100

'Yes, straight to where the sun sets. At first, the armourers thought he was a thief wanting to steal metal from their quarry. One turned back and followed him for almost half a day. Of course, we can't be sure he was Moses.'

There was a silence, while everyone considered what had been said.

Hobab ate a little meat. 'He's not on the road to Yz-Alcyon,' he said pensively, 'so if he doesn't get lost, and if he doesn't fall off a cliff, he might be able to go round the mountain to the Sea of Reeds. It's a long journey, though, and not easy for a man on his own.'

'He's going back to Egypt!' Zipporah and Sefoba cried in unison.

'Yes,' Jethro agreed. 'To Egypt, of course.'

' "Of course"?' Orma cut in. 'Why 'of course'? If he killed a man, why go back to Egypt to face punishment?'

Jethro clicked his tongue. 'Moses is on his way to Egypt. Right now, he could be on a boat in the middle of Pharaoh's sea.'

'If he can handle his camel,' Hobab said.

'You haven't answered my question,' Orma said. 'What will he do in Egypt?'

Hobab laughed. 'See Pharaoh, perhaps.'

They all looked at each other. Zipporah suspected that, beneath his mockery, her brother had another thought in mind. 'You know something more,' she said angrily.

'Don't make those lioness eyes at me, sister,' Hobab said.

Jethro raised his hand to silence them. He nodded at Hobab. 'Tell us.'

101

It had happened the day before Moses disappeared. At the hour when the sun was about to reach its zenith, Hobab's caravan had met some Akkadian merchants returning from Egypt with a long column of about a hundred heavily laden camels and an equal number of others that were not yet fully grown. They were on their way back to the opulent cities on the banks of the Euphrates, which they had left a year earlier. The pack-saddles on the camels' backs were overflowing with fabrics, graven stones, wood from the land of Cush, even cane boats such as were only made in the land of Pharaoh.

As was the custom, both caravans had halted and pitched their tents for the night. Then they had sat down to drink and exchange news. When the merchants discovered that the armourers were with Hobab's caravan, they had been keen to buy weapons with long iron blades, and were disappointed to learn that everything had been sold in the markets of Moab and Edom.

'I was as disappointed as they were.' Hobab sighed. 'I'd have liked to exchange the weapons for some of the young animals they were offering. Grey-haired she-camels from the delta of the Great River, Iterou, far more beautiful than ours. When they saw my disappointment they promised that one day they'd come this way and then we'd do business.'

'But what of Moses?'

'Ah, yes, Moses . . . He'd been with us for

102

nearly a moon. He sat down with us to drink milk with the merchants. He didn't say a word, didn't even seem curious about them, but he listened, even smiled when they made a joke. When everyone had spoken, he asked if they had any news of the sacred cities to the north of the Great River. 'Yes,' one man said. 'Every day new walls of stone go up, palaces for the living and the dead, and the slaves are working harder than ever under the whip of the new pharaoh. He's young, but he's more terrible than any pharaoh before him.' 'A young pharaoh?' Moses asked. 'Are you sure Pharaoh is young?' 'The people in Egypt say that the last flood of the Great River designated him. He's been destroying the statues of the previous pharaoh.' Hearing that, Moses stiffened. He questioned the other man as if he'd forgotten us. 'Did you see that with your own eyes or is it just hearsay?' 'No, no,' the old merchant said. 'I saw it. I was in the city of the kings during the last great flood.'

'The merchant explained how he had travelled along the Great River, Iterou, as far as Waset, the city of the kings, to sell the blue stones from the mountains of Aram that were prized as jewels by the princesses of Egypt. When he got there, he discovered that he would be unable to trade before the following season. Pharaoh had just succeeded his aged wife, who was also his aunt and had been pharaoh before him, and strangers were not allowed inside the palaces.'

'What are you saying?' Jethro exclaimed. 'His wife was a pharaoh?'

'That was what the merchant said,' Hobab

103

said, amused. 'The new pharaoh was first the nephew then the husband of the old pharaoh, who was a woman. He mentioned her name, but I couldn't repeat it.'

'A woman?' Jethro repeated, amazed.

'Yes.' Hobab laughed. 'But listen to this. Before she became pharaoh, this woman was the daughter of one pharaoh and the wife of another, who was her brother. May Horeb laugh with us, Father! That's how the rulers are in the land of the Great River, Iterou.'

'But what of Moses?'

'Well, none of this seemed to surprise him. What did surprise him was when the merchant of Akkad said the people of Waset hadn't seen any more of Pharaoh's former wife, that she'd been confined in a palace of the dead but hadn't been given the tomb to which she was entitled.'

Moses had stood up, gripping his staff. He was pale and his eyes were shining. He had asked the merchant if he knew the Egyptian language. When the other man said yes, he had questioned him in it. His voice was harsher now, and he spoke more quickly. The merchant answered, sometimes at length, with the respect that traders display in their dealings with those in authority.

Hobab and his men might have taken offence at being excluded from the conversation because it was conducted in a language they did not understand. But they were discovering a new Moses, confident, authoritative, solemn — emotional, too — and nobody had protested.

'When they stopped talking,' Hobab said, 'it was as if Moses had swallowed poison.'

'And you have no idea what the merchant was saying?' Orma asked, no longer feigning indifference.

'As I said, he spoke the language of Egypt.'

'Didn't you ask Moses what had upset him?' Sefoba asked.

'I didn't like to.'

'And the merchant,' Orma insisted. 'You could have questioned him afterwards — '

'Hobab did right,' Jethro cut in.

'Moses isn't a man to question,' Zipporah said, stony-faced. 'He says what he wishes you to know. He showed us that.'

Hobab threw her a sharp look, then smiled and nodded. 'You're right, sister. Anyway, he sat for a while in thought, then stood up and apologized for speaking in a language we couldn't understand. 'I know I've been rude,' he said, 'but my knowledge of the language of Midian is still poor, and I wanted to be sure I understood what I heard.' He bade us goodnight and the next day at dawn he was gone.'

'Hm!' Jethro said. 'That was only a pretext. Moses knows our language well now.'

'What does that mean?'

Hobab looked directly at Zipporah. 'It means that whatever he heard from the merchant, he wanted to keep to himself.'

The She-Pharaoh's Son

The summit of Horeb's mountain had long since vanished, shrouded in the clouds that moved endlessly southwards like ash. From time to time, Zipporah had to pull her veil across her face to protect it from the sand and dust rising off the road. She held tight to the jar of beer balanced on her shoulder. The folds of her tunic flapped around her hips and thighs. She leaned forward to resist the fury of the wind.

On coming over a crest of scrub-covered rock, she found herself below the village of the armourers. Cradled in the hollow of a long fault that snaked from cliff to cliff at the foot of the mountain, it was shaped like a vast oval. Its walls of rough brick and roofs of palm leaves covered with earth blended into the rocks and ravines around it. But the courtyard, five or six times as large as Jethro's, was alive with noise and activity, visible through the smoke of the fires and forges, whose stench caught Zipporah by the throat. The smoke curled in the wind, as if rolled round an invisible finger, then dispersed into the turbulent clouds.

The perimeter wall, on to which all the houses backed, had only one opening: a heavy wooden door coated with earth. The village was really a small fortress, closed to all except those whom the armourers wished to enter: they were anxious to guard the secrets of making the precious weapons from iron that were much sought-after by rulers from the Euphrates to the Iterou.

Between the gusts of wind that flattened the thornbushes, Zipporah heard the first blows and turned on to a path in which the recent rains had left gullies. Immediately, the grave, piercing sound of a ram's horn rang out, announcing her approach. She continued her descent, pushing back her shawl so that her face was clearly visible. When she reached the foot of the slope, she walked past the pen where the mules were kept, powerful, long-haired beasts, capable of carrying heavy loads of wood or ferrous rock from dawn to dusk.

The door in the perimeter wall opened, and two men came out, clutching long iron swords. The door closed behind them. Zipporah took a few steps forward.

'Zipporah! Daughter of Jethro!' the shorter and fatter of the two men cried, his toothless mouth open in a wide smile, revealing his pink tongue and gums. 'Welcome to the armourers' village.'

'Greetings, Ewi-Tsour. May Horeb preserve your smile.'

Ewi-Tsour stared at the jar of beer on Zipporah's shoulder. 'Zipporah! What a joy it is to see you! Especially as you never come empty-handed.' He laughed and slapped his companion's shoulder. 'Relieve Zipporah of her burden.' Then he turned. 'Open the door!' he cried. 'The daughter of Jethro the sage wishes to regale us with her father's beer.'

107

A moment later, Zipporah was crossing the great courtyard. Wives and handmaids appeared in doorways. Children came running, recognizing her and calling to her, jostling each other to hold her hand. She reached inside her tunic, took some honey cakes from a canvas sack and distributed them amid cries of delight.

Ewi-Tsour shook his head. 'You certainly know how to make yourself loved,' he said, with pretended mockery, and chased away the children.

'My father asked me to tell you that we have jars of honey for you.'

'He is wise and good,' Ewi-Tsour said approvingly, screwing up his eyes. 'But you didn't come here just to give us beer and honey.'

In a few words, Zipporah explained the reason for her visit. Ewi-Tsour nodded and pointed towards the north end of the huge courtyard. 'Follow me,' he said.

The furnaces stood in the eastern curve. Like silos used for storing grain and oil, each was covered with a thick layer of red clay but had an opening at the top, like the neck of a jar, from which emerged coils of brown smoke and, from time to time, sputtering flames, so bright they were almost transparent. All around, men were moving, pushing hollowed canes through the holes at the base of the furnaces then blowing hard into them. In front of a larger hole, from which a beak of charred pottery protruded, two men in leather tunics were using long stakes with flat ends to guide a glowing thread of molten iron into a hollowed stone.

Twelve paces away, under a vast canopy, other armourers, also dressed in leather but with their arms bare and glistening with sweat, were beating ingots that lay on burning embers with sledgehammers. The sound was so loud that Zipporah felt as if it were going through her chest. She was tempted to put her fingers in her ears, but did not. The stench of burnt earth was so strong that she could barely breathe. From time to time, sparks spat from the furnaces, butterflies of fire that the wind dispersed into the grey sky.

Ewi-Tsour saw her face. 'You're out of luck,' he shouted to make himself heard. 'It's really stinking today! The boys are making coal in the well.'

He pointed to a small group of young men bustling around a brick coping from which coils of thick brown smoke poured. He smiled, showing his pink gums, then led her to a half-open door. Beyond it, men sat on the floor of a large room, polishing iron blades with sand and strips of ox hide that dripped with grease. When Zipporah entered they looked up. The greetings over, Ewi-Tsour turned to one of the men, half of whose face had been consumed by fire. The skin on that side was taut, cracked in places and strewn with monstrous, hardened swellings, making unrecognizable what had once been lips, cheek, temple, eyelid and ear. As the man's beard grew only on the intact part of his face, he was like a creature with two heads, one of which resembled something from the underworld.

109

'Elchem,' Ewi-Tsour said, 'Jethro's daughter wants you to tell her where you saw the stranger from Egypt.'

'You told Hobab, my brother,' Zipporah said, holding the gaze of the man's one eye. 'He thinks that when you saw Moses he was heading towards Egypt.'

Elchem grunted in assent. Ewi-Tsour made a gesture of encouragement. The man turned, so that only the undamaged side of his face was visible. 'Yes, I talked to Hobab,' he said. His voice surprised Zipporah: it was youthful and clear. 'I followed the stranger. He was leading his camel away from the roads. I thought he was a thief. There are often thieves lurking around our quarries. But he went past the quarries. Your brother Hobab thought he was going north, hoping to cross the desert to the land of the Great Flood. It can be done, if you're brave. But he must have given up because I saw him again the day before yesterday, on the road to Yz-Alcyon.'

'You saw him?'

Elchem nodded, stretching his lips into what must once have been a beautiful smile. 'He was a thousand paces from me. He wasn't on his camel, but walking next to it.'

'That's a long way from here,' Zipporah murmured.

The man stared at her insistently with his single eye. 'The sky was grey, it was windy, and I have only one eye. But, as everyone will tell you, it's a good one. It was him, believe me, daughter of Jethro. Ask them.' He indicated his

110

companions, who grunted in agreement.

'Have no fear,' Ewi-Tsour said. 'Elchem's words are as solid as the metal we make.'

'He was bare-chested, like an Egyptian,' Elchem went on. 'None of us would travel like that, especially not in such cold weather.'

'I believe you, Elchem. I'm just surprised. So, will he be back now on my father's land?'

'No, he wasn't going towards Jethro's domain. He was heading for the sea. For the great cliffs.'

A big smile appeared on Zipporah's face. 'Of course!' She gave a joyful laugh and, in a gesture that impressed the rough armourers, she bowed, seized Elchem's hands and lifted them to her brow. 'May Horeb give you rest from his wrath, Elchem.'

★　★　★

She heard Moses' voice. A low murmur, like a hum. She came to a halt on the path, a few paces from the terrace outside the cave. She had to catch her breath before she could allow Moses to see her.

She took a few steps back, until she touched the cliff. Below, on the beach, the sea, alternately flashing green and grey with spindrift, made a crunching sound as it washed over the shingle.

She closed her eyes and placed her palms flat against the rock. The wind was blowing, hard and relentless, sometimes bringing Moses' voice to her loud and clear, sometimes obscuring it. She realized he was not speaking the language of Midian. The sounds he made were long, urgent

111

yet gentle. His voice was suddenly very close. She opened her eyes.

He was there, three or four cubits from her, advancing towards the edge of the terrace and the void beyond, eyes closed, forearms — adorned with the heavy gold bracelets — held out in front of him, palms open. She almost screamed in terror at the thought of him toppling over into the void.

He stopped a few steps from the edge and stood there in a curious posture, his chest thrown out and his back arched. His eyes still closed, he resumed speaking, more ardently this time, as if he was trying to project his prayer beyond the sea.

He's speaking the language of Egypt, she thought. He's praying to the gods of Egypt!

He was not yet aware of her presence. She felt ashamed to be watching him like this, but she was too fascinated to leave — fascinated by his face, by the new clarity of his features. She had never seen Moses' face like this. He had shaved! Clumsily, though — there were cuts on his cheeks and chin.

For the first time in her life she was looking at a man without a beard. Moses' face was youthful and vulnerable. She lowered her eyes, thinking how soft those exposed cheeks, chin and neck would feel if she touched them with her fingertips.

Suddenly Moses crossed his arms over his chest. The bracelets jangled and flashed in the sun. His voice became lower, almost inaudible, until it ceased altogether.

112

Silence enveloped them, broken only by the wind and the surf.

Not daring to look at him again, Zipporah moved away from the cliff. Trying not to dislodge any stones, she began to climb up the path.

'Zipporah!' Moses' voice echoed behind her in the cold wind. The voice she knew, the voice he used when he spoke the language of Midian. 'Don't go!'

She pulled her shawl tight over her chest and turned. His bare face was even more unsettling; his nose seemed stronger, his jaw broader, his eyes darker. He reached out a gold-circled arm. The memory of the man in her dream came back to her, sending through her a shiver of fear and desire.

'I'm happy to see you,' Moses said gently, taking a step towards her.

She struggled to hold his gaze, incapable of movement.

'Oh,' Moses said, laughing and touching his cheeks, 'my face has startled you. It's an Egyptian custom. You must be clean-shaven to address Amon.'

He laughed again, which gave Zipporah the courage to look at him. She stammered an apology for disturbing him at prayer. He indicated with a gesture that it was of no importance. 'You knew where to find me,' he said. He did not seem surprised.

'We were afraid you'd left for Egypt.'

'Your brother must be angry. It was not polite of me to disappear.'

'No, he isn't!' To herself Zipporah's voice

113

sounded too loud and sharp. 'Neither is my father, nor I . . . '

She was afraid. Afraid he wouldn't find her beautiful enough, afraid her skin was too dark, afraid of her Cushite face. Moses had become a stranger again, an unknown man, with bare cheeks and a prince's bracelets.

'The whole household has been hoping you would return,' she said, almost swallowing the words.

Twilight was approaching. On the horizon, a cloudless strip of sky was turning red. Reflections shimmered on the sea like thick pools of blood.

'It's true,' Moses said. 'I wanted to leave for Egypt, but I had no idea of the route. I led the camel your father gave me into a quicksand, but he struggled out, then refused to go any further north. I listened to him, and we came back here. The truth is, I have no desire to go to the land of the great Maat.' He made a violent, angry gesture, and turned to look at the reddening horizon. He shook his head. 'There's nothing for me there,' he said, as if he was talking to himself.

'Why come back to this cave and not to my father's domain?' Zipporah asked.

He glanced at her, but did not reply immediately. Then he said, 'Come, don't stay on the path. I have water if you're thirsty.' The gold glittered on his arm as he pointed to the cave. Only now did he become aware of his bracelets. He took them off. 'I had to speak to Amon, the god of Pharaoh and my mother,' he explained. 'It was easier to do so here than in your father's

114

house; I might have offended Jethro, and the altar to Horeb where he makes his offerings.'

He reached the far end of the terrace. His sack and staff were there, and so was the painted casket. He opened it and put the gold bracelets inside. He was no longer hiding anything from her, Zipporah thought, but that did nothing to calm either the fear or the desire that were at war in her blood. The light was fading quickly. The horizon was aflame, like the armourers' fires. Soon, it would be dark. There was still time for her to go home. She knew the way well enough, even in the dark. To stay here with Moses would be a significant step, and the thought made her tremble. But modesty and shame made her tremble more. She lowered her eyes, turned her hands and looked at her palms.

Moses came closer. 'It's late to start back to your father's house,' he said, 'but I'm sure you know the way, even at night. I could go with you.'

She looked up at him. They stood together in silence, aware that every moment contained a promise.

Moses was the first to speak. 'Stay with me,' he whispered. 'I want you to know who I really am.'

'Why?' Zipporah saw the pulse beating under the bare skin of his neck. It was still not too late — if she could find the strength — to turn away and go back up the path to the top of the cliff. She thought one last time of her sisters and Jethro. Especially Jethro. She wished he were here to encourage her.

'Because only you might understand,' Moses

said, and his voice sounded as it had when he was praying to Pharaoh's god.

Zipporah lowered her eyes. There was another silence, heavier than before.

Then she broke the spell. 'It's getting cold,' she said briskly, stepping aside. 'We must light a fire and get the wood ready before night comes.'

★ ★ ★

'The Akkadian merchant I met with your brother Hobab told me my mother was dead,' Moses began. 'The woman I always called my mother, although I didn't come from her womb. I never saw my true mother's face. I don't even know her name.'

The flames were high and whirled in the wind, which beat against the cliff. Beyond the shifting shadows on the walls of the cave, the darkness was total. There were no stars in the sky. The night was empty of life. It was as though they were the last man and woman left alive in the world, both protected and lost in their halo of quivering light suspended between earth and sky. The murmur of the surf faded. Moses spoke calmly, hesitating only when a word escaped him or emotion made his voice throb. Wrapped in a thick blanket that smelt of sand and camels, Zipporah listened. From time to time, she stoked the fire, adding a branch to the dancing flames.

Some years earlier, the name of the pharaoh who ruled over the land of the Great River, Iterou, was Thutmose-Aakheperkare. He was considered one of the wisest and most powerful of the Divine Sons and Protectors of Maat. Thanks to his alliance with Amon, the greatest of the gods, the river's floods had never failed to bring abundant harvests. He was a great warrior, who conquered lands to the north and south, and regained the strength and wealth that his forefathers had lost. With the labour of Hebrew slaves, he had enlarged palaces and temples, building whole cities from the sand and mountains.

Until the day it became clear that the descendants of Abraham and Joseph were multiplying in proportion to their ever-increasing burden. Pharaoh had to listen constantly to his counsellors' fears. 'What will happen when the Hebrews are equal in number to the people of the Great River, Iterou? What will happen if they become aware of their own strength? If war comes, they'll side with our enemies. If we're wise, we'll destroy the seeds of revolt before they bear fruit. Let us exhaust them in work! Let us stop them multiplying!'

So it was that Thutmose-Aakheperkare decided that the throats of all the first-born sons of the Hebrews should be cut at birth.

How to describe the cries, the tears, the weeping of women already big with child? Many hid, or lied to save their sons. Others came up with subterfuges to avoid the little boys being put to death. Among them was the woman who bore Moses. 'Who she was, where she lived, how I was found — even today I know none of those things. But I know that the woman I called my mother did not give birth to me.'

117

Here, Moses paused for a long time. Her face burning, Zipporah did not move.

'The woman I knew as my mother was the beloved daughter of Thutmose-Aakheperkare,' Moses resumed coldly. 'Hatshepsut. Mother Hatshepsut, I called her. As far back as I can remember, her face calmed my tantrums and nurtured my childish pleasures. It was the face of a wise, gentle sovereign.'

As soon as his beloved daughter was born, Thutmose-Aakheperkare had wanted to make her a queen, but the priests opposed him. So, after much manoeuvring, Pharaoh had given her a husband: his own son by another wife. A weak man who would succeed him as Thutmose II.

'That way, my mother could rule the country without attracting the wrath of the priests. But she knew her frail husband couldn't give her a son. I suppose that was why she disobeyed her father's orders, took a Hebrew baby to her breast and pretended he had come from her womb through the will of Isis and Nephtys — which made me the son of Pharaoh.'

So, Zipporah thought, clasping her hands to stop them shaking, Moses was indeed what Orma had first thought him: a prince. Nor could she doubt any longer that he was the man in her dream, a man like no other.

'Mother Hatshepsut was as tender to me as a mother could be. I can still feel the touch of her lips on my brow and the memory of her scent in my nostrils. Where I came from, only she and one of her handmaids knew. It was easy enough to convince her husband, whom she despised,

118

that I was his son. But to lie to Pharaoh, her father, before he died and climbed into Amon's boat was more difficult . . . I was given the name Moses. Nothing was too splendid for me. I was taught everything that one 'appointed by Amon' had to know: written words, the order of the stars, time and the seasons. I was taught to love and be loved. I was taught to fight, to command, and to despise everything that was not the will of the rulers and gods of the Great River, Iterou.'

Moses looked at Zipporah, but she averted her eyes. He waited a little, as if drawing his memories from the wind and the surf.

'I lived and thought not only like the son of Hatshepsut and Pharaoh but also like a man of the Great River. Occasionally, when I went to admire some new column or temple, I saw slaves. I didn't think of them as men and women. They were Hebrews, and they were slaves. Hatred and intrigue opened my eyes and led me to the truth.'

Thutmose II had died young. Moses, now a man, felt no sorrow at his death. He looked with indifference at the corpse on Amon's boat. But as soon as the stones of the tomb were sealed into place, the palaces and temples came alive with plots. Hatshepsut, radiantly beautiful and confident — as nobody had been since her father — of the help and support of the priests of Amon, advanced under the sun in male garb, clasping to her chest the sceptres of Osiris, the whip and the gold crook. The tiara of the kings of Upper and Lower Egypt was placed on her golden wig. The priests of Osiris muttered, but bent their heads and knees.

The abundant harvests that followed earned her the trust and gratitude of the people, which increased the anger of the nobles, who hated her because she was a woman. In the hope of pacifying them, she married her nephew, a young man the same age as Moses, promising that when the time came he would become Thutmose III. But what should have been a guarantee of peace became a further source of hatred.

'How could it have been otherwise? Thutmose is strong and handsome, loved by the priests and feared by the soldiers. He and I played the same games and were taught by the same masters. We fought together and prayed to Amon together. Suddenly we were both in my mother's room, I as her son and he as her husband! It was all too obvious which of us she loved. The corridors of the palace were buzzing with rumour and suspicion. Thutmose was told that he would never become the Divine Son and Protector of Maat because my mother Hatshepsut was manoeuvring for me to be the one designated by Amon. Of course, he believed it.'

It was known that Thutmose II had been weak. Doubts were cast on Moses' paternity. An investigation was launched. The handmaids were questioned — presumably under torture — about the men who might have shared Hatshepsut's bed. No lover was discovered — but an even greater secret came to light.

One day Thutmose summoned Moses to the great hall of his palace. They had often eaten there together, enjoying the dancers and

120

magicians. That day the room, with its high columns, was empty but for the throne of Thutmose. Armed guards stood behind every door. On his brow, Hatshepsut's young husband wore a gold serpent, the royal insignia of Ka. His eyes sparkled with joy and venom.

Moses stepped forward.

'Come no further!' Thutmose commanded, in his high-pitched voice. 'I know who you are.'

'Who I am?' Moses asked, surprised. 'What do you mean, brother?'

'I'm not your brother!' Thutmose screamed. 'Never say that word again!'

'What do you mean, Thutmose? Why are you so angry?'

'Be quiet. The priests have consulted Hemet, Khnoum and Thot. They've also questioned one of your mother's handmaids . . . ' He laughed sardonically. 'Your 'Mother Hatshepsut', my devoted wife, Divine Daughter of Amon, Queen of Upper and Lower Egypt! This is the conclusion they've come to. You're no one, Moses.'

At that moment Moses had realized that those who had been plotting against Hatshepsut had found the weapon they had been looking for. He waited for Thutmose to stop laughing. 'I have never claimed to be what you are, Thutmose,' he declared calmly.

'Quiet!' Thutmose's cheeks were flushed, and he was gripping the arms of his throne so tightly that his knuckles were white. 'Slave! Slave, and son of a slave! You're a Hebrew, a son of the multitude, a blemish on my palace! That's what

121

you are. Hatshepsut never gave birth to you. You're a lie, a Hebrew first-born who has no right to live!'

Moses was stunned, but when he tried to ask questions, Thutmose screamed more insults and called the guards. That night, Moses was thrown into the prisoners' pit.

'After a few days,' Moses said, taking the wood from Zipporah and putting it on the fire, 'they led me to a building site to the south of the Great River, Iterou, where they put me to work among the slaves — my own people, although I couldn't understand their language. It was there that I killed Mem P'ta, the architect and overseer. I had to flee without seeing my mother Hatshepsut again. I had no idea what had happened to her until we met the merchant from Akkad and he told us. 'In the land of the Great River, Iterou, Pharaoh is again a man! The name Thutmose the Third is divine. The name Hatshepsut has been banished. The stones on which it is written have been broken, her statues have been overturned and her temples destroyed. When she died, she was given no boat to take her to Amon.''

Zipporah shivered. Moses had fallen silent after these last words. She heard him sobbing. He had got to his feet, and was standing with his face half in shadow. Now he turned his back to her, walked to the edge of the cliff and faced the night and the wind.

'I grew up and was loved,' he cried, 'but knew nothing of the slaves who built the palaces where I slept. I thought I was someone I wasn't. I'm no one! Thutmose was right. But my people . . . Oh, my people! How can they live as they do? How can they bear it?'

Zipporah stood up. The blanket fell from her shoulders, but she was hardly aware of the cold. Moses turned to her. In the light of the flames, tears glistened on his cheeks and in his eyes. He flung his arms wide as if he were about to shout again, but at that moment there was a loud rumble, like a roll of drums, not from the sea, it seemed, but from the depths of the cave. It was a dense, fierce, powerful sound, and when it came a second time they cried out in fright. Then it stopped.

'Horeb!' Zipporah whispered, in a strangled voice.

It returned again, like a lament deep within the cliff. This time, it seemed that the rocks themselves trembled in response.

'What is it?' Moses asked tonelessly.

'Horeb,' Zipporah repeated, in a more soothing tone. 'Horeb is speaking. Horeb is angry.'

With a grimace, Moses turned to the darkness, then back to Zipporah. She had crossed her hands below her chest, palms open, and closed her eyes. Neither said anything. They listened to the noise of the wind and the surf.

They kept listening, but now, in the darkness, from where Horeb's anger had sounded, they were aware only of a vast emptiness. The rumbling did not return.

Zipporah relaxed. 'Tonight,' she said, smiling, 'his rage was brief. Perhaps he heard you and was answering you. Perhaps your rage is his.'

Moses looked at her suspiciously. Was she mocking him? 'Horeb is not my god. I have no god. Who is the god of the Hebrews? I don't know him.'

'I saw you praying for the woman who was your mother,' Zipporah countered gently.

Moses shrugged, and the tension left his face. 'I wasn't praying to Amon. I was praying to her.'

Now she did not know what to say. She felt the cold of the wind through her tunic. She thought how warm she would feel if he held her in his arms. But when he took a few steps towards her, she retreated instinctively.

He stopped. 'Now you know who I am. I haven't hidden anything from you. My soul is as naked as my face.'

She retreated, until her back touched the rock. 'What about me?' she said. 'Do you know who I am?'

'Jethro's daughter.'

She laughed, and held out her arms, their colour blending into the darkness. 'With skin like this? Can you really think so?'

Before she could shrink away, he imprisoned her fingers and drew her to him. 'You are Zipporah the Cushite, the woman Moses saved from the hands of the shepherds at the well of Irmna. You are the woman who always knows where to find me, the woman who brought me food without knowing who I was.'

★   ★   ★

They were standing flat against the wall, breathing rapidly, their faces distorted by the flickering flames. In spite of the sharp edges of rock digging into her, Zipporah was aware of nothing but Moses' body pressed to hers. She had wanted what was happening now with as much fear and passion as others wanted to live and die happy. She thought of pushing him away, but that would have been to lie to herself.

'You know who I am,' she heard him say again. 'Oh, Zipporah, don't look at me as if I were a prince of Egypt — don't be like your sister! I have nothing. I'm a Hebrew with no god and no family. Your father gave me my first camel and my first flock. You are rich, and I am nothing but the reflection I see in your eyes. You are the woman who desires my kiss and I thirst for you.' Moses' fierce breath was like a wind fanning a flame. He was right: she was the woman who desired his kiss — and she could not help thinking of him as a prince, a powerful man, a pharaoh's son, and of how different they were: how he was fair and she was dark — dark, and even weaker than the Hebrews.

Moses touched her lips lightly with his fingers, as he had once before, in this cave, on the day she had been overwhelmed by the sight of him. She wanted to say, 'No, Moses. It's a sin. I've never been touched by a man.'

She could feel his member pressed against her belly, and could hold back no longer. Urgently, she pulled Moses' face to hers, and her lips parted beneath his . . . If Horeb had rumbled at that moment, she would not have heard him.

★ ★ ★

They were lying on the blanket. The flames were less bright now, but they could still see each other.

'I see you,' Moses murmured. 'Your skin is no longer as black as the night.'

She was kissing him as if their kisses could wipe away the tears forming in her eyes.

Moses removed the brooches to loosen her tunic, kissed the hollow of her shoulder, and placed his bare cheek on the tender curve of her breast. She pushed him away, hungry for the skin she could feel beneath her fingers. She closed her eyes.

Moses undressed her, heedless of the icy wind. He, too, closed his eyes. 'I see you with my fingers,' he said. He caressed her hips and belly and thighs as if he were sculpting them.

Zipporah felt and saw Moses' slender fingers, his princely hands giving shape to his desire.

He leaned over her. 'I see you with my lips,' he said. 'You are my light.'

She saw his luminous brow, his lips kissing the hollow between her breasts, searching for the nipples, parting her thighs and drawing his pleasure, like water from a well.

She gave herself to him, gripping his shoulders, then placing her hands on the small of his back, crying out to catch her breath. There was a pain that lasted an instant, and then he was inside her. Fire spread through her chest, and she felt a sharp yet tender mixture of pain and pleasure as Moses bent over her, whispering words she could neither hear nor understand.

126

She gripped his thighs and buttocks as she had gripped the man in her dream. Then, in a moan the wind carried away, they at last breathed in unison.

★ ★ ★

That night, coming together and moving apart, exhausted but not sated, they barely slept. When dawn came, the wind was still blowing, and Horeb's mountain was still disgorging turbulent clouds like smoke from a forge, but between the clouds the sky was blue.

Zipporah was the first to rise. She washed in the cave with water from the gourd, out of sight of Moses. Soon she was the same woman she had been when she had arrived the night before.

Below, on the beach, the surf was also the same, although the sea was transparent now. In the light of day, the hollow formed by the terrace and the cave seemed as tiny as a nest. Moses and Zipporah were merely a man and a woman lost in the immensity.

Moses had crept up behind her. Now he put his arms round her waist. He was still naked. 'I'm going to see Jethro,' he said, his mouth close to her ear. 'I'm going to speak to him and ask him to give me his most precious daughter.'

Zipporah did not move, did not reply. She did not stroke the arms that embraced her, or lean against the body that had left the imprint of its desire on her skin. She kept her eyes fixed on the horizon. Somewhere out there was the shore of Egypt, although she could not see it. She remained motionless and silent — so much so that Moses took away his arms and moved to look at her, anxiety clear on his brow.

'What were you saying to your god yesterday?' she asked. Without taking her eyes off the sea, she held out her hand, brushed it lightly over Moses' chest, stroked his stomach, slid her fingertips over his member, then took his hand in hers and squeezed it.

'Yesterday,' she said, very gently, 'you were praying for your mother. I'd like to know the words you cast on the sea.'

'I'm not sure I could say them in the language of Midian.'

'Yes, you can.'

He hesitated. She gave his hand an impatient little shake. His body close to hers, Moses turned his eyes towards Egypt and said,

'I am perfect,
I am living in the truth,
I am pure, I am pure,
Here are my hands, here on my palms is my
    heart,
It is pure, it is pure.
Let this heart be weighed in the balance of
    truth,
I am nourished by truth,
I have not known the hardness of the heart,
I have given cool water to whoever was
thirsty, wheat to whoever needed it, linen to
    whoever walked naked.
O forms of Eternity, let this heart be
weighed in the balance of truth.'

Zipporah's eyes filled with tears. Without letting go of her hand, Moses moved closer to her so that their bodies touched. 'It isn't that I worship Amon, or any of the other gods of Egypt. I no longer belong to them and their heaven is no longer for me. This prayer is spoken as the boat takes the dead person towards the heaven of rebirth. My mother Hatshepsut was faithful to Amon.'

A limpid tear ran down Zipporah's cheek, perfectly transparent against her dark skin in the light. She waited until there was no longer a knot in her throat. 'My mother died on that sea as she led me to the arms of Jethro,' she whispered.

Moses waited for her to say more.

'You were right to want to return to Egypt,' she said. 'Your place is there.'

He could not have been more astonished if she had struck him. He let go of her hand, and stepped back. 'What are you saying?'

She did not reply, merely smiled.

'My place is here, Zipporah, with you and your father. What is there for me in Egypt?'

'When you killed Mem P'ta, you began your battle against Pharaoh,' she said, in a clear voice, the voice Orma disliked so much. 'You have to continue.'

Moses stared at her, uncomprehending, pain spreading over his features. 'Are you driving me away? After last night? I told you, I'm going with you to see Jethro. This very morning, on the camel he gave me. I'll talk to him. I'm going to pitch my tent again beneath the sycamore on the road to Epha . . . '

She shook her head.

Moses held out his arm in the direction of Jethro's domain. ''Jethro,' I'll say, 'give me your daughter Zipporah as a wife. She is the seed of my future life. I will be your son and will give you back a hundredfold all you have given me.''

'Moses — '

'I'll build up my flock. I'll go to every pasture in Midian. I'll sell the animals next winter. We'll have several tents. You will be Zipporah, the wife of Moses, a respected woman. No one will ever again mutter about the Cushite. No one will ever again dare raise his hand to you.'

She pressed both hands against his chest. 'Moses! You know who you are now. You are not no one, as your false brother in Egypt claimed. You are a Hebrew. A son of Abraham and Joseph.'

'Why should that matter to you?' he cried. 'You aren't a Hebrew!'

She saw terror in his golden eyes. How could such fear have been instilled in a man like him? She dug her nails into Moses' chest and pushed her hips against his. 'Last night,' she breathed, 'when you were screaming into the wind, you weren't weeping for your mother the Pharaoh. You were crying out in anger against the suffering of the slaves. That was what Horeb heard.'

'I don't know what you're talking about! Horeb isn't my god — he doesn't know me.'

'Don't blaspheme! You know nothing about Horeb. He is wrathful and he is just. And you were born among the slaves, even though

130

you acquired the knowledge and strength of Pharaoh. Why else did you kill the architect?'

Moses pushed her away. 'Nonsense!' he cried. 'You know nothing of the power of Pharaoh. You know nothing of the cruelty of Thutmose! It's impossible to fight the one Amon designates!'

'I know that you must put on your gold bracelets and go among those who are your people. You must hold back the whip that strikes them.'

'I killed a man because I was angry, and I ran away like a little boy. That's the truth. There is no other. No man can hold back Pharaoh's whip. You don't know what you're talking about!'

She let him shout and said nothing. Her silence increased his fury.

'I told you, I'm not a prince. I thought you had more sense than your sister. Don't you want to know the man I am?' Moses' cries echoed against the cliff.

Zipporah seized his wrists. 'I *do* know the man you are! I saw you in a dream before I even met you. I know who you are and who you can become. Your future is not here among the pastures of Midian.'

Suddenly Moses' anger faded, and he laughed long, loud and mockingly. He raised Zipporah's hands to his lips and kissed them. 'If your father didn't place such trust in you, I'd think the woman I want as my wife is not only a Cushite but also a little mad.'

Zipporah pulled away abruptly, her eyes as dark as her skin. 'If you don't believe me, there's no point in your going back to see my father.'

131

'Zipporah, how can you be so sure of my future?'

'As I said, I saw you in a dream. You are one of those who save life when it's in danger of being extinguished.'

An ironic smile played on Moses' lips. 'Tell me about your dream.'

'You wouldn't understand.' She walked past him to set off up the cliff path.

Moses put his hand on her belly to stop her. 'Don't send me away. Tell me the dream. Let me go to your father.'

She pushed his arm away, gently, and could not stop herself stroking his cheek, where the beard was starting to grow back. 'First, you must understand who you are.'

'I know who I am! I'm no one. Those who flee Pharaoh lose even their shadow.'

'So I, too, am no one. My skin is the colour of shadows and, although you've possessed me, we will never be husband and wife. Shadows don't marry.'

The Wrath of Horeb

'Is that what you told him? That you're not going to marry him?'

There was incredulity in Sefoba's voice — as there was, too, in Jethro's gaze, along with a touch of reproach, which the old sage tried to soften.

When she had returned, Zipporah had seen everyone looking up at the clouds massing around the summit of Horeb's mountain. She had gone straight to her father and told him the truth about Moses, how he had been Pharaoh's son and had then been banished as a Hebrew, thanks to his false brother's hatred and jealousy.

'His anger against Pharaoh's injustice is greater than he thinks,' she had added. 'Just thinking about the sufferings inflicted on the slaves makes him scream with rage. And when he screamed, Horeb rumbled with him. But he knows nothing of Horeb and he's afraid.'

Her sisters had come running to listen to her, and Jethro had not ordered them away.

'Did you sleep there?' Orma had asked. 'In the cave? Next to him?'

Zipporah had looked directly at Jethro. 'He wanted me,' she had replied, her voice as strong as ever, 'and I was happy to let him take me.'

They were all speechless with astonishment.

'Moses is like any other man,' she went on. 'I know that. I see it in his face and sense it when

133

I'm close to him. But he doesn't yet know his own strength. He dwells on his past in Pharaoh's house. He is blind to the future.'

Jethro looked steadily at his daughter. Zipporah saw embarrassment, joy, disapproval and even hope in his gaze. She was ready to listen to his judgement, perhaps even to obey it — but he did not have time to utter a word. Orma was already on her feet, her lips white.

'Listen to her! How dare she talk like that — she, who has just cast a blemish on us? Father, how can you let her say such things? She offered herself to the Egyptian, and you say nothing.'

Now Sefoba, too, stood up, tears in her eyes. For once, she could not understand Zipporah, and thought Orma's anger justified. Jethro was not looking at them. Suddenly he seemed made of stone, his mouth hidden by his beard, his eyelids closed and smooth as ivory.

Orma took this silence as weakness. 'I was the first!' she shouted angrily. 'I told you I knew he was a prince. Here, under the canopy, Father, I told you — you heard me! I said he was lying when he claimed to be a slave. As soon as he appeared at the well of Irmna, I knew. And Zipporah and you humiliated me by believing his lie.'

In the courtyard, the handmaids turned but did not dare to approach. They were more worried than curious, and even alarmed by Orma's strident voice, as though the wrath of Horeb had descended to earth in a mass of black clouds.

134

Zipporah stood up. Her hands were shaking, and her throat was dry. Orma's hatred was a living thing, a wild beast. She felt it clinging to her face and chest, tearing at her body, wiping out the memory of Moses' caresses. And she, too, was beginning to feel hatred. She made as if to respond, but Orma screamed louder than before: 'Quiet! Every word you say is a blemish on this household. You are a blemish on all of us! That's why Horeb is angry!'

'Silence!' Jethro's voice rang out. He had raised his arms with a strength that belied his frail body. 'Silence, girl!' he thundered. 'Close your mouth before yet more hatred issues from it!'

Orma swayed, as though Jethro had slapped her. In the stunned silence that followed, she let out a strange moan, clearly the prelude to a flood of tears.

Sefoba bit her lip and threw an anguished glance at Zipporah, who had covered her mouth with her hands. Never before had the two sisters seen Jethro like this: his eyes and cheeks were hollow with rage, the skin at his temples so taut it was transparent and as pale as the bones beneath.

'Stop this foolish whining,' he said, pointing imperiously at Orma. 'Don't use Horeb's name to me! Don't speak of his wrath. You know nothing about it.' He pointed now at the mountain.

All eyes in the courtyard turned to the threatening summit, which had jarred their nerves since dawn.

Orma moaned again. Her knees gave way, and she collapsed on the cushions. Neither Sefoba nor Zipporah dared touch her. Nobody in the courtyard moved.

Jethro towered over his huddled daughter. 'You are the child of my loins, but you are my shame. You have nothing in you but envy and spite.'

Although her shoulders heaved with sobs, Orma was not ready to admit defeat. Moving with the speed of a young lioness, she clutched her father's knees and kissed them passionately. 'Don't be unjust, Father.'

Jethro seized her shoulder and pushed her away. Orma clung tighter. 'Stop this,' he growled.

'Zipporah fornicates with the Egyptian without being married to him and I'm the one in the wrong? Is that your justice, Father?'

'My justice is something you can't understand.'

Orma let out a sharp cry, and let go of him as if a snake had bitten her, an insane laugh distorting her beautiful face. 'The only reason Zipporah opened her thighs to Moses was to take him from me! I was the first to recognize him for what he was. And I was the one he chose! I saw it in his eyes!'

'No,' Zipporah cried. 'No, you're lying!'

A crack suddenly rent the air. The summit of Horeb's mountain was like a thousand mouths of fire spitting white and yellow clouds into the endless sky where they were twisted by an unseen hand. Screams echoed through the

136

courtyard as the rumbling increased in volume and intensity.

'Horeb! Horeb!'

Sefoba rushed into Zipporah's arms, while Orma clutched Jethro's legs. This time, he looked up at the fearsome convulsions of the mountain and calmly put his arm round her shoulders. The ground shook. Another rumble echoed across the desert. Blackness flecked with incandescent jets of flame poured from the mouth of the mountain.

'Horeb's fire! Horeb's fire!'

Some clung together, joining their tears and terror. Others ran like insects or fell to their knees. The animals squealed and pushed over the cane fences round their pens. Red streaks glistened in the blackness that now covered the mountain. A grey light was spreading over Midian, draining it of colour and shadow.

Sefoba was trembling and crying. 'Horeb's fire!' she muttered.

Jethro held out his free arm and pulled her to him. 'Horeb's wrath,' he corrected her softly.

Zipporah looked at him.

He nodded. 'He awaits our offerings.'

Zipporah could hear no fear in his voice, no anxiety, but rather a curious satisfaction.

★ ★ ★

All day, Horeb continued to rumble. Ash rolled down the slopes of the mountain towards the sea, fires sprang up, and here and there bushes burst into flame. The stinking air grew thick with

137

dust, which smothered the flames and choked young birds in their nests. Fortunately, just before the close of day, a violent wind rose in the east, and the clouds from the mountain were blown towards Egypt.

In the west, the sun was hidden, and a strange shadow spread over the land that was neither night nor twilight. The streaks flowing down from the top of the mountain had come to a standstill and turned to mud from which smoke rose, and small explosions glittered — a monster batting its thousand eyelids as it fell asleep. Above, the mouth of the mountain was still incandescent, still wide open to the turbulent sky.

Moses reached Jethro's domain soon after the wind had risen, his beardless cheeks grey with dust, one hand gripping his staff, the other clinging to his camel's ashen fur. He had almost lost his way in the gloom and his eyes were wide with fear.

Hobab, who was repairing the ravaged fences with the help of Sefoba's husband, Sicheved, greeted him effusively. 'Horeb be praised! We were worried about you.'

They gave him water to wash, and wine, dates and cakes dipped in oil to take the taste of ashes from his mouth.

'You've come just in time,' Hobab said, when Moses had finished. 'Many of our animals took fright and ran away. We must find them before they die of thirst. Come with us. The others are with my father, helping him with his offerings and prayers to Horeb.'

Until nightfall, they searched for the mules and sheep. Whenever they caught an exhausted, trembling animal, they hobbled it and took up the search again. By the time it was too dark to continue, they had gone too far to return to Jethro's domain. Sicheved had been sensible enough to put a pack-saddle on his camel with canvas and posts to make a tent. They settled down for the night, and shared the gourd and dates Hobab had brought. The mountain had stopped rumbling, but its mouth still glowed red in the darkness, stoked by the wind. Hobab and Sicheved stood with their palms open, and offered up a prayer to Horeb. Moses listened, his body turned away, head tilted. A sharp, distant rumble seemed to answer them. More strongly than at any other time that day, Moses had the strange feeling that the mountain was alive, like a wild animal, but neither Hobab nor Sicheved flinched. Their calm impressed him. This had been a day when the whole world had seemed about to explode, yet they had gone about their work without showing any fear. It was not until later, as they sat outside the tent, that he asked the question he had held back: 'Why aren't you afraid? The mountain is still rumbling. The fire might spread and destroy everything.'

'That doesn't seem to be the will of Horeb,' Hobab replied. 'The wind has risen and is taking the ash out to sea. It won't harm the pastures or the wells. And the mountain has stopped spitting fire.'

In the darkness, Sicheved indicated the sky to the east. 'The stars are shining over Moab and

Canaan, a good sign. Whenever Horeb is angry and the sky is clear in the east, his rage passes and we're spared.'

Moses was astonished. Did it happen often? Sicheved and Hobab outdid each other in describing Horeb's most terrible rages, which had sometimes come close to destroying Midian.

'The only rages I've known have been gentle ones,' Sicheved said, in conclusion. 'They say it's thanks to Jethro and the justice he's brought to the kingdoms of Midian. Horeb is lenient with us.'

Hobab growled agreement.

'But why do Jethro and all of you sacrifice to Horeb and not to the god of Abraham?' Moses asked. 'Jethro claims that you're Hebrews, and even sons of the sons of Abraham.'

'You should ask him,' Hobab said. 'He's the sage.'

There was a long silence, broken suddenly by Sicheved's snoring. He had fallen asleep before he had had time to get inside the tent.

'Tomorrow,' Hobab said, in a low voice, as they lay down side by side, 'we'll go back, and you can speak to my father about Zipporah.' Moses sat up, but Hobab laid a hand on his shoulder. 'Have no fear, I'm happy with your choice. I love Zipporah. Like everyone else, I thought she would never find a husband. Nothing could please me more than to have you as my brother. I know you'll make her happy. Even if she isn't always the easiest of women.'

Moses sighed. 'Think again, Hobab. Zipporah doesn't want me. When I told her I'd go to your

140

father and ask for her hand, she said no. And now I don't know what to do. I'm at fault with her, your father and all of you. But she's the only woman I want.'

Hobab laughed. 'Be patient. Zipporah loves to do things in her own way. You mustn't doubt that all she wants is you. My father, too. It's rare for Zipporah and him to disagree, and she always obeys him in the end.'

Moses sighed again, unconvinced.

'Speak to my father tomorrow,' Hobab insisted. 'He will command. He seems the most amiable of men, but once he's made his mind up, he's resolute. And he's certainly made up his mind about Orma.' Hobab chuckled. 'He's told the handmaids to calm her with kindness, cakes and sweet drinks. But then I'll have to escort her to Reba, the son of the King of Sheba, the man she should have married moons ago. Pity me, Moses. I'm the one who'll have to listen to her complaints day and night. She'll talk about you, you can be sure of that. She'll talk until she's breathless. But I tell you this. You won't have Jethro's most beautiful daughter in your bed, and you're lucky. May Horeb forgive Reba much in advance! Nor will you have the gentlest of Jethro's daughters — she's already married, and her husband is right here, snoring away. The one who's left is the wisest and liveliest. You'll be kept so busy you won't have time for anyone else.'

Moses could not help joining in his laughter.

★ ★ ★

141

The wind from the east did not subside, and the mountain rumbled less frequently. Finally the sun broke through the clouds, creating a strange half-light, as if the sky in the west were dirty and bloodstained.

Tirelessly, Jethro had performed sacrifice after sacrifice. By his request, Zipporah had stayed at his side, assisting him in offering barley and wine, grinding the flour, baking the cakes according to the rites, slicing the fruit, refilling the oil pitchers. She left only when he slit the throats of the year's lambs and calves and cut open the chests of twenty doves.

She did not stop thinking about Moses for a moment. She knew that Hobab had welcomed him and that he had gone with him and Sefoba's husband to search for the escaped animals. She was full of gratitude towards her elder brother. It was his own discreet way of showing everyone his trust in, and affection for, Pharaoh's son.

She knew Moses had returned, and had again pitched his tent beneath the sycamore. She feared she would not be able to resist the desire to go to him. She was told how Orma had shamed Hobab as they were setting off to see Reba. As they passed Moses' tent, a tearful Orma had begged him loudly to follow her. Moses had looked at her without a word, made a gesture of reassurance, and gone back into his tent. Then he had left with Sicheved to visit the wells and clear them of ash.

Finally, on the third morning — the mountain had stopped rumbling the previous day — Sefoba joined Zipporah as she and the

142

handmaids were washing clothes. Pink-cheeked and smiling, Sefoba knelt beside her, and placed on a basket the tunic they had woven for Moses. 'You look exhausted. I'll take over.'

Zipporah returned her gaze. 'From the rings under your eyes, you're as tired as I am.'

Sefoba chuckled. 'Sicheved came back last night after dark. He was hungry, thirsty and grumpy. Men! Horeb rumbles and spits, but we don't look after them well enough! I had to spend all night reassuring him of my love.'

They burst out laughing. Then Sefoba took Zipporah's hand and placed it on the tunic. 'Moses is back,' she whispered. 'He's with Father now. Rest now, make yourself beautiful, and, when they call you, go to him with this tunic.'

Zipporah stiffened.

'Come on!' Sefoba murmured. 'Forget what you told us. Horeb's wrath has come and gone. We're all going to be happy.'

★ ★ ★

Jethro greeted Moses as best he could, given that his domain was still in disarray. He sat him down beside him beneath the canopy, and asked the handmaids to bring pitchers of beer, goblets and food. They ate and drank, watching the white clouds around the summit of the mountain rising straight into the sky, where the wind continued to push them westwards.

Jethro looked tired and drawn, but there was a sly gleam in his eyes. Pharaoh would soon see his

143

sky grow dark, and perhaps he would not have such rich harvests. Had Moses seen such things when he lived in the land of the Great River, Iterou?

Moses evaded the question: he wanted to talk about Zipporah. But after three sentences the words he had prepared failed him. 'I thought I'd made progress in the language of Midian,' he said, ashamed. 'But as soon as I have something important to say, all that comes out of my mouth is noise.'

'Let me speak then,' Jethro said, laughing. 'I have something to ask you.' He looked Moses in the eyes, his own shining so brightly it was as if they still smarted from the smoke of his offerings to Horeb. 'I know what is in your heart. Zipporah told me. She has also told me about the life you led in Pharaoh's house.'

Moses tried to interrupt, but Jethro silenced him with a gesture. 'Let me tell you this. Nothing I have learned surprises or displeases me. There are things a father prefers not to know, which I shall simply forget. Zipporah is the jewel of my heart, and, as Orma so cruelly remarked, it has made me an unjust father. You have seen only three of my daughters here. I have four others who live with their husbands in the kingdoms of Midian. They'll all tell you I love them dearly, that I give them everything they deserve to have. But Zipporah is special.'

He sighed, drank some beer, and again looked up at the mountain. He nodded and his mouth quivered in an inaudible murmur. Moses

144

wondered if he was praying, or if he was a little drunk. But then the old man looked straight at him, with the eyes of a man who has seen much in his life, and Moses was surprised to see that they were moist with emotion.

'I remember that day as if it were yesterday — the day the boat brought them to our shore, her mother and Zipporah. Horeb wanted me to be there. I rarely went to the seashore, but that day Hobab, who was still only a little boy, wanted to fish. From the top of the cliff, we saw a boat lying overturned on the shingle and, in the middle of the beach, what looked like a heap of black seaweed. The Cushite mother, exhausted as she was, had taken the child on her back and, with the strength of a lioness, had crawled across the shingle to get away from the waves. She died before she could utter a word, but with her eyes she told me everything she needed to say. Her daughter was not much bigger than my hand. She was bawling with hunger and thirst . . .

'It was the saddest day of my life, and the most beautiful. My beloved wife had been dead for many years. And now Horeb was providing me with the opportunity to give life.

'I held the baby to my chest. Swallows were circling overhead. I said, 'Your name will be Zipporah — Little Bird.''

Jethro paused as if the silence might reduce the power of his memories.

'In her way, Zipporah became flesh of my flesh. I brought her up like my own daughters, just as if she had been the fruit of my loins. I

145

gave her everything I could — food, jewellery, trust and knowledge. Knowledge, above all. Even when she was a child she was wiser and more perceptive than her sisters — and even Hobab. Apart from Orma, everyone felt for her what I felt. Nobody was jealous. Alas, Zipporah's skin is black. The men of Midian are men of Midian. Their prejudices blind them more than the sun. How could they recognize her worth?'

'Jethro!' Moses interrupted, picking up his stick, which he had placed across his knees, and shaking it. 'Jethro! When I saved your daughters from the hands of the shepherds, I hadn't even noticed Zipporah, hadn't seen whether she was beautiful or ugly, hadn't seen what colour her skin or her eyes were. But the moment I saw her, may your god strike me dead if I lie, my one hope was to have her as my wife. It was as though she cast a spell over me, like one of Pharaoh's court magicians. When she looks at me, I feel confident. When she's by my side, not even the iciest winds can chill me. When she's far from me, I'm cold and weak. My sleep is filled with nightmares so I spend nights with my eyes open, thinking about her. It isn't me you have to convince, Jethro, it's her. Zipporah doesn't want me. Ask her.'

Jethro curled his thick beard with his thin fingers. 'Listening to you, my boy, I take note of two things: that you are now much more fluent in our language than you think, but that you still know nothing about women. Anyone would think you had never met any in Pharaoh's house.'

Moses lowered his eyes.

Jethro summoned a handmaid. 'Ask my daughter Zipporah to join us.'

Moses became agitated, opening and closing his mouth like a fish, which made Jethro laugh. 'Trust what my eyes tell me. My daughter Zipporah looks at you as she has never looked at any other man. Her one desire is to be your wife. She'll tell you so herself.'

★ ★ ★

'You're right, Father,' Zipporah replied curtly when Jethro asked her the question. 'I have no other desire than to be Moses' wife. It's a necessity, if I don't want to remain a *naditre*, a fallow woman, as they say in Midian, and bring shame on you.'

'Good!' Jethro cried, slapping his thigh. 'Your wedding feast will be soon, then.'

'No.'

'Oh?'

'For the moment, it cannot be.' Zipporah's face was as hard as her words.

'Oh . . . ' Jethro repeated, although he did not seem upset. 'Sit down, I beg you, and tell me why.'

Without looking at Moses, who was rolling his staff nervously between his hands, Zipporah knelt on a cushion. 'Why must I explain to you what you already know, Father?'

'Does Moses also know your reasons?'

'Moses knows. But he thinks he is a shadow. He cannot walk in the footsteps of what he has

147

been, but neither does he want to embrace his destiny. What good would a Cushite be to him? And what good would one more shadow be to a Cushite? What a burden!'

Twice already, Moses had tightened his grip on his staff, as though he were about to stand up and leave. He had hoped for Jethro's support, but the old sage seemed to take a wicked pleasure in his daughter's replies. Hobab had been wrong: Jethro was not going to force Zipporah to his will. He played with his beard and observed: 'You're hard, daughter.'

'She isn't hard, Jethro — she isn't thinking properly!' Moses cried. ' 'Go to Pharaoh,' she says, 'and tell him that what he's doing to the Hebrew slaves is unjust!' But if I show myself to Pharaoh, he'll kill me! I won't have time to open my mouth. The slaves themselves don't fight Pharaoh, even though there are thousands of them, they submit to him. Who am I to help them? Why should I succeed where all others fail?'

'Because you're Moses!' Zipporah cried. 'Not only the son of a slave woman, but also the son of the Queen of Egypt.'

Moses waved his staff as if he wanted to break it in two, and roared almost as loudly as Horeb: 'Jethro! Tell your daughter she's wrong! Thutmose refused Amon's boat to the woman who was my mother. He's had all her statues torn down. Why should he listen to me? What would the Hebrews gain from my making him even angrier?'

'There is truth and wisdom in what you

148

say,' Jethro admitted.

'Of course!' Moses exclaimed in relief.

Zipporah remained impassive.

Jethro was silent for a while. 'What do you think of that, daughter?' he asked her at last, tilting his head.

Zipporah turned to face Moses. She seemed as determined as ever, but there was tenderness in her eyes now. 'There are always reasons not to do what we fear. Often they seem wise, but anything bred by fear is always evil. Lift your eyes to the summit of the mountain, Moses, and see in which direction Horeb is sending the clouds of his wrath.'

'Horeb isn't my god,' Moses said irritably.

'That's true,' Jethro said, having nodded at each of Zipporah's sentences. 'Horeb isn't your god. He's our god, the god of the sons of Abraham and those who suffer Pharaoh's whip.'

Moses flushed and lowered his head.

Zipporah took his hand. 'Moses, I had a dream, and for moons I searched for its meaning. When you arrived, I understood it. Horeb rumbled to greet your arrival among us. He is speaking to you.'

'Is that so?' Moses mocked. 'Who am I listening to now? Jethro's wise daughter or a superstitious old woman?'

Zipporah rose to her full height, lips quivering. 'Listen to this, then: as long as I live, no man other than you will touch me or be my husband. But you will only be Jethro's son-in-law the day you set off on the road to Egypt.'

'You know it cannot be!' he cried.

Jethro quickly took them both by the hand. 'Hush now, hush . . . Why assert today what may prove false tomorrow? Life is made of time, and so is love.'

The First-born

Jethro had told them to take their time, and it was a strange time that now began. For more than a year, Zipporah and Moses alternated between quarrels and peace.

At first, they avoided each other for days on end. Then, one night when the moon was full, the earth shook again and Jethro's household was in panic. Everyone rushed out into the darkness, eyes and ears alert. There was rumbling, but it was weak. The summit of the mountain was surrounded by a halo of pink light. Everyone feared that Horeb's wrath had returned, and the men remained watchful. Moses was standing outside his tent, beneath the sycamore. He did not see Zipporah until she was quite close to him.

Neither said a word, but stood with their faces lifted towards the mountain.

'Listen!' Zipporah said at last, in a low voice. 'Listen! Horeb is speaking to you.'

Moses laughed deep in his throat and turned to her. They were both trembling with desire. Moses stroked the line of Zipporah's lips. 'It's your mouth that's speaking to me. That's what I want to hear. Its silence consumes my nights.'

Moses moved his fingers from her lips to her neck, then to the hollow of her throat. Zipporah seized his wrist as if to push him away, but instead she clung to him and received his kiss as

151

if it were the breath of life.

Before long, their caresses impelled them inside the tent, bodies entwined, heedless of anything that was not their love.

In the morning, Sefoba guessed that Moses and her sister had been overcome with passion and reproached her. Zipporah answered that it was perhaps their passion that had appeased Horeb. Moses had woken at dawn and, finding himself alone, had rushed out of the tent, calling Zipporah's name, scattering the birds in the sycamore, to find that the sky was a limpid blue. A few wisps of smoke hovered over the summit of the mountain. Horeb had stopped rumbling. Never had Midian seemed more peaceful.

Before nightfall, Moses went to see Jethro and asked him the question he had put to Hobab on the day the ash had fallen. 'Why do you sacrifice to Horeb rather than the God of Abraham, if you are his sons?'

Jethro paused a moment for reflection, and replied with another question: 'What do you know of the God of Abraham and Noah?'

'Only what I heard from the Hebrews in Egypt — that He had abandoned them.'

Jethro sighed. 'He abandoned us because we were no longer worthy of His trust. A long time ago, He offered a covenant to Abraham. 'Go,' He told him. 'I will make you a great nation. I will uphold this covenant between myself and you, your children and all their children . . . ' Abraham obeyed and gave birth to sons and nations. There was a time when everywhere, from horizon to horizon, men and women were

152

protected by the God of Abraham, whom they called the Everlasting. But generations passed and as much hatred and wickedness grew up as there are nations, sons and brothers. In return for His covenant, they offered the God of Abraham only sand. So the Everlasting withdrew, full of wrath. That is all we have left of Him now. The wrath that rumbles over our heads, the wrath we call Horeb.'

Jethro closed his eyes, raised his hands, palms open, then clapped them together and nodded vigorously.

'That is the truth. All we have left of our ancestors' great covenant with the Everlasting, who brought them out of nothing, is darkness and wrath. With every day that passes, Horeb's wrath feeds on our sins. He demands justice and righteousness. He watches us impatiently. He knows our past, but he also knows the future that awaits us. He sees that we are advancing into darkness. In his impatience, he rumbles to shake us out of our torpor. All he receives in return is fear, but what he wants is courage and dignity.'

Jethro had become so impassioned that Moses felt afraid. In the sage of Midian's words he heard an echo of Zipporah's. He could no longer be in any doubt that father and daughter thought as one.

★   ★   ★

At the end of spring, Zipporah announced that she was with child. Jethro was the only one to take the news in his stride. The others, including

153

Sefoba and Hobab, all urged her to accept Moses as her husband so that she would not bring a child into the world alone.

'Alone?' Zipporah would reply. 'My mother was much more alone than I when she put me into the boat that brought us to Midian. I have all of you. I have my father Jethro.' When they objected, she would continue, 'Moses has been entrusted with a great task. Who knows if he will be able to fulfil it? It is a heavy task, a terrible one. But my promise remains: the day he sets out for Egypt, I will be his wife.'

They would respond with assertions that Moses would never have the courage.

'He's no coward,' she would retort. 'The only reason he refuses to return to Egypt is that he doesn't yet know who he is. Perhaps he will when he sees his child.'

Meanwhile Moses fretted and fumed. Despite the desire that set his body aflame, he did not dare approach Zipporah for fear of her reproaches. He was told that she was in good health, and that her belly was swelling. Then he would hear of things she had said about him that sent him flying into a rage, and he would set off with his flock and be away for many days. But he always missed Zipporah. He would come back and lurk near Jethro's domain in the hope of seeing her. Then, when he had, he would retreat to his tent, tense with desire, his beloved's new silhouette imprinted on his mind: she was still straight and tall, but with a round belly. He would spend all night thinking of the face he had glimpsed, her skin bronze in the evening sun, her almond eyes, the delicacy of her nostrils. He would clench his fists and moan like a caged beast, desperate for her heavy breasts and the curve of her back.

Whenever Hobab and Sicheved, with whom he often shared his meals, plied him with questions, he would reply: 'I'm becoming skilful as a shepherd. Is there anything wrong with that? Do the women of Midian despise shepherds? What more could a mother expect for her children than a good shepherd to watch over them?'

They would laugh and joke about what women did and didn't want. Sicheved would mock Sefoba, who was always waking him in the middle of the night to make sure he was still devoted to her.

But these moments of gaiety did not last long, and Moses would soon become grim again. 'There is no man alive,' he would mutter darkly, 'who could rise up against Pharaoh and defeat him. Of course I could take the road to the west with my beautiful Cushite wife. We'd be captured before we even reached the banks of the Great River, Iterou. Much good that would do the Hebrews! Is that my great destiny — to lead my wife into the lions' den?'

One dawn, at the end of his tether, before anyone had risen, he went and knelt by the side of Zipporah's bed. She woke up and saw him. His beard had grown again: it was thicker than ever and cut in the Midianite fashion. He looked quite different now from the man who had possessed her in the cave.

Without a word, she smiled and placed his hand on her soft, taut skin, beneath which life throbbed. Moses savoured the caresses he had so long awaited. It was a moment of pure joy. But then they became awkward with each other again.

'Whenever you want to see my belly,' Zipporah whispered, 'there's no need to roam the pastures with your flock. Just come to me.'

'But we are in sin,' Moses said. 'I cannot even share a meal with your father. He's always saying that no one acts justly now, that no one behaves as his ancestors did . . .'

Zipporah could not help laughing. 'Oh, Jethro's ancestors sinned.' She told him the story of how Abraham had persuaded Pharaoh that Sarah was his sister. 'He, too, was afraid of Pharaoh. And Pharaoh was so attracted to Sarah that he didn't want any other woman, even though he had spent just one night with her.'

'And what did he do when he learned the truth?'

'He expelled Abraham and Sarah from Egypt, cursing them for his lost happiness. But Abraham was never punished by his God for that sin, even though it's one of the worst anyone can commit.'

Moses was so astonished that he asked Zipporah to tell him everything she knew about Abraham. And so it was that they often came together early in the morning or at twilight, before and after the day's work. Moses would stroke Zipporah's belly while she told him what Jethro had taught her about the Hebrews. Moses

156

could hardly believe what he heard. Sometimes he doubted Zipporah's words, thinking she was either embellishing the truth or making it darker to provoke him, and he would run to Jethro. 'Is it true,' he would ask, 'that Noah and his household were the only people left alive on earth? Is that possible?'

Jethro would laugh and nod. 'Listen to my daughter,' he would reply. 'Listen to my daughter.'

But Moses would return with other questions. 'Zipporah says that Lot had sons from his daughters? Can that be true?'

Or it was Abraham's anger with his father Terah that he found hard to accept. Or the jealousy of Joseph's brothers. That after Joseph was sold to Potiphar, he had become almost a brother to Pharaoh and saved Egypt from famine shook him most.

To each of his questions, Jethro would give the same reply: 'Listen to my daughter.'

Zipporah was pleased that Moses was interested in the stories. To her father, though, she expressed her impatience: 'He listens, but does nothing. His child is about to be born and he still hasn't decided to be what he must be.'

'You must be patient,' Jethro would say to calm her. 'He's listening and learning. Time is doing its work in his head as it is in your womb.'

One day, Zipporah broke off in the middle of a story. Her eyes were wide, her body shook and she could hardly breathe. She cried out in pain and Moses leaped to his feet. She regained her breath and mustered enough strength to smile

— he looked so pale and lost. 'Call Sefoba,' she said. 'Call the handmaids.'

Soon the old woman who acted as midwife was growling orders in the courtyard. Sefoba and the handmaids held Zipporah over the bricks of labour until the sun was more than half-way across the sky.

Moses, Hobab, Sicheved and a few others took their places with Jethro and drank beer and wine. Through the walls they could hear Zipporah's moans. Moses' brow glistened with sweat. With each cry, he swallowed a mouthful of wine. By the time Zipporah's cries were joined by a baby's, he was in a drunken sleep and did not hear anything.

★ ★ ★

The boy was resting, tiny and pink, between Zipporah's breasts. He had her broad face, but Moses' skin.

'That's good,' Zipporah said huskily. 'The more he resembles Moses, the better.' She fell asleep easily.

In the morning, Jethro came to see her. He seized her hands, his eyes bright with joy.

'It is you,' she said to him, 'who will choose the name of my son and will cut his foreskin, according to the tradition of Midian.'

'The name is easy,' Jethro replied, lifting the child. 'We'll call him Gershom — the Stranger.'

When Moses learned that his son would have to lose a piece of himself on Horeb's altar, he protested, 'Do you want to kill him when he's

158

just opened his eyes? Do you want to make him impotent?'

'They did it to me when I was born,' Jethro replied. 'As you can see, I'm still alive and I've had seven girls and a boy.'

Moses was not appeased. Jethro explained that the God of Abraham had demanded that His covenant be inscribed in the skin of all His sons. 'We still do it in Midian because it's the last link we have with our ancestors.'

'That doesn't apply to my son. I'm not from Midian — Zipporah even less so.'

He went to see Zipporah. 'You can't do that to my son,' he told her.

'Who are you to speak in the name of your son?' Zipporah replied angrily. 'Do you think that because you took your pleasure between my thighs you can decide his fate? Until you are my husband, my father Jethro will be a father to the child of my womb.'

Moses felt so ashamed that for a hundred days he stayed away from Jethro's domain and did not see Gershom.

With tears in his eyes, he watched the circumcision from a distance and heard Jethro cry the name of his first-born before the altar of Horeb: *Stranger! Stranger!* Each time he echoed the voice of the sage of the kings of Midian, repeating Gershom's name as if he were clasping his son to his chest.

The Bride of Blood

Zipporah learned how to be a mother. Gershom filled her nights with cries and tears that she calmed, and her days with grimaces that gradually turned into smiles. She learned to fasten her tunic so that she could carry her child with her at all times, to guess when he was hungry or thirsty from the touch of his skin, to think of him at every moment, to share his joys and fears. The other women were always with her, advising her, sometimes reproaching her gently.

All this female hustle and bustle kept Moses at a distance. Zipporah never asked for him to approach her or their child. For several moons, they seemed to ignore each other. Just once Sefoba remarked, with a touch of sharpness in her voice, that Gershom's name suited him all too well. 'Stranger! He's certainly a stranger to his father. It's almost as if he'd been born through the good graces of one of Horeb's angels.'

The handmaids chuckled. Her eyes darker than her skin, Zipporah silenced them. After that, Sefoba had to grumble at night to her husband. Sicheved would advise her to be as patient as Jethro and her sister.

'They know what they're doing. Moses is the best of men. Things will change, you'll see. Even Hobab makes a joke of it. 'According to Moses,'

160

he says, 'there's no man alive who can rise up against Pharaoh. What he doesn't know is that there's no man alive who can go against the will of my father and Zipporah!''

But if any found fault with the unusual conditions in which Gershom was being raised, they did so far from the ears of Jethro and his daughter.

Winter came. Once again it was time to trade. Moses set off with the other men to Edom, Moab and Canaan. Ewi-Tsour, the head of the armourers, joined the caravan, his carts so heavily laden with bone-handled knives, curved daggers and long hammers that each required four mules to pull it.

When their return was announced, Zipporah climbed on to a silo to see the dust raised by their caravan in the distance. Then, like all the wives in the household, she hurried to make herself beautiful. She put on a bright yellow tunic, embroidered with a red and blue woollen design in the shape of a bird's wings. She adorned herself with necklaces and bracelets and, for once, used kohl to make her eyes sparkle. Sefoba, splendid beneath her long veil, brought her a piece of amber. Zipporah rubbed her wrist with it, breathed in its heavy, spicy odour and put it away in a linen pouch.

'Why not scent yourself straight away?' Sefoba protested.

Zipporah laughed tenderly. 'Moses isn't here yet and I don't know what he has in mind. But, if need be, my hips and thighs will smell of amber for him.'

161

For three days, Jethro's domain came alive with banquets, dances and games. The air smelt of bindweed, coriander and dill. Chirruping like flights of curlews, the young handmaids filled the big jars with bitter milk and beer, and mixed the wine with rosemary and date juice. The older handmaids took the gazelles that had been killed in the desert, stuffed them with almonds, pomegranates and grapes, skewered them on long pikes and left them to turn over low fires for a whole day. Ten more fires were lit to bake honey cakes, pies filled with dates, barley and lambs' entrails, *kippu* broth and crusty biscuits baked in sheep fat until they were golden.

Hobab, Sicheved and the armourers were proud of how much they had sold. In Canaan and Edom, on the other side of the great deserts of the Negev and Shour, many feared raids by Pharaoh's soldiers, and the rich and powerful masters of the cities of Boçra, Kir and Tamar had stocked up with arms and animals without quibbling over prices. Even Moses, who had set out with his meagre flock, did not return empty-handed.

No sooner had he pitched his tent beneath the sycamore than he rushed to Jethro's domain. He found Zipporah outside her room, fussing over Gershom's cradle with the handmaids. The sight of the woman who was not his wife took his breath away.

Zipporah was as slender as she had been before her son's birth. In addition, there was a

162

calm about her, which gave her body a stronger outline, her hips and breasts an extra fullness. Her thick hair was cut short, emphasizing the refinement of her features, the breadth of her temples, the elegant curve of her cheekbones. Everything about her testified to a new, serene strength. Even her lips, rounded in a tranquil smile, seemed shaped by the words she had whispered to soothe her child.

She greeted Moses formally and ordered the handmaids to leave. Then she lifted Gershom out of his tiny bed and, for the first time, placed him in Moses' arms. Moses laughed, purred like a tamed beast, and swung Gershom in his arms, surprised by the size of the baby wriggling between his palms. 'I seem to have been gone for so long that my son should be able to stand and say his father's name,' he joked.

Zipporah nodded, and withdrew to the doorway. They both felt awkward. They did not know what to do with their eyes or their bodies, and could not bring themselves to utter the words they had murmured to each other while they were apart. Moses tried to put his son back into the cradle. He was clumsy, and Zipporah went to help him. As she did so, she brushed against him with a little laugh that made them both tremble. Hurriedly, Moses searched in the canvas sack he was carrying over his shoulder and took out a long, narrow length of cloth, on which thick purple alternated with thinner indigo stripes that shone like bronze. 'In the great cities of Canaan, like Guerar or Beersheba, the noblest women wear these round their heads.

163

It suits them well enough, though to my taste their skins were too light. I immediately thought of you and bought one.'

As he placed the cloth in Zipporah's hands, their fingers touched. He squeezed hers and raised them to his lips. Zipporah had to use all her willpower to resist the desire to fall into his arms, demand his caresses and smell on his neck the almost forgotten scent of love. 'Go to my father,' she stammered. 'He's longing to see you.'

Moses tried to draw her to him, but she pulled away gently to tend Gershom, who was wailing. She leaned over the wicker cradle and began to sing to him. She broke off to look up at Moses. 'Go to Jethro.'

★   ★   ★

Jethro was beside himself with joy at the return of his son Hobab and son-in-law Sicheved. When Moses came to pay his respects, the old sage moved his scrawny body and patted the arm of the man who was not his daughter's husband as if he wanted to make sure he was alive. Moses placed a tall goblet of chiselled silver in front of him. 'You can use it either to make wine offerings to Horeb or to quench your thirst,' he said, with affectionate mockery.

'Both!' the old sage cried. 'May Horeb protect you.'

'There's also a young she-camel outside my tent to replace the one you gave me when I arrived.'

Much to the surprise of Hobab and Sicheved,

Jethro accepted the she-camel. His cheeks were turning red with the wine, and his eyes shone as he ran his fingers over the beautiful engravings on the goblet. Moses' gift delighted him. 'Did you meet any caravans coming from Egypt?' he asked, without any change of tone, after they had talked about the main events of the journey.

Hobab shook his head. 'No. The merchants who trade with Egypt have stopped passing through Canaan for fear of pillaging by Egyptian soldiers.'

Jethro nodded. 'That's why they passed this way while you were gone. It's a long way round Horeb's mountain, and you need good guides, but it seems to have become the surest route to reach the plains of the Great River, Iterou.'

He fell silent, and so did Hobab and Sicheved. They knew that Jethro had not questioned them further in order to arouse Moses' curiosity. But Moses simply rubbed his staff between his palms in the nonchalant gesture with which everyone was familiar. Jethro put down the silver goblet. He clicked his tongue and, in the tone he used for ceremonies, declared, 'This is what I've heard, my boy. According to the merchants, the land of the Great River, Iterou, is buzzing with rumours and plots. It's being whispered that the woman who was pharaoh is not dead. According to some, she's confined in one of her palaces. Others think her former husband is keeping her in her father's tomb. Apparently it isn't considered good to have been in the Queen's affections, or even her servant. The merchants also say that the lives of the Hebrew slaves have become harder than ever, with all the bricks they're forced to produce, all the stones they're forced to carry, all the walls they're forced to build. Hundreds are dying every day, and still Pharaoh's whip is not stayed.'

Moses was on his feet, his face ashen beneath the tan he had acquired on his long journey.

'I questioned these merchants as you would have done, my boy. I asked them if anyone in Egypt had mentioned a man named Moses. 'That's a name we never heard,' they replied. 'Even among the Hebrew slaves?' I asked. 'Who knows what names the slaves whisper to each other?' they replied. 'We're not allowed near them.''

Moses walked away.

'Moses,' Jethro called loudly, 'think of this. The woman who was your mother is alive, a victim of the same hatred that made you leave Egypt. If the Hebrews don't need you, she does. She has been humiliated by her own family for having made you a son of Pharaoh, and now she has but one hope left: to see your face before her eyes close. That much I know. She loved you, she gave you her name. You may not share ties of blood, but surely you are tied to her through the caresses she gave you in your childhood. And I know, too, that a man lives a better, freer life when he can say farewell to his mother.'

Moses had kept his back turned while Jethro was speaking. Now he wheeled round. 'Nobody has the right to tell me where my duty lies!' he yelled, brandishing his staff and pointing it at Horeb's mountain. 'Not even those rocks, stones

166

and sterile dust you take to be your god, Jethro!'
He strode to the other end of the courtyard, tunic flying, and disappeared. His departure was followed by a shocked silence.

A stunned Sicheved made as if to stand up. 'He can't be permitted to say such things.'

Calmly Jethro gestured to him to remain seated. 'All that shouting is like the squeak of a badly fitted door,' he said, smiling tenderly.

'But he's insulted Horeb,' Sicheved insisted.

'Unless it's his way of imploring his help.'

'What upsets me,' Hobab said sadly, 'is that he refuses to speak to us. He never once talked about Egypt or Zipporah during the journey, and now he runs away like a thief.'

'Because he thinks he is a thief!' Jethro cried. 'He thinks he stole what he is. He's fighting his own shadow and his own heart.' He went back to admiring the goblet Moses had given him. Hobab and Sicheved's disapproval was plain. The old sage rolled his eyes slyly and patted his son-in-law's thigh. 'Let time take its course. Horeb will respond to the insult if he feels the need. It's good that Moses is angry with him. That means he's realized that he himself lacks the power of eternity. Duty and shame are boiling in his heart like overheated barley soup. Now the herb of wrath has been added to the mixture. And Horeb knows all about wrath.'

★ ★ ★

Zipporah crept out of Jethro's domain, carrying her son in a basket. Laughter and the music of

167

flutes and drums could be heard from where the dancing continued. She had tied the cloth from Canaan round her head and it gleamed in the light of the torches. There was no fire outside Moses' tent. He was sitting on a worn cushion, motionless. When he heard her steps, he lifted his face to her, a face made hard by the moonlight. He watched in silence as she put down the basket. The child was barely visible in the darkness.

Without a word, Zipporah took a few steps away. 'Where are you going?' he asked, behind her.

'To find wood for the fire,' she replied, over her shoulder.

By the time she returned, Gershom had woken and was babbling in Moses' arms.

Zipporah lit the fire with the flame of an oil lamp. Then she unfastened her tunic and gave the child her breast. Moses watched her like a man who had woken from a troubled sleep. The flames rose, revealing Zipporah's beauty, the coppery tones of her face as she bent over the child, the silky colours of the cloth from Canaan shining like a diadem on her brow.

When Moses spoke, his voice was low, as if he was afraid he might frighten his son. 'Your father said what he had to say.'

Zipporah nodded. She took Gershom off her breast, deftly refastened her tunic and laid the child on her shoulder. Like a little animal, he pushed his head against her neck. Gently she rocked back and forth, humming quietly, so quietly that the vibration of her voice passed

168

from her body to Gershom's.

Moses did not take his eyes off her. Although his face was still filled with anxiety, he made a small gesture of approval. Time passed. He pointed to Jethro's domain, where the music and the sounds of merriment could still be heard. 'Why didn't you stay and enjoy the celebration with them?' he asked.

Zipporah gave a beautiful smile that glowed in the firelight, and kissed the child's hand. 'Because you're here.'

'Does that mean you finally agree to be Moses' wife?'

She shook her head, still smiling. 'No.'

Moses closed his eyes and clenched his fists against his chest. Zipporah thought he was about to fly into a rage. When he opened his eyes again, he stared at the fire as if he wanted to throw himself into it.

They remained like that for some time, patient and quiet, waiting for their child to fall asleep. Just once, Moses reached out to put more wood on the fire. Sparks flew up into the branches of the sycamore. Gershom drifted into sleep, and Zipporah laid him in his basket. Then she knelt beside Moses and embraced him. 'There hasn't been a night that I haven't fallen asleep thinking about you,' she said softly, her lips close to his ear, 'and there hasn't been a day that Gershom has opened his eyes without my whispering his father's name to him.'

'So why do you still refuse me? Anyone would think we were at war.'

She put her hand over his mouth, pressed her

169

lips to his neck and ran her fingers feverishly over his body. She stood up and drew him with her, kissing his chest through the tunic. 'Zipporah! Zipporah!' Moses muttered, as much in supplication as in protest. She kissed him with an urgency that made them both sway, and pushed him inside the tent. In no time at all, she had undressed him. When she took hold of his member he made as if to push her away.

'You did that to Murti the handmaid,' she said. 'Will you do it to me?'

'You knew?'

'That morning, when she left your tent, I was outside.'

She had stepped away from him. He took hold of her and now, in turn, undressed her, his hands and mouth aching for her. He fell to his knees and pulled her down until she was lying beneath him.

Gasping, Zipporah offered him the scent of amber on her thighs and loins with as much impatience as those in her father's domain were devouring the feast.

★ ★ ★

Later, they lay together, their bodies entwined.

'You and your father are both wrong,' Moses said. 'Why should I confront Pharaoh to see my mother Hatshepsut? Perhaps, among thousands of slaves, my real mother is also alive. She's the one I should support, not the woman who stole her child. But she's lost among the suffering multitude, like a grain of sand in the desert

170

. . . Besides, Thutmose would be only too pleased to capture me and use me to add to Hatshepsut's humiliation.'

Zipporah did not answer.

'In Edom, Moab and Canaan,' Moses went on, 'they are preparing for war with Pharaoh. They're being forced into it and they dread it. You must realize, Zipporah, that whole nations tremble before the might of Pharaoh, yet you and your father keep telling me to go to Thutmose and ask him to lessen the suffering of the Hebrews. It's absurd.'

Still, Zipporah said nothing. She listened to her child sleeping. Her silence disconcerted Moses. He waited for a moment, then sat up. 'It isn't my death I fear,' he said, 'but the use Thutmose will make of it. What good will my corpse be to you and Gershom? I don't understand you. You are my wife, but for one word. Why are you so determined not to say it?'

Zipporah stroked his belly and chest. 'Because,' she said quietly, the gentleness in her voice softening her reproach, 'you are not yet the man who is worthy to be my husband. The man I saw in my dream.'

Moses sighed in exasperation, and fell back on to the bed. Zipporah continued to caress him. 'What you say is sensible.' She kissed his shoulders, chin and eyes. 'And you think that everything that isn't sensible must be madness. And yet, sensible as you are, you aren't at peace.'

Aware of his desire rising, Moses tried to push her away. 'The only reason I'm not at peace is because we are in sin. To everyone in Midian, to

171

everyone in your father's house, we are in sin.'

Zipporah sat astride him and drew him into her. 'How do you know you're in sin when you don't believe in the wrath of Horeb and won't obey his will?'

★ ★ ★

Less than a moon later, Zipporah announced to Moses that her blood had not come, and that for a second time he was going to be a father.

He opened his arms and clasped her to him. 'We are in sin,' he whispered in her ear.

Zipporah pressed her brow to his neck. 'My will is the will of Horeb. Listen to him!'

Moses pushed her away gently, and turned, face set, to Horeb's mountain, as if he were sizing up an enemy before battle.

The next day, Sicheved came running and announced that Moses had taken down his tent and set off with his flock, his mule and his two she-camels in the direction of the mountain.

Jethro greeted the news with a smile, but he was alone in doing so. The next day, Hobab himself returned from the western pastures. Jethro asked him if he had seen Moses on the way to the mountain.

'I was on my way back here yesterday when our paths crossed. I accompanied him until nightfall, trying to warn him of the dangers that awaited him. He didn't speak, but he made it clear that he would prefer to be alone.'

'That's good,' Jethro said.

'How can you say that?' Hobab retorted, with

172

a vigour that surprised his father. 'The pastures on the mountain are wretched, and the slopes are dangerous for sheep and camels alike.'

'He isn't going there to feed his flock,' Jethro replied.

'Then you should have stopped him. It's madness to let him leave like that.'

Jethro dismissed him with a flick of his sleeve.

'He doesn't know his way about the mountain,' Hobab persisted. 'He doesn't know where to find springs. He's sure to get lost . . . '

Jethro put his hand on his son's shoulder and pointed at the vaporous clouds swirling around the summit of Horeb. 'Calm yourself. Horeb will protect him. He'll find his way.'

Hobab shrugged gloomily, unconvinced by his father's assurance.

A few days later, Moses had still not returned. Zipporah spent all her time with Gershom. Not once did she join Jethro when he made his offerings.

'Is Zipporah ill?' he asked Sefoba, when she brought him his morning meal.

'If it's an illness to keep your mouth shut and hold back your tears out of pride then, yes, she's ill.'

'But why?'

'Oh, Father!' Sefoba said angrily. 'Moses has gone, she's with child again and still has no husband. Even the handmaids are wondering what will become of her. It's all because of your stubbornness.'

'Enough!' Jethro cried. 'When Moses came to ask me for her hand, she refused, not I.'

'But I know that if you hadn't supported and encouraged her in this madness, we would have broken bread at their wedding feast long before now.'

Days passed, and nights, and more days, and still Moses did not return. Anxiety spread through the household. All eyes were on the mountain, and each day that passed they feared that Horeb might vent his wrath.

Every morning, at first light, Zipporah went outside and looked up at the mass of sulphurous matter on the mountain, hoping it would not roll down the slopes and set the air on fire. Her belly was growing, a token of the life Moses had left within her, but also a relentless measure of the time that had passed since his departure.

One afternoon, as she was encouraging Gershom's first faltering steps, Sefoba joined her, all smiles. Zipporah got to her feet, ready to receive the good news. But the words she heard were not those for which she had been hoping. The reason for Sefoba's joy was that she, too, was with child.

'I've waited so long,' she laughed, 'and, believe me, I haven't only waited. But nothing happened while you . . . ' Sefoba picked up Gershom and covered him with kisses. 'I was afraid I was sterile, like Abraham's wife.'

She was jubilant, but Zipporah could not muster the strength to share her joy. Her own disappointment was too great. She clutched at Sefoba's shoulders like a drowning woman and burst into tears.

The next morning, as she was going out to

look at the summit of the mountain, Hobab came to her side. 'The sky has never been so clear since Moses left,' he remarked, in a puzzled tone.

They were silent for a moment.

'Where can he be?' Hobab murmured. He pointed at the mountain, a thin smile on his lips, the same smile he had worn when they had played and worked together as children. 'You watch the summit and I the slopes. If he ever makes a fire, we may be lucky enough to see the smoke.'

'He won't make a fire,' Zipporah replied, looking haggard. 'Even here he never made one outside his tent.'

Hobab looked at her as if he resented the slightest criticism of Moses.

She turned to him, eyes bright and lips quivering. 'In any case, he didn't take anything with him to make a fire, I'm sure of it.'

Hobab put his arm round her shoulders. 'There are mouths of fire on the mountain,' he said calmly. 'The flames come out through faults in the rock. You have only to throw twigs and dry grass into them to keep warm when the nights are cold.'

The following morning, Hobab joined her again, and they stood watching the night withdraw slowly from the slopes. He took Zipporah's hand. 'Why don't you go to our father at Horeb's altar and help him with the morning offerings?'

Zipporah assented with a squeeze of her fingers.

Jethro was delighted to see her, but unable to hide his anxiety. Moses had been on the mountain for far too long.

* * *

Spring passed and summer came, but the heat was still bearable. Not once did Horeb's mountain rumble, and its summit remained serenely clear. The barley harvest was the best in many years, the flocks were not affected by illness, and the caravans, which now passed more regularly on the road to Epha, came back rich from the sale of incense in Egypt. The merchants bought everything the armourers had to sell without counting the cost.

Although — as they were to remember later — the sky over Midian had never been so radiant, it was as if a dark, invisible cloud weighed over Jethro's domain. Laughter was rare, there were no more feasts, and everyone was grim-faced.

Jethro flew into a violent rage when he discovered that the oldest handmaids were weaving mourning garments, which he ordered to be pulled apart and burnt. But he could not fight thoughts and silences. Who could believe now that Moses was still alive?

'Would you be able to find his tracks on the mountain?' Zipporah asked Hobab one morning.

Hobab hesitated. He looked down at Zipporah's belly, heavy with child, and sighed. 'It would have been easier a while ago. But now? Who knows how far he climbed? He might be on the other side, where there are no springs.'

'What if he's hurt and unable to return? What if he's waiting for us to come to his rescue? I've spent days and nights imagining him like that.'

Hobab looked at the mountain for a long time, as if it were an animal lying in his path. He knew what his Cushite sister did not dare say. If Moses had died, whether by accident, hunger or thirst, his body must be found before it was devoured by wild beasts. He nodded. 'It's time we knew.'

Seven days later, he returned. What he had to report was distressing.

At the western end of the mountain, he had found half of Moses' flock, wandering unattended. Then, over a distance of five hundred cubits, he had seen the faults and ravines strewn with the corpses of the rest of the sheep, eaten by wild animals and birds of prey.

'The flock must have scattered in all directions with nobody to stop them.'

He had continued his ascent, calling Moses' name until he was hoarse. At twilight, barely half-way up, where the dusty slopes were full of stones, fallen rocks and thornbushes, he had seen the tent. 'What remained of it. The poles were broken and the canvas had been torn to shreds by the wind.'

Hobab had been unable to go on without risking his own life.

'Did you see his mule or camel?' Jethro asked.

'Neither.' He knew what his father was thinking. 'There's nothing up there, Father. Not a blade of grass, not a trickle of water.'

Jethro glared at him. 'Think again, son. There

isn't nothing up there. There is Horeb!'

The sage of the kings of Midian could no longer tear himself away from Horeb's altar. Assisted most often by Zipporah, he performed all the rites scrupulously, making ever richer offerings. He sacrificed ten of the finest sheep in his flock, two heifers and a young calf. Hobab, seeing his father squander his wealth on a man who was neither a son, a brother nor even a husband, did not protest. Sicheved even gave his father-in-law animals from his own flock to be offered to Horeb in his name.

Soon the courtyard and the surrounding pastures were covered with the thick black smoke of burning meat. They all went about holding their noses, but nobody complained. Then, in the hottest part of one day, Zipporah felt the first pains, and the linen and bricks were prepared.

The delivery was much quicker than Gershom's had been. The sun had barely touched the horizon when she gave a final cry. Sefoba, who herself was big with child, came out into the courtyard and announced that Zipporah had given birth to a boy. But before the midwife had even cut the cord and placed the baby between Zipporah's breasts, the sound of cries arose — cries so violent, so terrible, that all the handmaids who had assisted trembled. Zipporah, her body still burning from the effort of labour, sat up with a groan. Sefoba opened the door.

'He's here!' a handmaid cried. 'He's here!'

Zipporah fell back, the newly born child

178

against her mouth. An icy wave went through her body, freezing the sweat on her skin.

'Moses is here!' Hobab, Sicheved and the young shepherds yelled all together. 'He's here! He's alive! Moses! Moses is alive.'

'He came with you,' Zipporah murmured, against her child's little cheek. 'Your father came with you.'

★ ★ ★

'His mule brought him back!' Hobab said, laughing. 'It found its way all by itself with him lying on it. It's not in a much better state than he is — shivering with fever and thirst.'

'He's breathing,' Sicheved cried, 'but he won't open his eyes! How can he possibly be alive? How long is it since he last drank anything?'

Sefoba was weeping profusely. 'You wouldn't recognize him,' she muttered. 'His tunic is in shreds. Oh, Zipporah, he looks as if he's made of dust! But he's alive.'

Jethro's eyes were bright and his beard shook as he listened to everyone. 'Horeb has brought him back to us,' he kept repeating. 'I told you he would.'

Although her back still hurt from the labour, Zipporah wanted to go to the room where Moses had been laid, but the old handmaid forbade her. 'Your place is here,' she said, putting the freshly swaddled baby down beside her. 'Moses is alive. I'm going to see to him now. Trust me, be happy and sleep. You can see your Moses tomorrow.'

But soon after daybreak the next morning,

179

when Zipporah went with the child in her arms to see Moses, she had to bite her lips to stop herself crying out. He was so thin that the bones of his temples seemed about to break through his skin. He was covered with scratches, his lips were swollen, and in places his beard and hair had been burnt away. There were dark scabs on his arms, and pus oozed from his feet, soaking through the linen in which they were wrapped. When he breathed, she heard a sharp, painful whistle, as though his throat were torn.

Zipporah knelt and placed her hands on his burning brow. Moses shivered. She thought his dark eyelids were about to open, but it was only a symptom of the fever.

'The wounds on his feet and the scratches on his chest aren't as bad as they look,' the old woman said. 'They aren't deep and will heal soon. What worries me is his thirst. He must take sips only. He has a high fever and whatever he drinks evaporates too quickly.'

After a moment's thought, Zipporah asked for blankets to be brought, then undressed, lay down next to him, and demanded her child. The old woman refused.

'Make a broth of herbs and meat,' Zipporah ordered. 'Pass it through a sieve and let it cool.'

'You're going to kill him! A man mustn't touch a woman who's just given birth!'

'I'm not going to kill him. My warmth and the warmth of his newborn son will burn away his fever.' The old woman attempted to argue, but Zipporah cut her short. 'Do as I say.'

A moment later, the old woman returned with

Jethro and Sefoba, grumbling about blasphemy and calling on all the members of the household who had gathered outside the door to be witnesses.

Jethro silenced her and Hobab closed the door. In amazement, they looked at the curious spectacle of Zipporah, Moses and their son, forming a solid mass beneath the blankets. Jethro gave a dry little chuckle, and narrowed his tired eyes. 'Do as Zipporah asks,' he ordered the old handmaid.

She left, cursing. Sefoba helped Zipporah to soak a clean cloth in cold water from a pitcher, and Zipporah applied it to Moses' cracked lips. The water went into his mouth, and he swallowed with a little moan. At that moment, the baby woke up and cried to be fed. Sefoba wanted to pick him up, but Zipporah stopped her. 'Leave him. I'll give him what he wants.'

Jethro burst out laughing. 'Does my Cushite daughter plan to give birth to her husband after her child?'

★   ★   ★

It took Moses four days and four nights to fight the fever and delirium and finally come back to life. In all that time Zipporah did not leave his side, feeding him at the same time as their child, quenching his thirst and the fires of his memory.

In the middle of the third night, she was awoken by pain in her hand. Moses was clutching it, his eyes wide open. An oil lamp was burning in the room, but its light was too weak

181

for Zipporah to see if he had truly regained consciousness. With her free hand, she made sure that her child had not woken.

'They won't believe me!' Moses growled. 'They won't listen! They'll say, 'How dare you speak the name of Yahweh?'' Leaning on his elbow, he pulled Zipporah's hand so hard that she fell on top of him with a moan of pain. 'They'd believe anyone else!'

The door creaked open. Zipporah made out the figure of Hobab.

'He's woken! He's talking!' Hobab whispered, kneeling beside them. 'Moses!'

But Moses had already released Zipporah's wrist and fallen back into his feverish sleep.

Hobab saw her rubbing herself and grimacing. 'He's got his strength back, hasn't he?'

Zipporah smiled at him and stroked Moses' brow. He was breathing in rapid little gulps. 'Tomorrow he'll be even better.'

Beside her the child wailed. Zipporah drew his cradle to her. Hobab went back to his place on the bed outside the door.

Zipporah was right. The next day Moses was better. He woke during the night. Eyes wide, half frightened, half relieved, trying hard to see in the dark, he discovered Zipporah beside him. 'Zipporah?'

'Yes, Moses, it's me.'

He touched her, pressed his dry lips to her neck, and embraced her. 'I'm back, then.'

Tears welled in Zipporah's eyes. 'What was left of you came back on a mule.'

'Oh!' He shuddered, and Zipporah feared that

182

the fever was returning. 'He spoke to me,' he said, gripping her shoulders. 'He called me. He made me come to Him!'

Zipporah did not need to ask who he was talking about. She tried to push him away, but he would not let go of her.

'I must tell you. He made a fire come out of the mountain. 'Moses! Moses!' he called.'

He was agitated, his mouth and hands shaking. Zipporah placed her fingers on his lips. 'Not now. Tell me tomorrow. You need rest. You must eat and drink to have the strength to tell me.' To force him to be patient, she put the baby in his arms. 'He came from my womb as the mule entered the domain with you on its back.'

Eventually Moses calmed. He raised the child to his lips. 'I'll give this one his name. He'll be called Eliezer, 'God is my support'.'

Zipporah laughed, and relief spread through her like sudden intoxication. She hugged Moses and the child Eliezer.

'You were right,' Moses whispered in her ear. 'I must go back to Egypt. I know that now.'

★ ★ ★

The next day was a day such as nobody in Jethro's household had ever known.

Zipporah finally left Moses' bed. His matting and tunic were changed, he was shaved and scented, and at last, just before the sun reached its zenith, everyone was given permission to come and listen to him.

Jethro was there, sitting on the cushion he had

183

had carried into the room. Hobab and Sicheved were by his side, as was Sefoba, with Gershom on her knees, and Zipporah, cradling Eliezer. Sefoba squeezed Zipporah's hand. The others, the shepherds and handmaids, young and old, stood crowded in the doorway in such a tightly packed group that daylight barely penetrated the room. Moses' voice was not very strong, and they had to listen carefully.

'The flame appeared twenty paces from me. Real fire! I hadn't seen a fire since the one Zipporah lit for me beneath the sycamore. I had nothing at that point. My flock was gone, there was no milk left, no dates. I had nothing but the sandals on my feet. But there was the fire! I was so hungry that the only thing I could think about when I saw it was what I could roast on it. Then I realized that although the fire was real enough, the thornbush in front of it wasn't burning. How is this possible? I thought. Have I lost my mind? I went closer. The flames were real flames, I saw that with my own eyes, but the bush was untouched. The flames were blue and transparent, and they came directly out of the earth, with a soft, rumbling noise.'

Moses broke off, eyes lowered. The only sound in the room was his breathing. He lifted his face again, and touched his mouth, which still felt painful, with his thumb. His eyes came to rest on Zipporah, who did not flinch. Beside her, Jethro gave a nod, a sign of encouragement to continue.

'The flames were real flames, and I heard the voice. 'Moses! Moses! Here I am. Don't come too close. Take off your sandals. This earth is

184

sacred. I am the God of your father, I am the God of Abraham, the God of Isaac, the God of Jacob.''

Again, Moses fell silent, and this time he stared at those watching him as if the words he had uttered might cause laughter or shouts. Jethro's beard shook and he slapped his thigh with the palm of his hand.

'So what did you do?' a woman near the door asked impatiently.

'I covered my eyes,' Moses replied, miming the action. 'The flames may not have been burning the bush but they were searing my eyes.'

'Don't interrupt him,' Jethro grunted. 'Let him tell his story. The next person who speaks will have to leave.'

They all looked at Jethro reproachfully. But it was true that Moses was still weak, and if his story was as long as his absence had been, he would have to marshal his strength. They let him continue without further interruption.

He spoke of the anger in the voice: ''I have seen the whip falling on the shoulders of my people in Egypt. I have heard them cry out beneath the blows of the slave-drivers! I have come down to deliver them. Go, Moses! I am sending you to Pharaoh. Bring my people out of the land of Pharaoh. Bring the children of Israel out of Egypt. I shall deliver them from the hands of the Egyptians and lead them to a good, spacious land, a land flowing with milk and honey! Go! I am sending you to Pharaoh.''

'If I go to the Hebrew slaves,' a terrified Moses had replied, 'and say to them, 'The God of your

185

fathers has sent me to you,' they will ask, 'What is his name?' What shall I say?'

'*Ehye asher ehye*. I am that I am,' the voice had replied.

'But I was still reluctant,' Moses said. ' "They won't believe me!' I protested. 'They won't listen! They'll say, 'How dare you speak the name of Yahweh?' ' '

'Yet that is what you will say to the children of Israel,' the voice had replied.

Moses had said that he was no great speaker, that he was not fluent in the language of the sons of Abraham, and that there were certainly Hebrews who were wiser, cleverer and more confident than he, and who would be more suited for such an important mission.

'Why me?' he had groaned, just as he had when Zipporah kept telling him to return to Egypt.

Then the voice had exploded with anger. 'Who gave man a voice? Who makes him deaf or mute, sighted or blind? Who if not I, Yahweh? Go now! I shall be your mouth. I shall teach you what you do not know.'

And Yahweh had told Moses what would happen to him when he returned to Pharaoh Thutmose.

'I know the King of Egypt,' the voice of Yahweh had said. 'I know how hard his heart is. He will not let you go unless I force him to do so. I will strike Egypt with all my wonders.'

'I was even more frightened when I heard that,' Moses said. 'I gnashed my teeth. 'They won't believe me!' I begged. 'They won't listen!'

'Throw down your staff!' the voice said. So I did as I was told — like this.'

And Moses took the staff that everyone knew, the staff he had used to break the head of Houssenek's son, and threw it to the floor, in front of the handmaids.

The result was pandemonium. There on the ground was no longer a staff but a snake. And what a snake! It was very long — as long as the height of a man — and black all over. It lifted its head, blinked with its slit eyes, put out its tongue and hissed. They had all leaped to their feet: Zipporah with her baby in her arms, Sefoba, Hobab, Sicheved. Everyone was standing; the women were screaming, the children shouting. Only Jethro remained seated, laughing with his mouth wide open, his beard shaking with pleasure, while the snake, frightened by all the excitement, coiled like a whip, as if it might strike or escape.

'Don't let it get away!' Moses cried. 'I must pick it up by its tail!' But he was too weak to stand and he could not reach it. Sicheved threw a cushion at the beast, which retreated with a sinister rustle, and Moses was finally able to get his hand on it. There was a stunned 'Oh' followed by a breathless silence.

Moses was holding his staff once more. Not a snake, just his staff. There were more exclamations, more incredulous cries as, with a sigh, he laid the miraculous staff down by his side. But before they all went back to their places, hearts still pounding, Moses raised his right hand for everyone to see.

'Yahweh also made me put my hand in my chest. Believe it or not, it went right inside my body. When I took it out, it was white with leprosy. 'Put it back in your breast,' He said to me, and I did. When I took it out again, the leprosy had gone and it was as you see it now. I can't do that again, but it happened.'

In the stunned silence that followed, Jethro slapped his thigh. He took Zipporah's arm and forced her to resume her seat. 'Sit down,' he ordered everyone. 'Let Moses tell his story.'

In response to Moses' reluctance, the wrath of Yahweh had flared up, setting both his beard and his mind aflame and knocking him back against the rocks. 'Do as I command you!' Yahweh had thundered. 'Take your staff and go to Egypt. You will not be alone. Your brother Aaron the Levite will come to meet you. If you need someone to speak, he will. I shall be your mouth, he will be your mouth, if you want him, for you will be a god to him.'

Moses sighed and shook his head. 'How the mule brought me here, I don't know. Any more than I knew I had a brother named Aaron. I'm ashamed that I tried so hard to flee Yahweh's will. I couldn't help it. You all knew that Horeb was up there, but how was I to know?'

He seized his staff, provoking more cries of terror. Then, his tired face softened by a half-smile, he laid it on his thighs. He looked in turn at Zipporah and Jethro. 'Now we must get our children ready to set off on the road to Egypt.'

★　★　★

The days before departure were so full of activity that nobody had time to think about the imminent separation. Animals had to be chosen that would form Moses' and Zipporah's flock and provide them with milk and meat, be useful for trading, and make it seem that they were simply shepherds to any soldiers of Pharaoh they might meet on the way. The mules and camels had to be loaded with pack-saddles filled with grain, dates, jars of olives, linen, big gourds of water, and canvas and poles for tents.

Moses was so impatient that Hobab and Sicheved had only two days to make two cane baskets to be strapped to the backs of the camels. Strewn with cushions and covered with thick canopies, they offered good protection against the sun and would provide reasonable comfort for a long journey.

When Hobab showed his handiwork to Zipporah, he tried to convince her that he should go with her. 'Moses is still weak. He doesn't know the road. What will you do if you meet brigands?'

'Your place is here,' Zipporah replied. 'Our father Jethro needs you more than we do. Who will lead his flocks to Edom and Moab if you leave? Stay here, support him and find yourself a wife.'

Hobab became annoyed. 'Sicheved can take my place here. He knows as much as I do. And Jethro will be happy to know I'm with you.'

But still Zipporah refused, gently but firmly.

189

'We fear nothing, Hobab. Moses' God is protecting him. Do you think he's sending him to Pharaoh only to let him perish on the way?'

Reluctantly, Hobab bowed to his sister's wishes. After all, the road to Egypt was no longer so unsafe since caravans of Akkadian merchants had been using it. But he sought good guides to go with them, and had little difficulty in finding four young shepherds from among those who had followed Moses in previous winters.

Meanwhile, Murti and a half-dozen other handmaids came to see Zipporah. 'Let us go with you. We'll take care of your sons. Moses will soon be a king and you'll need handmaids.'

'Go and ask my father Jethro,' Zipporah replied. 'It's he who'll decide.'

Jethro granted them everything they wanted without listening to them. Handmaids were the last thing on his mind. For the first time in his long life, he was at a loss for words, unable to express his immense joy. He made Moses repeat over and over, for him alone, the words the Voice had spoken. And each time he clapped his hands and kissed Moses, his old body vibrant with jubilation. 'He's come back to us! The Everlasting hasn't forgotten our covenant. His wrath is no longer upon us. Yahweh is again reaching out His hand to the sons of Abraham.'

But it was not long before his joy was tinged with sorrow. The day before their departure, he grasped suddenly that Zipporah was leaving. She would no longer serve him his morning meals, would no longer be by his side for the offerings, would no longer listen patiently to his

190

endless learned chatter. All that day, he remained by her side, following her everywhere as she busied herself with the final preparations, watching her as if trying to imprint her face on his brain. His lips were frozen in a smile, but his beard shook and his eyes were too bright. He kept wanting to touch her, and he would put his hand on her arm, or brush against her shoulder or the back of her neck. Once, like a young man, he seized her by the waist. Zipporah took his fingers and kissed them with infinite tenderness. 'We'll meet again, Father. We'll meet again, I know. Your days will be tranquil now and at last you'll be able to become a very old man.'

Jethro's laughter echoed through the courtyard. 'May Yahweh hear your words. May the Everlasting listen to you,' he exclaimed.

At dawn on the day of departure, as she was feeding Eliezer, two hands closed over Zipporah's eyes. She had no difficulty recognizing their cool scent. 'Sefoba!'

Sefoba sat down beside her, then covered the child and Zipporah's legs with a magnificent blanket on which coloured stripes were interwoven with subtly drawn motifs.

'It's beautiful,' Zipporah breathed, taking Eliezer off her breast so that she could feel the cloth.

The child screamed. Sefoba took him and pressed him to her wet cheek. At this, Eliezer, surprised, fell silent.

Zipporah had spread out the blanket and could now see clearly the design that glittered in the morning light against a dark background. 'The tree of life.'

'Do you remember the beautiful fabric that Reba gave Orma?' Sefoba asked, cradling Eliezer. 'The one he tore the day after Moses arrived . . .'

Zipporah stroked the purple and gold birds, the ochre flowers, the indigo butterflies perching on the branches. 'I kept it for you under my bed.' Sefoba sniffed, overcome with emotion. 'I always knew that one day my Cushite sister would go away and leave me alone.'

While outside the noise of the animals being formed into a caravan increased, Zipporah and Sefoba held each other in a long embrace, into which they drew Eliezer and Gershom.

At last everything was ready, and the caravan prepared to leave Jethro's domain. Moses was in one of the cane baskets, Zipporah and her children in the other. The whole household bade them a last farewell with singing and shouting and the sound of flutes and drums. They set off across the great dusty plain. The baskets disappeared last, swaying in rhythm to the steps of the camels, their canopies fluttering in the wind from the sea, a wind that spread a calm over Midian such as no one had known for a very long time.

★ ★ ★

After four days on the road it happened. The camels had been relieved of their pack-saddles and the shepherds were pitching the tents. As was now his custom, Moses went off to erect an altar of stones to Yahweh, as Jethro had taught him. By the time he returned, the sun was low, the shadows were long and the light blinding. It seemed to Zipporah that there was something strange about the way he was walking, and she stood up to see better. 'Moses!' she cried.

At that moment, he stumbled and went down on one knee. If he had not been holding his staff, he would have fallen. He stood up again and resumed his unsteady walk. Zipporah ran to him and put her arms round him to stop him collapsing. 'What is it? What's the matter?'

He did not reply. His harsh breathing, his pale face, his closed eyes, his drawn lips reminded Zipporah of how he had been when he had come down from the mountain. The young shepherds came to her aid and, together, they laid Moses in the tent. Zipporah called for water and linen and put his head on her knees.

As she was cooling his brow, Moses opened his eyes. When he saw her bending over him, he grimaced. 'Yahweh is taking my breath from me,' he whispered. 'My chest is burning.'

He moaned and pressed his hands to his torso as if he wanted to tear out his lungs. Zipporah tore off the collar of his tunic and stifled a cry. His wounds, which for several days had been no more than light, barely visible scars, were now spread, scarlet and swollen, across Moses' torso. 'Am I still in sin?' he groaned. 'But what sin?'

Zipporah was so frightened she could not think clearly. She stroked Moses' face. 'No, there is no sin. I'll bandage your wounds.'

193

She called for the oils and unguents that the old handmaids had wisely packed in leather bags before their departure. Moses grasped her hand. 'How can we go to Egypt,' he asked, gathering all his strength, 'if Yahweh takes my life?'

Zipporah felt anger and fear well up inside her. 'No, it cannot be!' she cried. 'Yahweh has returned to bring goodness and justice. He cannot want you to die.'

For a moment, Moses lay there with his mouth wide open. Then his breath returned to him. 'Yahweh can do whatever He wishes,' he rasped.

'No!' Zipporah protested again. 'I know He wants you alive to see Pharaoh. What good would Moses' death be to Him now?'

She wanted to rise and beg the God of Moses, but the words she had spoken to Hobab came back to her: 'The Everlasting is protecting him. Do you think He's sending him to Pharaoh only to let him perish on the way?'

'Nothing has yet been accomplished,' she said aloud. 'It cannot be. I know you must live.'

But why did some of Horeb's anger remain in Yahweh? She had to think carefully, look beyond the pain and the wounds. What had they done wrong?

If only Jethro were here.

Moses shivered. 'Yahweh punishes injustice,' he moaned in a barely audible, almost delirious voice. 'He's trying to remind us of His covenant.'

Zipporah opened her eyes wide. 'The covenant!' she cried, tears of joy mixing with tears of terror. 'Moses, remember what the Everlasting

194

said: 'This will be the sign of the covenant between you and me.'"

But Moses no longer had the strength to listen and understand. Zipporah rushed out of the tent. 'Eliezer!' she shouted at the handmaids. 'Bring me my son, Eliezer! And a flint, the thinnest and sharpest you can find.'

When she returned, her son clasped in her arms, Moses opened his eyes. He was barely able to breathe.

'Pour mint and rosemary oil in this bowl,' she ordered. 'Murti, fetch me a flat stone. And you, bring boiling water. There's some on the fire — I saw it. The flint needs to be dipped in it. And bring more linen. There isn't enough.'

As she spoke, she took the swaddling clothes off the child. Eliezer's cries worried Moses even more than his own pain. 'What are you doing?' he muttered.

While the handmaids bustled around her, Zipporah placed Eliezer's naked little body on the flat stone, by Moses' side.

'What are you doing?' Moses panted.

Zipporah showed him the cutting edge of the flint and tenderly pinched Eliezer's tiny member. 'Your God said to Abraham: 'You will be circumcised as a sign of the covenant between us. From generation to generation every child must be circumcised when he is eight days old. My covenant will be in your flesh, an everlasting covenant between me and you.' Your son Eliezer is more than eight days old today, and neither you nor my father has circumcised him. The Everlasting has called you so that the covenant

195

between your people and Him may be reborn. But how can that be if your son does not bear the sign of it according to His will?'

With a steady, confident hand, as if she had been doing it all her life, Zipporah dipped the flint in the herb-scented oil and brought it down on her son's foreskin. The cry that Eliezer gave was not much louder than those he was already making.

Without waiting, she picked up her son and raised him above Moses. 'Lord Yahweh, God of Abraham, God of Isaac and Jacob, God of Moses! O Lord Yahweh, listen to Eliezer's cries. Your covenant is in his flesh, an everlasting covenant. Look, Lord Yahweh, Moses' son, his second son, has been circumcised according to your law. O Lord Yahweh, listen to the voice of Moses' wife Zipporah. I am only what I am, but receive my son, the son of Moses, among your people. Lord Yahweh, may the blood of Eliezer wipe out Moses' sin. You need him, and I need him. I who am his wife by the blood of Eliezer. O Lord Yahweh, I am your servant and, although my skin is black, I am your people.'

When she had finished, there was a curious silence that surprised them all until they realized that Eliezer had stopped crying.

Then Moses' breathing was heard, as violent as a gust of wind. It was as if life, in all its strength, was entering his chest.

Zipporah put Eliezer down near Moses' face. Moses' eyes were shut and he was taking great gulps of air. She pressed Eliezer's face to his father's cheek. For a brief moment, they breathed together. The child gave a cry, then another. Zipporah smiled. Murti and another handmaid, who was very young, burst out laughing. Zipporah held out Eliezer to them. 'Quick,' she said.

They hurried off with him, to anoint his wound with balm and wrap him in linen.

Zipporah's fingers and palm were red with blood. She lifted Moses' tunic, took hold of Moses' member as she had taken hold of her son's, and smeared it with her son's blood. Moses sat up, his chest rising and falling.

Zipporah did not give him time to ask questions. 'We have not spoken our marriage vows either,' she murmured, 'but, as I promised you, today is our wedding day. May the Everlasting see us and bless us, my beloved husband. You are the man I want, the man I have chosen. You are the husband of my dream, the man who saves me and carries me off, the man I have always wanted, the man I have waited for without knowing his face. Oh, Moses, you are the man you must be, and tonight will be our wedding night. I, Zipporah, the Cushite, a stranger in every land, from this moment I am your bride of blood. The sin is no more. Gershom and Eliezer have a father and a mother. I am your bride of blood, oh, my beloved husband.'

Moses smiled and, with great effort, held out his arms to her. Zipporah fell into them, lay down beside him, kissed his wounded chest and pressed her mouth to his until their breath was one.

★ ★ ★

When night fell, Zipporah saw, in the lamplight, that Moses' wounds had disappeared as miraculously as they had come. She caressed him and kissed his chest greedily, but he did not wake or make a sound. She laughed and fell asleep beside him, as exhausted as he was.

In the middle of the night, Moses woke her with his caresses. He had become Moses again, his desire reborn. 'Oh, my bride!' he whispered, hoarse with passion. 'My bride of blood who gives me life over and over again. Wake up, this is our wedding night.' He kissed her breasts, belly and thighs. 'You are my garden, my myrrh and honey, my nightly tonic, my black dove. Oh, Zipporah, you are my love and the words that save me.'

Their nuptial hour lasted until dawn.

Part Three
The Outcast Wife

Miriam and Aaron

These were happy days for Zipporah, days such as she had dreamed of for a long time. She was on her way to Egypt by the side of her beloved husband, and it was no longer a dream that was impelling her onward, but her impatience to do what had to be done in the land of Pharaoh. What did the monotony of the days matter, the endless swaying of the camels that made you feel seasick, the burning sun, the frozen nights? Each morning, when she looked at the grim plains stretching before her, she saw, rising on the horizon, the greatness of the mission Yahweh had entrusted to her husband. She had only to put her hand on Moses' wrist, chest or the back of his neck to be overwhelmed with joy. She had only to see her husband with her sons, or hear him groaning with pleasure in her arms, to be sure that he was like no other man. That everything about him, body and soul, represented hope.

And so the days passed, full of promise. But just as the happiness of those days should have reached fulfilment it came to an abrupt end.

★   ★   ★

Unable to cross the Sea of Reeds with their flock, they had to go round it. For five moons, they kept close to the desolate folds of the mountains, a land of dust and stones, devoid of shade. They moved ever westwards and still there was no sign of the Great River, Iterou.

Moses became restless. The slowness of the days and the length of the nights made him irritable. His sons' laughter and babbling no longer took the frown from his brow, no longer distracted him from his endless staring at the western horizon. Occasionally, Zipporah even sensed weariness in his caresses.

Soon not an evening went by without his being tormented with anxiety. The shepherds had never gone as far as Egypt — how could they be sure they were on the right road? They would smile. 'Have no fear, Moses. There's only one route, and you could have found it without us. You must journey towards the setting sun.'

Then Moses would find other reasons to torment himself. Would his brother Aaron come to meet him, as Yahweh had promised? How would he recognize him? How would they get to Waset, the queen of cities? How would they manage to see Pharaoh? Would the children of Israel accept him? Would they believe him? Would the Lord Yahweh speak to him again?

'I build altars, as your father taught me,' he would say to Zipporah. 'I call His name, I make offerings. But only the locusts answer me!'

'Trust in your God,' Zipporah would reply patiently. 'What have you to fear? Isn't the Everlasting the embodiment of will?'

Moses would nod, and laugh, and play with Gershom, drawing imaginary beasts for him in the sand. But his anxiety soon returned.

One day he even threw down his staff, as he had done in Jethro's domain, and again it turned into a snake. The handmaids screamed in terror, the shepherds laughed, and Gershom was full of admiration for a father capable of such wonders.

Then, one day, as they came over the top of a hill similar to hundreds of hills they had left behind them, the shepherds stopped dead and pointed. 'Egypt!' they cried.

Zipporah and Moses were already on their feet, gripping the handrails of their baskets. There, below them, as far as the eye could see, a line of green stretched across the ochre and grey immensity to the horizon, linking earth and heaven. Moses picked up Gershom and placed him on his shoulders. When his camel knelt to let him down, he swept Zipporah into his arms and danced with her, his cheeks wet with tears. That evening, his offering to Yahweh was a long one and the fire of their celebration blazed all night.

After another day's walk, the Great River, Iterou, appeared, cutting across the green expanse like a snake without head or tail. Then they were on the plain, and green stretched from north to south. It was there, between the desert and the unimaginable opulence of the land of Pharaoh, that a group of men came out to meet their caravan in the early-morning mist.

★　★　★

They were wearing wide beige tunics that covered them to their feet. Their faces were wrapped in turbans that left only their eyes

203

visible, and they all held staffs. They came to a standstill in the path of the flock. The shepherds whistled, and the caravan halted.

The newcomers pushed aside the sheep and walked up to where the camels stood. A smile was already hovering on Moses' lips. Zipporah took Eliezer in her arms. Here at last is his unknown brother, she thought. She, too, was ready to smile, to share the joy that was about to overtake Moses. But a sudden twinge of fear made her hug Eliezer a little tighter and carefully adjust his coloured turban before she made her camel kneel.

The newcomers walked briskly up to Moses' camel. He climbed out of the basket.

'Are you my brother Moses?' Zipporah heard a man's voice ask. 'Are you the one who has been sent back to us by the God of Abraham, the God of Jacob and Joseph?'

Moses was overcome. All he could do was open his arms and lift his staff.

'Yahweh, the God of the children of Israel, has visited me to announce your coming,' the man went on.

The accent was unfamiliar to Zipporah, but in the ease and authority of the voice, she could sense that this was a man accustomed to words and their power. By contrast, Moses' tone was humble. 'Yes, yes, of course,' he stammered, almost inaudibly. 'I'm Moses. How happy I am. A few days ago . . . Just a few days ago . . . Of course I'm Moses!'

For a brief moment, they stared at each other, astonished as much by their appearance as by the reality of what was happening to them. The shepherds and handmaids who pressed around Zipporah peered at the strangers, searching for their eyes in the folds of their turbans. And the strangers gazed back at them uneasily, gripping their staffs, as if still fearing a threat.

'And I am Aaron,' Aaron at last replied.

He took hold of the end of his turban and skilfully unrolled it to reveal his face. It was thin but impressive, with severe dark eyes, a red mouth and a thick beard. The brow was perhaps most like that of Moses, although it was higher and prematurely lined beneath the thick, curly hair. It was a face in which the flame of passion probably flared up quickly. It made Aaron seem older than Moses even though he was several years younger.

Moses at last gave full rein to his happiness, and threw his arms round his brother. The shepherds responded with cries of joy. Zipporah, with Eliezer resting against her chest, handed Gershom to Murti. But before they could reach Moses' side, one of Aaron's companions stepped forward and made the same movement as Aaron had with his turban. A flood of heavy, silky hair was released. The woman seized Moses' hands. 'Oh, Moses!' she exclaimed. 'What a happy day this is for me. I am your sister Miriam.'

Moses stood rooted to the spot, incapable of responding to her show of affection.

Zipporah was astonished to discover the reason for his silence. Miriam had a face of great and terrible beauty. Full, perfect lips, eyes shining with emotion and intelligence, smooth

205

brow, delicate nostrils: there was not a feature that lacked elegance or charm and, unlike Aaron, she seemed still young, even though she was perhaps fifteen or sixteen years older than Moses. But when the wind lifted her heavy hair, it revealed a disfiguring mark. A shiny purple scar ran down one side of her face. It was irregular, with raised edges, and wider between the temple and the eye, as if it had been beaten flat.

'I have a sister,' Moses stammered at last. 'Miriam, my sister. I didn't know I had a sister.' He burst into a great laugh, and pressed Miriam's hands to his cheeks. 'Of course, until a little while ago, I didn't know I had a brother either!'

Zipporah was perhaps the only person present to sense how awkward Moses felt beneath his effusiveness. Miriam and Aaron, though, were beside themselves with joy, and could not stop embracing him.

'It has come to pass, Moses.' Aaron raised his hands to heaven. 'Yahweh came to me and said, 'Get up and go to meet your brother Moses. Support him, for he will deliver the children of Israel from the yoke of Pharaoh.' We abandoned everything and left. 'You will find him in the desert,' He said, 'on the road to Meidoum.' We came and waited for you on the edge of the desert on the road to Meidoum, and here you are!'

Moses laughed. 'I kept asking myself, 'Will my brother come? Will I recognize him?' How foolish I was to be afraid! Zipporah mocked me,

206

and she was right again.'

'Would you believe it?' Miriam cut in, as if she had not heard what he said. She could not stop looking at him. 'I used to carry you in my arms when you were a child.'

Moses laughed again, but his eyes were serious. 'When I was a child?'

Aaron, meanwhile, had turned to the woman Moses had pointed out. When he saw her and Eliezer, he frowned and stared at them with eyes like coals. 'Zipporah?' he asked, before Miriam could answer Moses.

'Yes, Zipporah,' Moses echoed, fervently. 'Zipporah, my beloved, my bride of blood, may she be blessed. I owe her everything, even my life. This is my first-born son, Gershom. And this is my second son, whom I have called Eliezer, 'God is my support', because he came to me at the same time as the Voice of the Lord Yahweh.'

Zipporah was smiling, but Miriam, her penetrating gaze emphasized by the mark on her face, looked her up and down, as if she could see her naked beneath her clothes.

Aaron blinked incredulously. 'Your wife?' he said, turning to Moses.

Miriam took a step forward and pointed in the direction of the handmaid Murti, as if she still hoped there was some mistake.

Moses laughed uneasily and put his arm round Zipporah and Eliezer. 'The daughter of Jethro, sage and high priest of the kings of Midian. I owe him a great debt, too. Everything you see here, brother, this flock, these mules and camels, even the tunic on my body and the sandals on my feet, I owe to Jethro's generosity. These shepherds are from his household. But the greatest gift he has given me is his daughter. I tell you this: without Zipporah and Jethro, I wouldn't be Moses.'

He had tried to put warmth into this long speech, but Aaron and Miriam's response was glacial. 'So, you were among the Midianites,' Aaron said, 'and their priest is a Cushite?'

Moses laughed again, with a touch of mockery.

Zipporah also laughed. 'No, Aaron,' she said, her voice gentle and polite. 'Have no fear. My father Jethro is like all the Midianites, a son of Abraham and Ketourah.'

Both brother and sister looked surprised, but they smiled at Zipporah. She lowered her eyes, then regretted appearing too submissive.

Moses' hand tightened on her shoulder. In that pressure, she could sense his anxiety, the silent words that went from his body to hers: 'They don't know you yet. They have no idea. They're from Egypt and are accustomed to Pharaoh's whip. They'll soon forget their mistrust.'

'It's a long story,' he said. 'I'll tell you all about it. But let's be off. I'm anxious to reach Waset. We'll talk more on the way. We have much to learn from each other.'

Aaron acquiesced happily enough, but on Miriam's face, which had known such suffering, Zipporah saw disappointment and incomprehension. And new suffering. The joy of her reunion with her beloved brother, the brother

208

for whom she had waited all these years, had faded already.

★ ★ ★

For thirty days they walked southward, along damp, narrow paths away from the main roads. Zipporah had never seen landscape like this: a vast green expanse of fields, gardens and woods and, running through it, an enormous river, dotted with islands of dense foliage and countless boats, their sails gliding, like giant butterflies, on the strong current.

Some of the gardens and palm groves were so huge and luxuriant they could have provided food for the whole of one of Midian's kingdoms. Zipporah discovered fruit, grains and foliage she had never seen or tasted before. From time to time, between the cane hedges and the trunks of trees, fig, bay and palms loaded with dates, the walls of a city would appear. She would have liked to go closer but, each time, Aaron and Miriam would move the caravan away so that the curiosity of the inhabitants was not aroused.

'There are spies everywhere,' they explained. 'They'll soon see you aren't from Egypt. They'll run and tell Pharaoh's soldiers.'

More than once, Zipporah was tempted to say what she had repeated throughout the journey: 'Why be afraid, since you are acting according to the will of your God?' But she did not want to embarrass Moses and remained silent. In fact, she saw so little of her husband that to demand his attention might have exacerbated the tension within his brother and sister.

Moses had told Aaron that they would have much to say to each other. In fact, they became inseparable. At first they spoke in the basket, but the swaying of the camel made Aaron feel ill, so they rode side by side on mules, talking from morning until night. After a few days, Zipporah noticed that it was Aaron's dry clear voice she heard most, that he was doing all the talking, while Moses listened and nodded.

Whenever they pitched camp for the night, the brothers would go off together to sacrifice to Yahweh. Then they would eat separately from the others, Aaron still talking. Moses would not get back to his tent until the middle of the night when Zipporah was asleep. Aaron would wake them in the first light of dawn, anxious to perform the morning offerings with Moses as early as possible, for fear of being caught unawares by Pharaoh's soldiers or spies.

'Aaron is like your father, Jethro,' Moses had said to Zipporah in the first days. 'He wants to know everything about Yahweh's appearance to me in the fire. I have to repeat to him a hundred times what He said to me. He also wants me to know the history of the sons of Isaac and Jacob, especially what happened to Joseph. He's very like Jethro. But he's not as good a storyteller as you are!'

At that point he still found it amusing. But soon, Zipporah detected in him an increasing sadness and anxiety.

'I thought I already knew something of our past,' he said one day, 'but I realize now that I know very little. I also thought I knew about the sufferings of the Hebrews in this land and Pharaoh's wickedness, but I know nothing.'

She refrained from asking him any questions, and he did not ask for her help. In the evening, when the tents had been pitched, she would spend all her time with Gershom, Eliezer and the handmaids. It was rare now for Moses to spare his sons so much as a glance. And, surprisingly, just as rare for his sister Miriam to take any notice of them.

Murti was the first to express surprise. 'Isn't it strange that Moses' sister hardly ever comes to see your children? She made an appearance the other day but since then she's kept her distance.'

Zipporah remained impassive, pretending not to have heard.

'Is that typical of the women here?' Murti persisted resentfully. 'Keeping away from the children and the handmaids, even at night, and spending all day with her brothers and their companions, as if the rest of us had the plague?'

Zipporah forced herself to smile. 'We don't know each other. We're strangers. Don't forget, we've had Moses with us for a long time now. Miriam is greedy for her brother. She wants to make up for all she's missed.'

'Well,' Murti squealed, 'she's certainly doing that! If she could eat him, she would. I'm surprised she doesn't complain about him sleeping in your tent.'

'Could it be you're jealous yourself?' Zipporah teased her.

'Oh, no,' Murti cried. 'I know I sinned, but now Moses is my master and the man I admire. It's you I love.'

'Things will be better soon,' Zipporah said, stroking the back of her neck. 'Aaron won't have so much to say, and Moses will spend a little more time with us.'

'Do you think so?' Murti asked, skilfully turning Eliezer to rub his buttocks with powdered chalk. 'The day Aaron doesn't have much to say seems like a long way off.'

Zipporah laughed, but her lips were trembling. What was the point of revealing the pain gnawing at her heart before they had reached Waset? Murti's words were all too true.

One evening soon after they had set out together, Miriam had approached Zipporah's tent. With a veil concealing her right cheek, she had looked beautiful, but her smile was forced. Zipporah was unwrapping Eliezer's swaddling clothes. As she removed them from the chubby little body, she had waited for Miriam's reaction and had seen a look of terror on her sister-in-law's face.

Naked, Eliezer's descent could not be concealed. Miriam had wanted to make sure that he was circumcised, but what she saw was the colour of his skin. Unlike Gershom, Eliezer was more his mother's son than his father's. And the less he looked like a baby, the more his skin, although lighter than Zipporah's, acquired a soft, luminous blackness with a touch of brown. He looked like a little loaf of bread stuffed with herbs, the tender-hearted handmaids would say,

212

so crusty you could eat him all day.

But Miriam was not tender-hearted, and had no desire to eat Eliezer. She did not try to conceal her revulsion and anger. Without a word, she walked away, leaving her bitterness hanging in the air behind her.

Zipporah had no need of words to understand. Her life had taught her the aversion her skin could arouse in others. Miriam, imbued with the knowledge and tradition that her brother Aaron loved to talk about, could not have imagined that Moses, the Moses she seemed already to worship as a god, as Yahweh had foreseen, could have a son so unlike his own people.

⋆   ⋆   ⋆

'Waset is five days' walk from here,' Aaron announced one morning, as they were preparing to set off again. 'From this point, we must go on foot, without our flocks, camels or mules, and without shepherds or handmaids.'

'Why is that, brother?' Moses asked in surprise.

'If you approach the city of Pharaoh with this caravan, his soldiers will be upon us before nightfall. We are slaves. Slaves own nothing and don't have the right to own anything.'

Moses looked at those who had made the long journey with him and were staring at him now with disbelief on their faces.

Aaron anticipated his protest. 'They can go back down-river and wait in the place where we

213

met. They'll run no risk.'

'Wait for what?' one of the shepherds asked, anger in his voice.

'Wait until Moses and I have talked to Pharaoh and led our people out of Egypt.'

'That could be a long time,' Murti put in. 'My mistress and Moses' sons need their handmaids.'

'Among the Hebrews,' Miriam said harshly, 'wives and sons don't have handmaids. The wives take care of their children without help.'

Murti was about to answer, but Zipporah silenced her with a gesture. Moses threw her a glance, but also said nothing.

Zipporah smiled at Miriam and Aaron. 'Moses isn't a slave,' she said, calmly, 'and neither is his wife. He hasn't come to see Pharaoh so that he can lead the life of a slave, but in order to bring that life to an end.'

A curious silence ensued. Aaron and Miriam stared at Zipporah with as much astonishment as if they were seeing her for the first time.

Moses bent down and took Gershom in his arms. This simple gesture encouraged Zipporah to say what she had kept to herself for days. 'The Everlasting wants Moses to appear before Pharaoh. Do you think a pair of camels, a few mules and a flock of sheep will anger Him? Isn't it better for Moses to arrive among your people as he is — a free man who does not fear Pharaoh's power, his hatred and his whims? Do the Hebrew people think that the man who will free them is timid and submissive?'

Miriam and Aaron quivered with indignation.

'Daughter of Jethro!' Aaron cried. 'We know

214

our people and what they expect. It is presumptuous for a daughter of Midian to speak of the will of Yahweh.'

'Aaron, Miriam,' Moses intervened, with a smile on his lips but not in his eyes, 'I understand your anxiety and I am grateful to you for it. Remember, though, that I know Thutmose well. I know his roads and I know his power.'

'Of course,' Aaron agreed, less sure of his ground.

Moses placed his son in Zipporah's arms and again smiled coldly at his sister and brother. 'I don't doubt your great wisdom, Aaron, my brother, but the reason I'm here among you is that I listened to Zipporah. She is wise as I am not. Without Zipporah, I wouldn't be Moses. Her thoughts are my thoughts. That's why she became my wife.'

There was embarrassment on every face. Even Aaron lowered his head as a sign of humility. Only Miriam, her eyelid deformed by the throbbing of her scar, continued to stare at Zipporah with all the severity she could muster.

'Let's all go together to the slaves' village,' Moses said, in a conciliatory tone, 'and see if we're welcome there.'

That night, Moses came back to the tent earlier than usual and took Zipporah in his arms. They lay for a time in silence, savouring the simple tenderness.

'Don't be angry with them,' Moses murmured. 'Aaron knows who you are, but they still need a little more time to accept . . . ' He hesitated.

215

Zipporah finished the sentence for him: 'Accept your wife, even though she's a stranger.'

Moses laughed, and kissed Zipporah's temples and eyes. 'And, of course, Aaron has no love for the Midianites. He's prejudiced against them for learned reasons. He's convinced they sold our ancestor Joseph to Pharaoh.'

They both laughed but then, abruptly, Moses was serious. 'Things are becoming complicated.' He sighed. 'These are the people for whose sake I came. They have suffered, and suffering has moulded their minds. But they're strong and sincere. Give them time, and they'll learn to love you and judge you by the good you do for them.'

Zipporah thought of the way Miriam had looked at Eliezer and her. 'You mustn't fear my impatience,' she replied, as lightly as she could, and kissed Moses' neck as she liked to do. 'You mustn't fear anything. Not Aaron, not Miriam, not even Pharaoh. You are Moses. Your God has said to you, 'Go, I shall be with you.' How could I wish for any other joy than to be with you and our sons?'

Two Mothers

For two days they followed the river, which was still dense with boats. Brick houses with whitewashed walls and flat, square roofs, often with an upper floor, stood along the banks. They had many windows, which were wider than the doors of bedchambers in Midian. The spacious gardens were adorned with colonnaded monuments, planted with vines and trees, palm, pomegranate, fig and sycamore, and surrounded by brick walls, ten to fifteen cubits high.

The walls ran along wide, straight roads that led to even larger gardens, overflowing with fruit and vegetables. Everywhere men, women and children bustled. The men were beardless and bare-chested. The women wore short tunics held in below the breasts, their long, smooth, flowing black hair sometimes covered with straw hats. Slow-moving old men led heavily laden donkeys, while young men carried nets of freshly caught fish.

Further on, as they came closer to the queen of cities, the road left the riverbank, and they found themselves facing a vast expanse of palm groves between the river and the hills and ochre cliffs beyond which the desert began. And there, finally, rising into the blue sky, were the temples of Pharaoh.

There were about ten, the largest surrounded by smaller ones, as if they had given birth to

217

them. Seeming to grow out of the rock, their tops reaching high into the sky, they were so vast that, beside them, even the cliffs were mere hillocks. Their façades shimmered in the heat like oil against the transparent sky. The neatly laid brick road leading to them burned in the sun.

Zipporah remembered Moses' words about the splendour of Pharaoh's temples, but their size surpassed anything she could have imagined. Nothing here was on a human scale. Not even the stone monsters with the heads of men and the bodies of lions that stood guard before them.

Further on, beneath great pyramids, they could see vast building sites. Colonnades and needles of white limestone and walls carved and painted with thousands of figures rose on the façades of palaces hollowed out of the cliffs. There were unfinished monsters without wings, and statues without heads. In places, the roads became dirt paths, with bricks piled beside them. And everywhere the slaves swarmed, working, carrying, hammering, creating a din that swelled in the heat of the day and could be heard at the furthest reaches of the sites.

Moses, who was familiar with the spectacle, remained impassive. But Zipporah was no more able than the shepherds and handmaids to hold back an exclamation of admiration. Aaron, who had no doubt been expecting this reaction, pulled on the reins of his mule, turned to them and raised his emaciated face. He seemed even older now. He dismounted and waved his hand furiously in the direction of Pharaoh's temples.

218

'All of these things that are Pharaoh's, all of these things you admire, we built!' he cried. 'We, the children of Israel, the slaves. Pharaoh takes pride in what he has been building with our blood for generations. But look . . . '

Aaron ran to pick up two bricks that had been left by the side of the road, and rubbed them together vigorously. They crumbled to a fine dust, as if they were melting in his hands. 'Pharaoh builds, but what he builds is only dust,' he proclaimed. With a cry that might have been a laugh, he threw down the remnants of the bricks, which shattered at the camels' feet. 'One breath from the Lord Yahweh will be enough to sweep it all away,' he concluded scornfully.

All those who, a moment earlier, had been contemplating Pharaoh's extravagance with childlike amazement lowered their eyes. Zipporah glanced at Moses. He was looking admiringly at his brother. As the Everlasting had said: Aaron could speak.

★   ★   ★

The slaves' village sprawled at the bottom of a disused quarry. It was a maze of long, narrow alleys, surrounded by a wall three cubits thick and five cubits high. The houses were shanties of rough brick, built back to back. They all looked the same, each with a door and a hole in the roof through which smoke escaped from the hearth.

Moses ordered the shepherds to pitch their tents on one of the slopes of the quarry, where a caravan of merchants had already camped. Only

219

Murti and two other handmaids followed Zipporah as she set off behind her husband along a dirt path. Miriam looked at them, but said nothing. Aaron was walking proudly at the head of the little band. Moses was surprised that there was no sign of Pharaoh's soldiers.

'They hardly come here any more,' Aaron said. 'They know we have nowhere to go but these hovels. They come every two or three moons to count the pregnant women and the babies.'

Aaron and Miriam hurried along a dusty street that ran through the middle of the village, then turned into a warren of alleys filled with rubbish. They finally came out into a square, in the middle of which was a deep well with a cane roof. Children sat by it, the little girls washing clothes, the boys weaving mats from straw. They looked up as the newcomers appeared, recognized Miriam and Aaron, then leaped to their feet. 'They're here! Mother Yokeved, Aaron and Miriam are here!'

Alerted by the cries, a crowd filled the little square. There were shouts of joy. An old woman advanced towards Miriam, who smiled and tried to take her hand. 'Mother . . .'

But Yokeved walked past her and stopped a few paces from Moses.

Despite her age and the trials that had turned her thick hair white, she retained the beauty her daughter had inherited. Beneath the lines caused by exhaustion and suffering, her features were elegant and her eyes held a mixture of power, gentleness and a serenity that overwhelmed Zipporah. Mother Yokeved stood there, short of breath, lips parted, hands shaking, but with dignity and self-control. She shed no tears, and when she spoke, it was only to voice a name: 'Moses.'

It was not a cry, not a question, not an expression of doubt. Zipporah sensed that she was savouring the extraordinary joy of uttering her son's name after such a long time.

'Moses!'

He smiled, and nodded hesitantly. 'Yes, Mother, I am Moses.'

She returned his smile. 'I am Yokeved,' she murmured.

Only then did they cross the distance that separated them and embrace. Then, clasped in Moses' arms, her eyes closed on a sorrow that went beyond age, Yokeved gave a sob. 'Oh, my son, my first-born son!'

Zipporah realized she was holding Eliezer too tightly, and relaxed her grip a little.

The villagers pressed round them, filling the narrow space with a great clamour of voices. Moses took Yokeved by the hand and led her to Zipporah. 'My daughter!' Yokeved exclaimed joyfully. 'You are my daughter!'

Her eyes grew larger at the sight of Gershom and Eliezer, and her laugh was like a blessing. 'And here are my grandchildren!' she cried, opening her arms. 'My daughter and my grandchildren. May the Everlasting be praised!'

Zipporah had waited so long to hear these words. They warmed her heart like fire and, unlike Yokeved, she could not hold back a flood of tears. She almost dropped Eliezer when she clasped Yokeved's shoulders as she had never been able to embrace her own mother.

★   ★   ★

There followed ten days of joy and hope. Moses sacrificed half of the flock that they had brought from Midian. The women ground the remains of the grain. The air was filled with the smell of cooking, and makeshift tables were set up, while men posted themselves on the road to raise the alarm if Pharaoh's soldiers visited them. Sitting by the fires, Moses told his story. Whenever his voice grew blurred with exhaustion, Aaron continued, vigorously and in greater detail. When dawn broke, those who had to returned to the building sites to become slaves again, even though they had had only a few hours' rest.

But the next night other men, women and children slipped into the village and the little square in front of Yokeved's house. They, too, wanted to see and hear the man who had received the extraordinary promise from the Everlasting: 'I shall deliver them from the hands of the Egyptians, and lead them to a good, spacious land, a land flowing with milk and honey!''

The news spread through the building sites like the scent of flowers in spring. The slaves' faces, too, were like spring flowers, as if exhaustion no longer had any hold over them.

As the days passed, Zipporah hardly saw Moses, who was held back constantly by one group or another and rarely snatched more than a few hours' sleep. She spent her time with Yokeved, caring for her sons and doing women's work. Miriam spent little time with them. On the few occasions that she visited, she was distant and silent. She occupied herself with the village women or the newcomers, who treated her with respect and came to her for counsel.

Yokeved, whose one happiness was to look after Gershom and Eliezer, was unaware of Miriam's coldness towards Zipporah. She did not notice the severity of her gaze, the way she pursed her lips whenever Yokeved, with much laughter, kissed and stroked Eliezer's dark skin, or called Zipporah 'my daughter', which Zipporah loved to hear: 'Come now, my daughter.' 'Zipporah, my daughter, where are you, child?' The words flowed into her like honey, as if the promise that had been made to Moses of a more just world had already been kept.

★ ★ ★

Soon, a number of venerable old men arrived in the village. They were welcomed, and a family gave up its house to them. Zipporah realized that some had come a long distance, from the furthest building sites in Waset, both north and south. Moses' name had reached there, too, like a seed carried on the wind. She was delighted at first: everything was happening as the God of Moses had announced.

But one morning, as he was sharing his meal with Moses, Aaron said something that startled her. 'They'll all be here soon, Moses. They'll listen to you, and offer their opinion on the best way to see Pharaoh. Then we can decide what to do.'

His features drawn, dark shadows beneath his eyes, Moses glanced at him, distracted. 'Decide what to do?' he asked. 'What do you mean?'

'Decide on the best moment to approach Pharaoh. How to get to him. Many of those around him will try to stop us. We should agree too on what to say to him.'

Moses seemed surprised. 'Aren't there too many elders? How will they ever reach agreement?'

At this Aaron took offence, and told Moses that this was the only way for them to proceed. 'Our elders have always done this, and we must follow their example. Assemble them, listen to their advice and apply it. That's the way things have always been done. It is our law. Nothing is greater than the mission that awaits us, and we must carry it out according to custom. The elders will decide.'

When she heard this Zipporah froze. She could not believe her ears. Had Aaron forgotten the words of his God, which he himself had repeated endlessly? Hadn't the Lord Yahweh said to Moses, 'You will go, you and the elders of Israel, to the King of Egypt'? Hadn't He said, 'I will be with your mouth, I will instruct you on what you must do, and to your brother Aaron you will be a god'? Hadn't those been the words of the Voice on the mountain of Horeb? Surely everything had already been decided. As for the difficulty of approaching Thutmose, which so worried Aaron, Moses had simply to appear outside Pharaoh's palace, Zipporah was sure, and the guards would make themselves the instrument of the Lord Yahweh's will.

She was about to vent her irritation, but she remained silent. She hoped that Moses would look at her, but he merely agreed resignedly with what Aaron had said.

At that moment, Zipporah realized how tired her husband was by what had happened so far, and that Aaron's interventions were wearing down his spirit and his will.

Remorse gripped her. In the belief that Moses did not need his wife, surrounded as he was by acclaim and the outpouring of hope, she had been happy to surrender to Yokeved's gentle care. But now, with Moses plagued again by torment and doubt, she saw that she had abandoned him to Aaron's intransigence, his self-belief, his lust for power, which were destroying the confidence and authority Moses had acquired during their journey.

Zipporah wanted to avoid a confrontation with Aaron so she said nothing: soon she would find an opportunity to talk to Moses alone, she thought. But events were to overtake her.

★ ★ ★

In the middle of the afternoon, while Moses was asleep, children came running. 'They've caught one of Pharaoh's spies!' they cried.

The square filled with people. A short,

middle-aged man with thick eyebrows was dragged before Aaron. He was dressed in the tunic common to the Hebrews, but his hair, his mouth and, above all, his cheeks, with the merest shadow of a beard, indicated that he was Egyptian. Zipporah, who had approached with Yokeved, saw fear in his dark eyes. Those who held him were handling him roughly. When Aaron asked who he was, he rose to his full height and stared straight at him. It was clear to everyone that this was a man who had once been accustomed to being obeyed.

'Senemiah, guardian of the corridor to the mighty Hatshepsut,' he replied, with only the barest trace of an accent.

These words, and the composure with which they were uttered, silenced those who had been shouting a moment earlier. Even Aaron seemed impressed. He sought the support of Miriam, who was approaching him. She was taller than the Egyptian. She looked him up and down, then coolly lifted her hair to reveal her scar, as if she wanted the man to take a long, hard look at her. She gave a brief laugh, of indignation and contempt. 'You seem to have lost your way, spy. Your queen is no more.'

'She lives!' Senemiah protested. 'Her death is only a rumour spread by Thutmose. She lives, I swear it by Amon!'

'Don't swear on the name of your god here!' Aaron thundered.

Senemiah waved his hands as if to erase the words. 'Forgive me. Hatshepsut wishes you no harm.'

226

Miriam laughed again. 'I know Hatshepsut and I know what she wishes for us — if she still lives, as you claim.'

Senemiah looked at her in surprise — as did Zipporah and some of the others present. 'I'm not here to spy on you,' he said to Aaron. 'I've come to see Moses.'

A murmur of astonishment rippled through the square. Zipporah felt Yokeved's hand grip her arm. She turned to the old woman and saw that her face was distorted with fear. But before she could react, Moses' voice rang out, full of gaiety and warmth: 'Senemiah! My friend!'

Eyes still puffy from sleep, Moses hurried out of the house and, heedless of the others, ran to the newcomer. Everyone was rooted to the spot as Moses greeted the Egyptian, kissing and embracing him with cries of joy.

Eventually he became aware of the heavy silence around him. He looked at the faces, the mouths wide with astonishment, and smiled. 'Have no fear,' he said. 'Senemiah is a friend. He was my master when I was a child. He taught me many things. He scolded and chastised me, as a good teacher should.' He squeezed Senemiah's shoulder. 'Most important of all,' he said gravely, 'Senemiah risked his life to help me flee from Thutmose.'

His eyes sought Zipporah's. Gently, she disengaged herself from Yokeved's grip and went to him.

'Moses,' Miriam said, 'we have no friends among the Egyptians. They pretend to help us one day and betray us the next.'

227

'And why is he wearing Hebrew garments?' Aaron asked, with a grimace of mistrust.

'Because I'm fleeing Thutmose and his spies,' Senemiah replied curtly. 'And because it was the only way I could see Moses.'

'What do you want with him?' Miriam asked. 'Why should Moses make you brave enough to slip in among us like an eel?'

There were laughs and jeers.

Moses raised his hand, his face hard. 'I have said that Senemiah is my friend. Let him speak.'

Miriam closed her eyes, as if her brother had slapped her. Zipporah, fascinated, could not take her eyes off that severe, inscrutable face, on which the scar seemed to grow darker, to become a menacing living thing.

The elders had moved to surround Aaron, a majestic halo of white beards around him.

'Hatshepsut is alive,' Senemiah said to Moses urgently. 'She's waiting for you. She wishes to see you.'

Moses stifled a cry.

'It's a trap set by Pharaoh,' Miriam said, pointing at Senemiah. 'How do you know he isn't lying?'

Moses did not appear to hear her, any more than he felt Zipporah slip her hand into his. 'So it's true,' he murmured.

'Thutmose is keeping her prisoner in her palace. But she's alive. She wants to see you before she dies, Moses.'

The silence was now heavier than ever. Zipporah, still holding Moses' hand, felt his body shake. He seemed indifferent to the mood

228

of the crowd. He started when Miriam said, 'You can't go there. It's impossible.'

The elders nodded and murmured in agreement.

'Now is not the time,' Aaron said. 'It's over, Moses. You're no longer an Egyptian.'

Zipporah saw horror and incomprehension on the faces of the elders, of Aaron and Miriam, and of the villagers. How could Moses hesitate? How could he heed what the Egyptian had said?

But Moses looked at Senemiah. 'So she knows I came back?'

Senemiah nodded. 'She's known for more than a moon,' he said urgently. 'That's what keeps her alive. But we must leave without delay. Arrangements have been made for you to get into the villa tonight. Tomorrow it will be too late.'

'Moses!' Miriam cried. 'Why should you care about the woman who stole you from your mother Yokeved? The woman who stole your life and will be punished by Yahweh tomorrow.'

Moses recoiled. He became aware of Zipporah's hand in his and clutched it tightly.

Aaron stepped forward, his arm raised. 'Miriam is right, Moses. Have you forgotten your duty? What does the woman who was pharaoh matter to you? Your place is no longer with her.'

Around Aaron the old men muttered in agreement. 'It would be an insult to all of us,' one declared.

'An insult?' Moses snapped. 'An insult for me to see the woman who rescued me and kept me alive when I was a baby?' He raised his hand,

229

with Zipporah's still in it, and shook it angrily. 'Didn't my mother Yokeved prevent my murder, which Pharaoh had demanded? And didn't the love of another mother save me? Where is the insult in so much love, venerable elders?'

The only answer was an icy silence. Eyes aflame, Miriam put her fists together. Yokeved laid her hand over them, then turned to Aaron and the elders. 'Listen to the word of Moses. What he says is right. I entrusted my first-born to the river and prayed for a woman to find him. I prayed for her to love him as I loved him. Remember, Miriam. Calm your anger, my child. You prayed as I did. Listen to Moses. His mother Hatshepsut is going to meet her god, and she wants Moses' face in her eyes when she leaves. There is nothing wrong with that. It is only fair.'

'Nothing wrong?' an elder roared. 'What are you thinking of, woman? The Egyptian woman is going to meet her god, you say? But her god is lies and darkness, an insult to Yahweh!'

Moses was about to fly into a rage, but it was Zipporah who exploded: 'Are you all incapable of trust? The names of Moses and the Lord Yahweh spill from your mouths, but you might as well be drinking milk with stagnant water! For days, you've been intoxicated by Moses' words and the words Yahweh spoke to him. Oh, yes! You're drunk, but you're deaf, too! Do you think there is now one gesture Moses makes, one word he speaks, that hasn't been willed by the Lord Yahweh? The Everlasting said: 'Go, Moses! I am sending you to Pharaoh, I shall be with you, I shall be with your mouth . . . ' Do you think

230

those were idle words? For days, Moses has been telling you of the Lord Yahweh's will, but you behave as if his words were merely words. Don't you understand that what must take place began a long time ago, even before Moses reached the land of Midian? And that nothing can prevent it? You must have faith! If the Everlasting did not want Moses to go to his mother Hatshepsut, would she still be alive? Or do you not believe your God has such power?'

Her last words were greeted with astonishment and anger.

'How dare you speak to us like that, you who are not of our people?' cried Miriam. 'Do you think you can teach us anything, stranger? Don't you know that the people of your race bow down to Pharaoh and bear arms for him when he orders it?'

'Miriam!' Moses bellowed. 'Be careful what you say.'

'For too long you have let yourself be swayed by the dreams of Midian, brother,' Miriam retorted. Clearly she had no intention of keeping silent. 'They may have been sweet, but now you are among your people. Open your eyes, Moses, listen to the elders, free yourself of the errors you have been taught. The people of Midian weren't Joseph's people. They are not yours now.'

Zipporah could see how easily Moses might be swayed by his sister's argument and stepped in again. 'Don't let yourself be blinded, Moses,' she said. 'Do you really believe that the man who is to be a god to his brother Aaron could have taken a wife the Lord Yahweh did not want him

231

to take? When the Lord Yahweh turns his eyes on me, does He look through me, like the breeze blowing through a leafless tree? Am I, the wife of Moses, the mother of his sons, the woman who circumcised Eliezer, merely a shadow ignored by the Everlasting?'

All except Miriam lowered their eyes.

Moses turned to Senemiah. 'Take me to Hatshepsut.'

He was still holding Zipporah's hand.

★ ★ ★

Zipporah smelt the strange odour while they were still on the river, huddled in the bottom of the boat. It was a peppery, carnal, animal smell that both repelled and attracted her.

It was dark. The reflections of hundreds of torches and bowls of burning pitch undulated on the surface of the river. By their light, the walls and roofs of huge palaces could be seen, with gates and landing-stages and, at regular intervals, sculptures with painted faces and wide open eyes.

Senemiah murmured a few words in the Egyptian language, and the two oarsmen pointed the stem of the boat towards an area where no light shone.

'We're nearly there,' Moses whispered to Zipporah. 'Don't worry, all will be well.'

In the darkness, Zipporah replied with a smile.

'A sail!' Senemiah whispered suddenly.

Moses and Zipporah crouched lower in the

232

bottom of the boat. The two oarsmen did not pause as a felucca glided past along the other bank, going towards the southern part of the city. Zipporah saw figures dancing on the deck, while laughter, and the sound of flutes and drums echoed over the water.

A moment later, their own boat entered the dark area and the oarsmen rowed faster. Like a shadow within a shadow, the boat drew alongside a landing-stage. An animal yelped. Two figures loomed up and brought the boat to a standstill. Senemiah jumped out. 'Quick.'

Moses lifted Zipporah and set her down on the landing-stage. By the time he joined her, the boat was already pulling away. Zipporah felt Moses' hand on the small of her back. They broke into a run, their sandals slapping on the flagstones. She looked back to see the boat enter the blurred halo of the torches. The strange smell, more intense and pungent than ever, caught at the back of her throat. A door closed soundlessly behind them.

'Wait here,' Senemiah whispered.

He vanished into the night. Her eyes accustomed now to the dark, Zipporah realized they were in a vast garden. She could hear the murmuring of a fountain, and the rustling of foliage in the light breeze. She had to stop herself coughing: the odour had inflamed her throat, and left the taste of dust in her mouth.

'Frankincense,' Moses murmured. 'What you smell is frankincense,' he repeated. 'My mother Hatshepsut has always used it. It's obtained from trees in this garden — thirty of them. Apparently

Thutmose hasn't had the courage to remove them . . . '

Zipporah had no time to ask him the question that came to her lips. Footsteps approached, and a small lantern swayed before them.

'Come,' Senemiah whispered.

The garden was so large, they might easily have become lost in it if Senemiah had not been guiding them. They went through a door into an antechamber. It was a dark room, lit only by lanterns held by two young handmaids, who bowed low to Moses and whispered words that Zipporah did not understand. Ahead, Senemiah was opening another door, which was twice as high and had gold corners. They went through it into another antechamber, better lit this time, full of draperies and low columns supporting painted wooden sculptures of men and women in transparent tunics and necklaces of blue stones, their raised arms reaching up to the dark ceiling.

The smell here was stronger than ever, and the air was thick with blue smoke, but neither Senemiah nor the handmaids seemed to notice. He stepped across the purple rugs, went behind the columns and pulled aside a curtain. Light flooded across the floor. Senemiah bowed low and remained in that position.

Moses, his arm shaking, led Zipporah into the next room.

She pressed her hands to her mouth to stop herself crying out.

★ ★ ★

234

In the middle of a huge, bare room, Hatshepsut lay on a half-raised slab of green granite. She was naked, but for a gold plate laid over her pubes. Her body glistened with a thick film of frankincense oil the colour of amber, which covered every inch of her flesh. In the harsh glow of the torches, she looked as if she were made of bronze.

Her body showed the ravages of age, but her face, which she was straining to turn towards Moses and Zipporah, was surprisingly young. Her almond-shaped eyes, each with a thick black line under it, were so perfect, her brow — beneath a headdress of blue and red tufts and an ostrich-feather tassel — was so smooth, her chin so round and soft that Zipporah thought at first that she was wearing a mask. But the eyelids lowered, the mouth opened, a sigh emerged from Hatshepsut's throat and the illusion was shattered.

Opposite the woman who had been Pharaoh, on a slab identical to the one beneath her, lay a sculpture of painted wood, as naked as she was, but with a youthful body and, on its head, a leather cap adorned with the long twisting horns of a ram and two ostrich feathers. Around Hatshepsut, a few paces behind her, between the bowls of burning frankincense, a dozen handmaids stood with their heads bowed, motionless despite the overpowering smell.

Hatshepsut sighed again, and made a soft sound that vibrated in the air like a cry. Moses nodded and stepped forward. Zipporah,

235

overwhelmed by everything around her, remained rooted to the spot.

Moses stopped a few paces from the old woman's glistening body. 'It is I, Mother Hatshepsut,' he said. 'It's Moses.'

Hatshepsut's mouth fell open. Zipporah thought she was going to cry out. But no sound emerged and her mouth closed slowly. Zipporah realized, aghast, that Hatshepsut had laughed.

For a time, with her eyes fixed on Moses, the old woman's face again became a mask, although her chest continued to rise and fall violently, shimmering in the light of the torches. Her curiously short fingers moved against her hips. Zipporah wondered what she was feeling at that moment: pain or pleasure. Then her throat quivered, and she spoke: 'Amon is great, my son. He has given me your light so that I can join him.'

Moses gave a forced smile in agreement.

Hatshepsut regained her breath. 'Did you meet her?' she asked, her voice clearer now.

'Yes,' Moses replied.

'How lucky she is.'

They were talking about Yokeved, Zipporah thought.

Moses bent forward. 'I'm happy to see you, Mother Hatshepsut.'

Her face, which seemed not to belong to her body, quivered briefly with denial. 'I would have liked to be beautiful for you, son of my heart, but even frankincense cannot help Hatshepsut now.' She paused for breath. 'You, too, are different.'

236

Moses nodded. 'I am Moses the Hebrew.'

Hatshepsut made another of the grimaces that served as a smile. Zipporah was suddenly aware of the extraordinary complicity between Moses and the old woman, so evident in the way they looked at each other.

'Thutmose is cruel and cunning,' Hatshepsut whispered.

'I know.'

'More than you know. He won't yield.'

'He must.'

'He hates you.'

'He'll be weak.'

'May your God hear you.' Again she had to pause for breath. The only sound in the room was the sputtering of the incense. Suddenly, Hatshepsut's eyelids fluttered and she looked at Zipporah. 'Approach, daughter of Cush,' she said.

Moses was as startled as Zipporah. He turned to her and held out his hand. Hesitantly, Zipporah stepped forward.

'Here is my wife,' Moses said.

Hatshepsut's eyelids flickered in a sign of comprehension. She raised her hands a little, and the thick oil on her fingers shone. 'Wife of Moses, the frankincense comes from Cush. Hatshepsut has lived on it for a long time. Frankincense is Amon's gift to Hatshepsut. You are Amon's gift to Moses. But Moses no longer cares for Amon.' She was breathless now.

Appalled by what she was witnessing, nauseous from the smell, her temples throbbing, Zipporah could feel her legs give way beneath her. She stifled a moan and gripped Moses' tunic.

Hatshepsut closed her eyes to gather her strength. When she opened them again, she looked at Moses. 'I know you have returned. Thutmose knows it, too. Go now.'

Moses nodded. After a brief hesitation, he said a few words in Egyptian. Hatshepsut's eyes had lost the glimmer of life and were identical now to those of the statue opposite her.

★   ★   ★

As quickly as he had helped them to enter the palace, Senemiah hurried them out. Lantern in hand, he led them back into the garden.

Shaken by the sight of Hatshepsut, mouth dry from inhaling the frankincense fumes, Zipporah was relieved to be outside in the cool of the night. As Senemiah and Moses walked into the darkness, she stopped for a moment to take a deep breath.

In the blackness, she could discern Moses turning to her and heard him whisper, 'Zipporah!'

She rushed to follow him, but Senemiah's lantern was already too far away to light her steps and, forced to move slowly to avoid falling into the bushes, she was soon left behind. In a few seconds the halo of light from the lantern had moved further away, appearing and disappearing between what she imagined to be trees, a marker that confused more than it guided her. Worried now, she put out her hands in front of her to detect obstacles. 'Moses!' she called, in a low voice.

He did not hear her. She touched what she guessed to be a tree-trunk, moved away from it, and called again, louder this time. At that moment, much closer than she had imagined, the door leading to the river and the landing-stage opened with a creak. She heard cries. By the light of torches, she saw Moses raise his staff as if ready to fight. Men in leather helmets, armed with spears, surrounded him, hiding him from Zipporah's view. Senemiah's voice rose and Zipporah heard herself scream: 'Moses! Moses!'

She rushed to the door of the garden. She was only a few steps from it when a figure loomed up. She was stopped by a powerful arm, and a hand went over her mouth. She could feel the hardness of the muscles that held her tight against a man's chest, which was wet with river water. The stranger pulled her unceremoniously into the darkest part of the garden. From the landing-stage came more cries, and waving torches cast crazy shadows on the door. Suddenly it closed.

The garden was again shrouded in darkness. Zipporah, as angry as she was frightened, grasped her attacker's damp tunic and swung her other hand at him, scratching his shoulder and arm. For what seemed a long time, she twisted in vain until she was out of breath and forced to stop struggling.

'Calm yourself, Zipporah,' she heard the man whisper in her ear. 'I mean you no harm. I'm

Joshua, a friend of Aaron. Calm yourself!'

She let go of the tunic, and the stranger took his hand away from her mouth. 'Have no fear. I'm here to help you.'

She could not see his face, and could barely make out his figure, but his voice had told her that he was young. From the other side of the garden wall she could hear cries and the sound of weapons. Orange lights crossed the sky. Joshua took Zipporah by the elbow and tried to pull her away.

'We have to help Moses and Senemiah,' she protested.

Again Joshua put his hand over her mouth, this time gently, even a little shyly. 'Ssh! Don't shout. Follow me.'

He drew her to the wall and led her to the side of the garden opposite the door. There, he took her hand and put it on what felt like a round step. 'This is the base of a statue,' he whispered. 'Its arms are solid enough to stand on.' As she placed her foot on the pedestal, he added, 'Before you get to the top of the wall, there's a ledge you can hold on to.'

Groping her way, Zipporah climbed, vaguely aware that Joshua was climbing up the other side of the statue. When her eyes came level with the top of the wall, she was unable to restrain an exclamation.

Four large ships formed a semi-circle in front of Hatshepsut's palace, their bows and sterns lit by naphtha torches that glittered on the river. She saw Moses being pushed into a boat by soldiers. When it moved off from the

240

landing-stage, he remained standing.

Zipporah thought of Hatshepsut's words: 'I know you have returned. Thutmose knows it, too.'

Beside her, Joshua groaned. 'That's Pharaoh's way of summoning Moses to his palace. At least he knows Moses is a great man. He's sent four ships and a hundred soldiers to fetch him.'

Zipporah was surprised by how calm he was. In the reflected light of the naphtha flames, she saw his face properly for the first time. He was younger than she was, with candid eyes that had the same coppery glints as his short beard, and a pointed, determined chin. He raised his eyebrows, which made him look even younger. 'Didn't you yourself say that Moses has nothing to fear? The Lord Yahweh wants him to appear before Pharaoh.'

With his chin, Joshua indicated a number of small boats, filled with soldiers, that were escorting the vessel in which Moses stood as it headed towards the ships. 'That's for show. Pharaoh is trying to impress him.'

Zipporah did not reply. Her eyes had been drawn by a dark form lying motionless and abandoned on the landing-stage. 'Senemiah!'

The bloodstain on his tunic was visible in the dim light.

'Not so loud. Voices carry on the river.'

'They've killed him.'

'They had to kill someone,' Joshua replied. 'Better it should be the Egyptian.'

'He was Moses' friend!' Zipporah said indignantly.

241

Joshua grimaced. 'I'm sorry. I meant that if the soldiers had found you, they might have killed you instead. Pharaoh can't touch a hair of Moses' head, but the murder of his wife would have been a good way to undermine him.'

Zipporah watched the boat in which Moses stood, gripping his staff, as it came alongside one of the ships. With a pang, she watched him grasp the rope-ladder hanging against the hull. Whatever Joshua said and whatever she herself asserted, she could not help thinking that this might be the last time she saw her husband.

'Look who's there,' Joshua breathed.

As the soldiers pulled Moses on board, a familiar figure appeared on deck. 'Aaron!' He walked up to Moses and threw his arms around him. Then the soldiers separated them.

'The soldiers came to the village at nightfall,' Joshua explained. 'They went straight to Yokeved's house and asked for Aaron. Not Moses. They tied his wrists and took him away. I followed them.'

Orders rang out on the ships. They heard the heavy oars sliding through the rowlocks. There was a drumbeat, then another cry, and hundreds of oars lifted in unison and plunged into the dark water. Slowly at first, but soon building momentum, the ships moved out into the middle of the river and headed south. Moses and Aaron were soon out of sight. With the naphtha torches gone, Hatshepsut's palace was again plunged into darkness.

'What a strange smell,' Joshua said, wrinkling his nose as if he had just noticed it. 'What a strange place it is, too. Is this Hatshepsut's palace?'

Zipporah said nothing, unable to tear her eyes from the ships.

'Can you swim?' Joshua asked, taking her hand to gain her attention.

'Yes.'

'I have a little cane boat over there, downstream of the landing-stage. When I saw the soldiers push Aaron into a boat, I didn't hesitate. I had to come upstream, but this time it'll be easier. We'll just follow. There's no risk — cane boats are so small that at night people think they're drifting tree-trunks. Or crocodiles.'

'Crocodiles?'

Joshua chuckled. 'Have no fear. There aren't any here at this season.'

'How can you joke when Moses is in the hands of Pharaoh's soldiers?'

'I listened to you in the village. I liked what you said,' Joshua replied, with all the enthusiasm of youth, 'and the trust you placed in Moses. I believe you too. Moses will accomplish the mission for which Yahweh sent him among us, and our duty is to help him as best we can, not to fear our own shadows. That's what the old men find it hard to understand. But they'll come round.'

With a few words and a luminous smile, Joshua had dispelled the sadness and doubts that had troubled Zipporah since she had seen Moses among Pharaoh's soldiers. Even his farewell to Hatshepsut seemed far away now. 'Thank you.'

'What could be better than to know that the

world will soon be less unjust?' Joshua replied. Already he was squatting on top of the wall and sliding down the other side. 'Come, we must run.'

When they reached the cane boat, Joshua put his hand on Zipporah's shoulder. 'I should tell you,' he said, serious now, 'that not everyone in the village thinks as I do. Especially since the soldiers took the opportunity to ransack a few houses. One thing you can be sure of, Miriam will be furious.'

The Scar

Joshua was right. Miriam's anger was indeed terrible, as if she hoped single-handedly to equal the wrath of Horeb.

Zipporah and Joshua reached the village soon after dawn. As they advanced into the warren of alleys, they were greeted by silent, averted faces. When they reached the little square, Zipporah found the elders crouching on mats outside the houses. With pursed lips, lifting their staffs in their blotched and bony hands, they glanced coldly at Zipporah and Joshua.

If Joshua had not given her a friendly push forward, Zipporah might not have had the courage to go to Yokeved's door. Fortunately Yokeved greeted her with her usual tenderness. 'Zipporah, my daughter, you're back at last. How happy I am!' She kissed her. 'I have not feared for my sons, but for you, yes. Pharaoh's soldiers hate the people of Cush. I said to Joshua, 'Go and see if Zipporah needs you.' No one is more capable and devoted than him — and such a handsome boy!'

Yokeved hugged Joshua, making him blush like a capsicum. Before she asked what had become of Aaron and Moses, she urged Zipporah to go to her children. 'Gershom has been as good as a star of the Everlasting, but Eliezer is asking for you. The poor little prince can't bear to be apart from you.'

245

As Zipporah was comforting Eliezer, kissing away his tears, Miriam burst into the room. 'Well, daughter of Jethro,' she thundered, 'are you happy?'

Zipporah was so surprised that she sat up abruptly, almost dropping her child.

'Are you satisfied now?' Miriam went on, the venom of her words reflected in her eyes. 'My brothers are in Pharaoh's gaols.'

Her sharpness inflamed Zipporah. She passed Eliezer to Yokeved. Yokeved gave her a little sign of encouragement, as if to say: 'Stay calm, my daughter. Fear makes her talk like this.'

Although she had not thought she was capable of such moderation, Zipporah remained calm. 'You know what I believe, Miriam,' she replied curtly. 'Why should we quarrel about it?'

'Oh, it's easy for you. We are imprisoned, slaughtered, our houses destroyed, but you . . . ' Miriam addressed a malicious smile to Joshua, who lowered his eyes. 'There's always some kind soul ready to help you.'

Zipporah held her gaze, but did not reply.

'Miriam,' Yokeved intervened, 'anxiety is making you unjust, and injustice heals no wounds.'

Miriam glared at her, and seemed about to retort, but she contained herself and merely shrugged. Behind her, Zipporah noticed that the elders had got up from their mats and were standing in the doorway of the room, listening. 'My husband and Aaron will be back tonight,' she said. 'They aren't in gaol, they're appearing before Pharaoh.'

'How can you know that? The Egyptian betrayed them, as I told you he would. You made sure that Moses walked into the trap. But you always claim to know more than us.'

'The Egyptian didn't betray them, Miriam. He died at the hands of Pharaoh's soldiers.'

'It's true,' Joshua confirmed, his voice almost steady.

Miriam's exasperation grew. Her scar throbbed with the strength of an animal. She was so beautiful and so terrible that Zipporah had to turn away.

Clearly Miriam misunderstood this gesture. Zipporah heard her cry of annoyance, and her sandals scuffing the floor as she rushed out. Zipporah ran after her as far as the door. 'Miriam!' she cried, so angrily that the elders recoiled. 'When you see me, Zipporah the Cushite, the adopted daughter of Jethro, you see a stranger. A black woman who isn't the daughter of Abraham, or Jacob, or Joseph. All of that is true. But I'm not a creature of Pharaoh. I'm not your enemy. I'm your brother's wife.'

★　★　★

At twilight, a hubbub of voices arose: Moses and Aaron were back, and the whole village came out to welcome them. It was quite a while before Moses, half carried by the crowd, reached Yokeved's house and was able to clasp Zipporah in his arms. 'I was so afraid for you,' he whispered.

'Joshua took care of me. But Senemiah . . . '

247

'I know. He threw himself in front of the soldiers' spears. There was no need. He didn't understand that I wasn't afraid.'

'Pharaoh would have killed him anyway.'

'Alas, Thutmose has become cruel. He has no remorse. He's worse than his ancestors.'

Moses clasped her tighter. From the heaving of his chest, Zipporah grasped that the encounter with Pharaoh had been a failure.

'It's terrible,' he murmured. 'What can I say to them? They won't understand. Even Aaron doesn't understand.'

Zipporah did not have time to kiss him, or make a gesture of encouragement: the old and the young, the women and children, the men returning from the building sites, with hollow cheeks and muddy hands and feet, their bodies caked with dried blood where the ropes of the hoists and winches, the stakes and the stones had torn their skin, everyone was there, anxious to hear Moses. They tore him from her arms. 'Tell us, Moses, what Pharaoh said.'

Moses looked at them, eyes bright, and they knew that the news was bad. Their cries faded.

'Aaron will tell you,' Moses said. 'It was he who spoke to Pharaoh.'

Aaron told the story well, without omitting any detail: how they had been dragged before Thutmose's golden throne, how he, Aaron, had announced the will of Yahweh, and how Pharaoh had replied: 'Who is this Yahweh that I should listen to his voice and release my slaves? I know no king of that name. No one gives orders to me!' Moses would be glad to see the Hebrew rabble idle, he had cried.

Moses had lost his temper and had threatened Pharaoh with the wrath of Yahweh, the Everlasting, who would punish him with plague and sword if he persisted in his refusal to free the children of Israel.

Pharaoh had laughed. 'I know you, Moses! I know you very well. You were almost my brother. Even when that madwoman Hatshepsut dressed you in gold and called you her son, you were as timid as a sheep. And now you come to me in a slave's tunic and threaten me? I might die of laughter.'

To the outrage of those present — the viziers, the princes, the veiled girls — Moses had climbed the steps to Pharaoh's throne, seized Thutmose's wrist and lifted it above his head. 'In that case, Thutmose,' he had thundered, 'if you don't fear me, kill me. Raise your whip to me, the whip that has taken so many Hebrew lives. Come, brave Thutmose, wipe me from the surface of the world, since you are its god.'

Pharaoh had forced another laugh and ordered his guards to drag Moses away, but not to hurt him. 'It suits me to let you live. That way you'll see the results of the law I shall pass on your people. From tomorrow, those who make bricks will no longer be given straw. Let them go and find it! If they have feet to tread the mud, they also have hands to gather straw. Why can't they use them? But I want the same number of bricks as yesterday and the day before yesterday. Not one less, or the whip will crack.'

When Aaron came to the end of his story, there was silence.

* * *

That night, Moses did not come to bed until late, but he found her waiting for him. She took him in her arms and caressed him for a long time. For the first time, she felt her husband's tears on her chest. 'Remember,' she murmured. 'Remember the words of Yahweh on the mountain of Horeb. 'I know Pharaoh, he won't let you go, unless forced by my strong hand. I will stretch out my hand and strike Egypt with all my wonders. And Pharaoh's heart will harden.''

'I haven't forgotten,' Moses said, after a long pause. 'But who will believe these words after tonight? Who will believe them tomorrow when they have to search for straw? 'Oh, Moses, how well you have freed us from the yoke of Pharaoh!' That's what you'll hear, Zipporah. And what shall I answer?'

Moses was right. The next day hope had turned to despair and resentment. The work became harder, Pharaoh's whip sharper. The most exhausted returned in the evening, while the others had to press bricks all night.

'We should have consulted the elders about the best way to approach Pharaoh,' Aaron said.

'Why did you go to see Hatshepsut?' Miriam said. 'Pharaoh hates you all the more for it, and will not listen to you again.'

'It isn't me he has to listen to,' Moses retorted,

250

matching her anger. 'Don't you see? It's the voice of Yahweh he must hear through my mouth and Aaron's. That's how it must come to pass. And it is Yahweh's will to harden Pharaoh's heart against us.'

'So your wife says,' Miriam replied, 'but she isn't one of us. How can you listen to her? Who could believe that the Lord Yahweh wants to increase our burden? How could He, if He wants us to be free?'

It was then that a rumour sprang up in the village, and was spread by the elders: it was the fault of Moses' wife that Pharaoh had hardened his heart and refused to listen to Moses. How could Moses be the man chosen by the Everlasting? How could he be His mouth and His guide, if his wife was a daughter of Cush — the daughter of a people on whom Yahweh, as everyone knew, had not turned His eyes and with whom He had made no covenant?

When the rumour reached him, Moses waved his staff and threatened anyone who dared utter this lie to his face. 'She gave me life when I was a fugitive. She led me to the voice of Yahweh. She circumcised my son Eliezer when I had forgotten and Yahweh took my breath as punishment. Is this how you repay her?'

Behind his back, the elders muttered that Moses did not know enough of the history of his people to be certain where his duty lay. What was the value, in truth, of sons whose mother was not a daughter of Israel? Miriam no longer hid her disdain for Zipporah.

'Don't listen to them, my love,' Moses would

251

implore Zipporah, when they lay together at night. 'They are lost. They no longer know what they're saying, and I don't know how to fulfil the promise I made them.'

'We must listen to them,' Zipporah would whisper, returning his caresses. 'They don't love me. They're disappointed with your choice. I'm not the wife they would have wished for Moses. And it may be that Miriam is right — she and the elders, all of them. The Moses they need must belong to them more than he belongs to his wife.'

★ ★ ★

'Don't blame Miriam, Zipporah, my child,' Yokeved said tenderly to Zipporah one morning. 'Moses owes much to her. When I entrusted him to the river to protect him from the killing of the first-born, Miriam was a young handmaid in Hatshepsut's palace. Hatshepsut didn't share her father's hatred for the Hebrews. It was Miriam who pointed out to her the basket in which I had laid Moses. Everyone knew the queen had a weak husband who couldn't give her a son. When she saw Moses, she didn't hesitate long.' Yokeved laughed at the memory. But then her face became sombre. 'Alas, Hatshepsut grew old, and her power diminished. The lords of the palace tore each other apart. Thutmose remembered Moses' birth. He sought out all of Hatshepsut's old handmaids — '

'And found me.' Miriam's voice made them both jump. 'You're right, Mother, to tell my

252

brother's wife the story. She has no idea what it means to belong to the people of the Lord Yahweh under the yoke of Pharaoh.' Holding herself erect, Miriam walked up to Zipporah, her eyes burning and her voice like lava. 'Thutmose suspected that Moses had not come from his sister's womb. Everyone suspected it. And he found me. The soldiers took me to the cellars of the palace. For twenty days they interrogated me about the man they called Moses. At first, I replied, 'I don't know. Who is Moses?' The questions became blows. Then the blows became something else. After each one, they asked, 'Who is Moses? Whose womb bore him?' And I would say, 'What Moses? Who's called Moses?' Then they brought irons and braziers.' Miriam raised a hand to her scar. 'They thought that would be enough. But I said, 'What Moses? Why should I know that name?' '

Miriam unfastened her tunic and opened it, revealing her naked body to the two women. Zipporah gasped and her hand flew to her mouth. Miriam's chest, belly and thighs bore ten purple scars as disfiguring as the one on her face. They cut across her right breast, forming folds like old leather.

'This is what it means to belong to the people of Yahweh under the hand of Pharaoh,' Miriam roared. 'Look, daughter of Cush! Look at the mark of the slave! Do you understand now? You are only Moses' wife, and you must be content with that, for there are those among us who will never know kisses and caresses like those my brother lavishes on you.'

253

Part Four
Zipporah's Words

I had had a dream, and it had come true.

But it faded when I was faced with Miriam's body.

I had called on the god of my father Jethro: 'Who will be my god if not you?'

Moses' God had replied: 'I am here. I am Yahweh, He who is.'

And now, before Miriam's tortured body, Moses' God was forbidden to me. When I saw Miriam's belly and breasts, her ruined beauty, her violated flesh, my own flesh, intact, made for love, cast me back into the darkness of women with no ancestors.

Zipporah the stranger, Zipporah the wife who counted for nothing.

There was no need for Miriam to repeat the lesson: I had understood. Moses' wife could not raise her voice along with those who suffered the hatred of Pharaoh because they belonged to the people of Moses and Yahweh. Moses' wife was of no people, whether loathed or glorious. She was like the chaff that has been separated from the wheat.

Yahweh had appeared to Moses to make Himself heard by His people, and now Moses belonged to that people, just as Miriam's scars spoke for all the wounds endured by the children of Israel under the Egyptian yoke.

How insignificant Zipporah was in this

struggle. And how severe Miriam's words: they forbade me to receive my husband's love, or even to support him other than by keeping silent and taking my black body as far away from him as possible!

I moaned, still unaware of the days of blood and turmoil that awaited me. Unaware of the terrible loss I would suffer, a loss that is killing me now just as surely as the blood flowing from my gashed belly, the wound that gapes as much as Miriam's.

The Return

It took me many words and caresses to convince Moses that the wisest course for me was to return to Jethro's domain. His rage echoed through Yokeved's house and the streets of the village.

'Yahweh speaks for you as much as for the others!' he roared.

'Stay with me,' he implored. 'I'll fail without you.'

He went to the elders and cried, 'Would the Everlasting be the Everlasting if He supported only those who have the same skin colour as us? Do you think He will turn away from my sons because their mother is from Cush?'

But the elders did not relent: 'You are forgetting the covenant, Moses,' they replied, confident in their knowledge. 'The Everlasting holds out His hand to those He has elected to His covenant, not to others.'

That increased Moses' irritation. 'You were happy to forget the covenant and its demands in the days when Joseph was sold into the hands of Pharaoh.'

His rage was so violent that it was clear he knew that I would go. Then he turned his pain against me: 'Is this how you show your love for me? By running away? You, my bride of blood? Leaving me here to face the multitude, even weaker than I was in the desert when you gave me back my life?'

I had to calm him with kisses, intoxicating myself with them as if savouring honey that would soon be finished. I had to calm myself, too, to overcome my desire to grant him what he asked and say, 'Yes, of course I'll stay with you.'

But Miriam was before my eyes. The sight of her brought me to my senses.

Finally, one evening, after a day when the whip of Pharaoh had decimated a group of men who had been unable to supply the bricks demanded by the foremen, those returning to the village attacked Moses. 'Look, Moses, at the dead! May Yahweh see what you have done, you and your brother. You have made Pharaoh and his princes even more cruel. You have given them a sword with which to slay us. And you complain because you must lose your wife?'

Moses spent the following night standing on the ridge of the quarry overlooking the village. Fearing for him, Joshua and I had followed him. We crouched behind a rock and heard him calling to Yahweh at the top of his voice: 'Why did you send me? Since I came to Pharaoh to speak in your name, he has mistreated your people and you have not delivered them. Why must I go on, if all I can do is make things worse?'

He was shouting so loudly, he could be heard down in the village. What could not be heard, either by the villagers or by Moses, was Yahweh's answer.

When dawn broke, Joshua told me what Aaron and the elders were saying: 'The Everlasting

260

won't answer Moses. He is impure because of the Cushite woman. Yahweh won't appear to him until he's resolved this.'

I could wait no longer. I ordered my handmaid Murti to rouse the shepherds. 'Tell them to prepare my camels and what we need for the journey. Tomorrow at dawn we set out for Midian.'

Moses did not protest. In fact, he did not dare look at me. He took his sons in his arms and held them for a long time.

His caresses that night were different from those I had known before. It was I who was leaving, yet Moses was distancing himself from me, like a man about to leave on a long journey.

When the time came to say farewell, only Yokeved and Joshua had tears in their eyes.

For two whole days, I did not open my mouth. If I could have stopped breathing, I would have. If my skin had been light, everyone would have seen my face flush red with humiliation. I had become Zipporah, the outcast wife.

Two terrible days.

Then, as we were going north along the Great River, Iterou, I heard my name called. There were so many boats on the river, I didn't see him at first. It was Joshua! He was waving his arms excitedly and laughing. A moment later, he stood before me. 'I hoped I'd catch up with you! I jumped into a boat as soon as I could. They are much quicker than horses and mules.'

'Are you planning to flee Egypt for Midian?'

My voice was sharper than I had intended. But Joshua laughed and kneaded my hands.

'Yahweh has answered Moses! Yesterday. Yahweh spoke to him! He said, 'You will see what I am going to do to Pharaoh. The king of Egypt may endure but my hand will prevail! He will surrender, he will expel my people, he will not want to hear their name spoken! I will lead you to the land over which I have raised my hand, the land I gave to Abraham, Isaac and Jacob. You will see! I will harden Pharaoh's heart and I will multiply my signs and wonders.''

Joshua was shaking with joy. Was he aware that, to me, his words were like a slap in the face?

Of course I could not help but rejoice. At least, the Lord Yahweh was not leaving Moses in torment.

But my heart was heavy as I listened to Joshua. No sooner had I turned my back than Yahweh had spoken to my husband! Was He punishing me because I had not been convinced that my departure was a good thing? Did He want to show me that Miriam was right?

Was He, too, saying, 'Let's rid ourselves of this Cushite'?

My eyes filled with tears. Joshua guessed what was tormenting me. 'No, no! You're wrong, I'm sure of it.' He kissed me, took me in his arms, tried to fire me with his enthusiasm. 'Moses will lead us. The elders won't doubt him any more. And you will see him again. I know it. We, too, shall see each other again. I know it as well as if it were written in those clouds.' He pointed to a long line of vapour hanging over the northern horizon.

I tried to laugh with him. 'Can you read?'

'Of course! I can read and write almost as well as Aaron. And not the writings of Pharaoh, the writings of our elders.'

'Be a valued friend to Moses, then,' I murmured, giving him one last kiss. 'Watch over him, love him, and don't let Aaron be the only one to instruct him.'

★ ★ ★

The winter rains had just begun when I saw again the low, whitewashed walls of the well of Irmna.

Throughout the journey from Egypt I had been brooding on my woes, but now the sight of the rough bricks surrounding my father's domain was like a caress. The joy of returning home soothed me. I clasped Eliezer and Gershom to me and whispered, 'We're home!'

Gershom, who was starting to put names to things, recognized the great sycamore on the road to Epha and Eliezer clapped his hands when he saw the pen full of mules, kids and rams.

Of course, it was all a far cry from the splendour of Egypt. Here, the green of the oases was merely a patch in the immensity of the desert, whereas the green banks of the Great River, Iterou, filled the horizon from one end of the earth to the other. But here the bricks that had been used to build the walls and houses had been made with joy, the joy of constructing and harbouring the simple delights of peace, affection and justice.

263

My heart was pounding at the thought of the cries of joy that would greet me as soon as my children and I had passed through the heavy door with its bronze fittings. And that was exactly what happened.

Sefoba came running with a little girl in her arms, shouting as loudly as though the roofs were on fire. My brother Hobab lifted me off the ground as if I were still a child. My father Jethro raised his arms to heaven and blessed the Everlasting for letting him see his daughter Zipporah again. The handmaids made so much noise with their screams of joy that they frightened Gershom and Eliezer. There was much kissing and hugging, much laughter, many tears, and a banquet like those I had known in the old days when I had helped prepare them for my father's guests.

It was only then, sitting beneath the canopy on comfortable cushions, that Jethro, in his usual gentle manner, asked me, 'And why have you returned, daughter? Is Moses well?'

It took me all that evening, all the next day and beyond to tell him everything that had happened in the land of Pharaoh.

As was his custom, Jethro listened attentively, then asked a thousand questions. Why had Moses done this? How had Aaron said that? Were the slaves' houses real houses? What was the correct name for the resin Queen Hatshepsut smeared on her body? 'Oh, may Yahweh bless me, what horror!' he would exclaim, after each answer I gave.

That was the only judgement he made,

although he questioned me again and again about Miriam and the elders.

He also sent for Eliezer, to see with his own eyes the circumcision his daughter had performed. He stroked his grandson's member tenderly, gripped my hand and, with fingers that were now twisted with age, squeezed it until it hurt. 'May the Everlasting bless you, daughter!' he cried. 'May He bless you to the end of time. What an extraordinary thing! Quite extraordinary, I tell you, and something we'll always remember.'

When I finally told him about my departure, how Joshua had caught up with me and the advice I had given him, my father clapped his hands. 'That's my Zipporah! I'm proud of you, my daughter. For this and for everything else you've told me, I'm proud of you.'

Over the next two or three days, I reacquainted myself with life in the domain. Sefoba and the handmaids wanted to know everything I could tell them about the strange things I had seen in the land of Pharaoh. Then, as he used to whenever he wanted to tell me something important, Jethro asked me to serve him his first meal of the day.

As I was putting down the pitcher of milk, he pointed to the cushions. 'Sit next to me, daughter.'

With a wink of a crumpled eyelid, he indicated the summit of Horeb's mountain. 'There hasn't been a rumble since you and Moses left. Not the slightest rumble since the great quarrel with your sister and Moses.' He chuckled, and clicked his tongue. 'Do you know she's a queen now? The lady Orma, they call her, the lady Orma, wife of Reba, the King of Sheba. Still as beautiful, still as scatterbrained and just as much a creature of whim. She loves power. She loves it so much that she terrifies all who come near her. Even the armourers fear her. Who would believe she is Jethro's daughter? She may come and visit you. Or she may not. She still bears you a grudge. On the other hand she might be happy to hear that you've left Moses, and then she won't be able to resist coming here and showing off her wealth and her handmaids . . .'

The look he gave me told me that that was of no importance and that he had something quite different to tell me. He drank his milk slowly before he resumed talking.

'Moses is on the right road, the road that Yahweh has shown him. He is committed to it. He is performing the task he came here to find.' My father made a gesture that encompassed his domain and Horeb's mountain. 'I know what you're thinking, daughter. Aaron and Miriam, his brother and sister, rejected you. Your Cushite skin has become the banner of their jealousy. The elders of Moses' people rejected you. It's possible that even the Everlasting has rejected you. That's what you're thinking.'

He shook his head and raised an eyebrow, just as he had in the old days when he reprimanded me for making a mistake in writing.

'Zipporah, you are finer and stronger than the resentment you feel. Don't let the appearance of things and the pain in your heart make you

266

believe that it is night when the sun has risen. What are the children of Israel today? Suffering victims, who for years have been regarded by Pharaoh as nothing more than pairs of feet and hands. They have no idea how much they know. Their hearts have been hardened by suffering. They go from one misfortune to another, like flies trapped in a pitcher who have no idea that its neck is wide open. They see a strange woman and cry, 'Oh, how horrible, she isn't like us! Her skin is black. The Lord Yahweh has covered her with darkness. Let's keep away from her!' It's as if they saw an unknown flower and the first question they asked was 'Is it poisonous?' Zipporah, my child, don't forget that they have lost their way because Pharaoh's whip and the hard labour to which they are condemned have killed the innocence they once had when they were in Yahweh's heart. Miriam is right. The only reason some of them are still standing, still holding their heads high, as men and women should, is because they cling to their wounds, as a climber clings to the rocks on Horeb's mountain.' He laid his hand on my thigh.

'Slaves are slaves in their hearts as much as in their bodies. Just as it will take them time to escape Pharaoh's whip, it will take them time to loosen the knots he has tied in their minds. But the Everlasting knows about time. They are on the march behind Moses. Do not doubt it, daughter. And that young man, Joshua, was right. You will see your husband again. Have faith, Zipporah, my sweet. Let Yahweh's time give birth to life.'

267

I listened to my father Jethro's wisdom and I let time take its course. A strange time.

At first all I could do was wait. Moons passed, and I watched Gershom and Eliezer grow. Hundreds of dawns when the name of Moses was on my lips, and my concern for him in the offerings I made to the Lord Yahweh. And there were just as many nights when my desire for him, my hunger for him, woke me in tears.

A year went by without any news from Egypt.

'Have the Akkadian merchants disappeared?' my father would grumble.

'The caravans have started going through Moab and Edom again,' my brother Hobab explained. 'Those lands are more prosperous than ever. They are the places to buy and sell.'

Nevertheless, at the height of summer, a caravan leader came to ask permission to draw water from the well of Irmna. Jethro lost no time in questioning him about his journey and his business. The man raised his arms to heaven and cried that he had just come from Egypt, where he had lost almost all his goods because chaos reigned there.

'Oh!' my father exclaimed, with a smile. 'Tell us about it.'

And so it was that we learned of the wonders the Lord Yahweh had brought to the land of Pharaoh by the hand of Moses.

'One minute, the Great River, Iterou, turned to blood,' the merchant said, rolling his eyes, 'and when it turned to water again, the fish were dead. Can you believe it? It's true, though. What a stench! Even the sand of the desert stank of it! But that's not all. No sooner was that pestilence over than the land was covered with frogs. They swelled in the sun and exploded. Then it stank again. Wait, I haven't finished! Gnats, hail, boils, locusts — each new season brought down another calamity on Pharaoh's head. How can anyone trade in such a land? When I ran away with what I had left, you couldn't see the sun any more. For three days, the whole country was covered with clouds. Three days of darkness! Can you believe it? If I hadn't seen it with my own eyes, I wouldn't believe it myself.'

Jethro laughed, a sound so joyful that the merchant took offence.

When he caught his breath again, my father threw me a look, as if to say, 'You see, daughter! I was right, wasn't I?' I had to hold my hands tightly together to stop them shaking.

Serious again, Jethro turned back to the merchant. 'What is Pharaoh doing to overcome these misfortunes?' he asked.

'As far as anyone knows, nothing at all. He's told the people these things will pass. They're just magic tricks and his priests will deal with them.'

'Oh!' Jethro said, with a sardonic grin, and winked at me.

'I agree with you.' The merchant snorted. 'Maybe this magic will pass but Pharaoh is in danger of passing with it!'

'And does anyone know why these things are happening? There's a reason for ordinary things so there must also be a reason for the extraordinary ones.'

'Some say it's because Pharaoh's god, Amon, is angry with him for rising up against the former pharaoh, his wife and aunt, who was protected by Amon. Others say it's because of the slaves. But how could slaves perform such wonders? All they do is stamp mud to make bricks.'

The next day, Jethro summoned the household beneath his canopy and told them of the wonders taking place in Egypt. Moses' name was again on everyone's lips, and I was the centre of attention.

'Oh, how proud and happy you must be to be Moses' wife and the mother of his sons!'

Indeed I was. And all the sadder to be separated from him by such a long distance.

Other caravans came. Now the merchants were fleeing Egypt, and each one who passed rolled his eyes in terror and told of new wonders.

'The slaves have found themselves a leader who's almost a god. His name is Moses, and he's inflicting these wounds on Pharaoh because he wants to lead the children of Israel out of Egypt.'

All over Midian, people were remembering that Moses had been welcomed to Jethro's house and become his son-in-law, the husband of Jethro's Cushite daughter. Visitors flocked to hear news of Egypt from Jethro's mouth. Each time, my father sent for Gershom and Eliezer and made them sit on the cushions beside him.

'These are my grandchildren, the sons of Moses and my daughter Zipporah. It is good for

270

them to learn what their father is accomplishing beyond the sea.'

And he would launch again into the story of the river of blood, the gnats, the hail, the boils, the locusts, the darkness . . . He would take his own staff, brandish it and bring it down between the cushions.

'Your father Moses is hearing the voice of Yahweh. And this is what it says. 'Go to Pharaoh and tell him: Be just, King of Egypt. Free the slaves from their labour, allow them to leave your land.' Pharaoh laughs. His beardless mouth curls wickedly. He sits on his gold throne, with snakes on his head, his eyes dark with scorn. 'No!' he says to Moses. 'Make bricks for me, slave rabble.' Then Moses points his staff — like this — at the dust and suddenly the wind rises. Without warning. In the north, in the south, whoosh! An icy, rasping wind! Pharaoh runs out on to the terrace of his magnificent garden, and sees the clouds massing. Thunder crashes. Lightning splits the sky, and hail falls until it covers all of Pharaoh's green land.'

'What's hail, Grandfather?' Gershom would ask, delighted to be scared.

And we would laugh and be happy. Like Eliezer and Gershom, we wanted to be told over and over again about the wonders my husband was performing.

'Soon,' everyone said to me, 'you will be a queen like Orma. Greater even than her.'

To this I would reply, 'Moses is neither a king nor a prince. To his people, Moses is the voice of their God. And I am here.'

271

One day, however, Eliezer, who was beginning to know how to use words, asked, 'What's my father Moses like? Is he old and white like you, Grandfather? Or is he like Mother, black, with no beard?'

The handmaids laughed until they cried. I cried without laughing.

Jethro had been right. Yahweh's time was doing its work. Moses was accomplishing his task. But the time was passing slowly. Moses had been gone for so long that my son had forgotten his face.

With all the wonders Moses was performing, there was one I did not believe would ever come to pass: that we would be reunited. That I would once again kiss his neck as I had loved to do. That I would see him clasp his sons to his breast.

★ ★ ★

At the end of the following winter, a piece of news reached us that was more remarkable than any that had gone before.

The slaves had finally set out from Egypt. They had left the marshes and the villages. Thousands of them. Men and women of all ages, the strong and the weak, all the children of Israel! The other slaves, too, those captured in wars of conquest. Pharaoh's building sites were now as silent as if time had stood still.

Moses had led these thousands of people to the Sea of Reeds, and Thutmose had set off in pursuit with his army. By the time the slaves reached the shore, a storm was gathering and the spears of Pharaoh's soldiers could already be seen in the valleys leading to the sea. Moses had plunged his staff into the waves and the waters had opened before him. The Sea of Reeds split in two! The waves stopped, and the seabed became a path to the opposite shore.

The thousands of slaves who were following Moses rushed in. When they reached the other side, they saw the waves join again and engulf Pharaoh's war chariots. They were free!

For the first time in many years, I thought of my dream. I saw the water opening before me, the boat plunging between the huge liquid walls. I saw the cliffs of water threatening to join together, like the edges of a wound, and swallow me.

And there, on the dried-up seabed, I saw a man holding out his arms to me and giving back to me the breath that the waves were trying to take from me. Moses, although I did not know then that it was.

The man the Lord Yahweh would appoint to give back the breath of freedom to his people.

My father Jethro was watching me. He saw the look in my eyes, my trembling body, my hands kneading my sons' shoulders. He guessed my thoughts. 'Did I not tell you?' he asked softly. 'They are on their way. Yahweh is moving time on. We'll have more news soon. A new story is beginning.' Tears welled from his eyes, rolled down through his wrinkles and disappeared into his beard. 'Tomorrow,' he said, 'we will go to the sea. I want to see if anything about it has changed.'

But the next day, before we reached the cliffs, of which I had so many memories, we saw a man wrapped in a heavy woollen coat covered thickly with dust, his face masked by a hood pulled down over his brow, sitting on an exhausted ass. He looked like a forlorn brigand. But when he saw me with Gershom and Eliezer he jumped down and rushed to me. 'Zipporah!' His hood fell back. 'Zipporah!'

He was shouting and waving his arms. I recognized the voice before the face, which had grown thin, the beard matted with dust and sea spray.

'Joshua!'

He laughed and hugged me. It was like an anticipation of Moses' body, and it made me tremble.

The Days of Blood
and Turmoil

And so began the days of blood and turmoil.

Joshua told us that Moses and his multitude had pitched their tents in a desert plain called Rephidim, just five days' walk from Jethro's domain. 'Less, if you run,' he said, pointing to the folds in Horeb's mountain, which were almost white in the mist that shrouded the west.

I had imagined Moses a long way off and he was so close!

'I've come to fetch you, Zipporah,' Joshua went on. 'You, too, Jethro. Moses needs you. His mother, Yokeved, is dead and he's at the end of his tether. Nothing is as it should be. They quarrel, they grumble, they're hungry and thirsty, they have no pasture for the animals . . . If it isn't hunger and thirst they complain about, then they're tired of putting up and taking down the tents. The desert is too empty for them, the rocks too hot, the land of milk and honey too far. It's as if they've brought the chaos of Egypt with them. One man even complained that they were no longer under the whip of Pharaoh — 'At least then we had food and drink and shade!' he said. If I hadn't held him back, Moses would have cracked the man's skull with his staff. 'What shall I do with all of you? I lead you out of Egypt, and now you look as if you

275

want to stone me!' He was shouting so loudly, you could have heard him from here. Apart from that, Aaron and Miriam want to be in charge. Yahweh speaks to Moses and counsels him, but Aaron tells him that he doesn't understand the words. He quarrels with and about everything. The confusion only increases everyone's discontent. Now it seems the Amalekites are sending an army against us and we have no weapons. Moses said to me, 'Run to Jethro. He'll take you to see the armourers.''

Here Jethro nodded. His mind was made up, I knew.

'We'll leave at dawn. Rest, Joshua. My son Hobab will go to the armourers. Their leader, Ewi-Tsour, will supply you with iron swords.' He winked at me. 'Anything Zipporah asks of him, he'll supply double if he can. Meanwhile, Sicheved will divide my flocks. He'll keep half here, and care for my house, and the other half we'll take to Moses.'

If I could have done so, I would have set off immediately.

I spoke to Gershom and Eliezer. 'We're going to see your father Moses again.'

'Will he do wonders for us with his staff?'

Laughing for joy, I assured them he would.

★   ★   ★

May the Everlasting forgive me, but Joshua was right: his people had brought the chaos of Egypt with them when they crossed the Sea of Reeds.

There were tents as far as the eye could see,

276

and smoke, and a constant din, and rubbish stinking in the sun, and a swarming multitude of people and animals, thousands of faces, sombre old men, sad children, anxious women, people dying, others being born. A multitude that covered the fields of dry grass on the edge of the desert and seemed lost somewhere between yesterday and tomorrow. By the time we arrived, the noise, already shattering to our ears, had been made even louder by the battle with the Amalekites, which had begun the day before on the northern edge of the camp.

It was there that I saw Moses again. I was so astonished that I remained rooted to the spot. Astonished, perhaps even terrified.

He was standing on a big flat rock overlooking the fray. The shields and spears of the Amalekites glinted in the sun. The only weapons we could see in the hands of Yahweh's fighters were sticks and stones. The ground was strewn with corpses. Moses, on his rock, was raising his arms to heaven and brandishing his staff.

As I stood there speechless, Jethro pointed him out to the children. 'There's your father. The man with his arms held high is Moses.'

Eliezer, frightened by everything he saw around him, gripped Gershom's arm with both hands.

'Why does he have his hands in the air like that?' Gershom asked.

We were to find out later: if Moses brought down his arms, the Amalekites were victorious; if he kept them up, they were routed.

'Look at Hobab and Joshua!' Gershom cried.

They were descending the slope towards the battle, followed by Ewi-Tsour and his armourers, who had consented to come with us. We heard the cries that greeted them. The mules were unloaded in a trice, and iron swords shone in the hands of the Hebrews.

I saw Aaron climb on to the rock to support Moses' right arm. Another man, whom I didn't know, did the same with the left.

The battle went on until evening.

So it was that on the day of my return I did not meet my husband.

When night fell, Joshua was victorious, and when he returned to the camp, he was acclaimed with songs.

Scented with amber and adorned with jewels, I dressed in my most beautiful tunic. Holding my two sons close, I waited for Moses outside the newly pitched tent. My heart was pounding so hard that I was afraid everyone would hear it.

As Moses was late, thanking Yahweh with Aaron, hundreds passed before us. They wanted to know the truth of the rumour that had spread from one end of the camp to the other even more swiftly than the announcement of victory over the Amalekites: Moses' wife was back.

And, yes, there was a stranger, as black of skin as they had said. A daughter of Cush.

At last we heard cries, trumpets, ram's horns, drums, singing. My sons knew what that meant. 'Here's our father Moses!' they cried, leaping up and down. 'Here he is!'

A mass of people was climbing towards us. The crowd parted.

Lord Yahweh, what had you done to my husband? He was walking towards us, but tottering like an old man. Older, it seemed, than my father Jethro. He was supported by Aaron and Miriam, both upright and strong, the gleam of victory in their eyes.

Gershom and Eliezer were stunned into silence. My throat dried, and a shiver went down my back.

My husband, my beloved. My Moses.

He looked so exhausted.

'What have they done to you?' I murmured. 'How is this possible?'

'Is that my father?' Gershom said.

His voice reached Moses, who opened his eyes wide. With all his remaining strength, he rose to his full height.

Regally, Aaron and Miriam moved aside to let him greet us.

All around, the multitude of the people of Yahweh watched us.

They saw Eliezer in his father's arms, which shook so hard he could barely carry the boy. Zipporah, her black cheeks glistening with the tears that streamed down them. Gershom, clinging to his father's waist and burying his face in his belly. That was what they saw. Moses' family.

'You're here!' Moses said. 'At last!'

His voice was weak, but everyone heard him. In the camp, the noise had died away. No more singing. No more drums, horns or cheers. Silence.

Silence in recognition of the fact that Moses'

family was reunited.

Then Jethro, in his old voice, cried, 'Moses, Moses, my son. Glory to you, glory to Yahweh! May He be praised for all eternity, and you too!'

Joshua blew his trumpet, and the noise of the camp resumed.

My father Jethro kissed Moses. 'I've brought enough for a victory feast. Tonight, those who fought will eat their fill.'

Moses was still holding my hand. He laughed — a laugh I recognized. 'Let us go to the great council tent,' he said. 'You can meet the elders.'

I walked by his side, leading my sons by the hand.

Miriam stepped in front of me, barring the way. 'No! You may not enter. The council tent is forbidden to women, especially foreign women. It's not like the land of Pharaoh here, still less like Midian. Women must know their place. They aren't involved in the affairs of men. If your husband wishes to see you, he will come to your tent.'

★ ★ ★

He came. In the middle of the night, supported by Joshua. I laid him on my bed.

Like a blind man, he touched my face, brow and lips with his fingertips. 'At last you came,' he said, with a smile in his voice. 'My bride of blood, my beloved Cushite.'

I was glad it was dark and he couldn't see my despair.

He fell asleep before I could answer him. So

280

quickly, so suddenly, that I took fright. I felt as if I had a corpse beside me. I almost cried out, almost called for help. At last, he sighed, and his chest rose and fell beneath my hand.

He was sighing in his sleep. The sigh of a man who dreams despite his fatigue.

I lay down next to him, weeping. 'Moses!' I cried, holding him close. 'Moses!'

This was the end of Zipporah the strong. At that moment I knew it.

Now and for ever, I was Zipporah the weak. The weakest of the weak.

I didn't yet know how weak I was, how incapable of sustaining and nurturing life. But I knew I was powerless. I would have had to be Moses to resist the madness of the multitude. The madness of their exodus and their hope. I would have had to be Miriam, Aaron, Joshua, to be one of the people of Yahweh. To have endured the yoke of Pharaoh for generations, and bear the marks on my body and in my heart.

Later, feeling calmer, I studied my husband's face by the light of the lantern.

There were so many lines on it: long, hard lines on his brow, disappearing beneath his hair, deeper over his eyebrows. Lines on his temples, meeting at the corners of his eyes, like rivers flowing into the sea. Lines on his nose, his lips, his eyelids, his chin . . . As if Moses, my beloved, had to have as many lines on his face as there were men, women and children in the unruly people he led.

★ ★ ★

281

He woke abruptly before dawn. He was surprised to see me there. I kissed his eyelids and his lines. I kissed his neck. And then, gently, he pushed me away. 'I have to get up. They're waiting for me.'

'Who?'

'All of them. They're waiting for me outside the tent.'

I didn't understand. I went with him, and I saw.

There they were, long columns of them. Two hundred, three hundred? A thousand? Who could have counted them? There they were, waiting, all wanting to pass in front of Moses with their complaints.

'My tent companion has moved his goat. It's right under my nose now, and it stinks. Order him to tether it somewhere else.'

'They stole the stone my wife uses for grinding barley. It was a good stone, the best. Here, there's nothing but dust and the stones are useless. What can we do?'

'Moses, the tents of the tribes are scattered all over the camp and nobody knows where anybody is. We can't do anything in this chaos.'

'Moses, the women are giving birth without midwives because there aren't enough. Children are being born without anyone knowing when to cut the cord. What should we do?'

'Someone stole the cushion I brought with me from Egypt. I know who it was. Will you tell him to give it back, Moses?'

I understood now why Moses was so exhausted. It wasn't from keeping his arms in the air during the battle against the Amalekites.

I ran to Jethro. 'Go and see Moses, Father! He needs your wise counsel!'

That evening, in the council tent, Jethro said, 'Have you gone mad, Moses? Do you want to lose everything? They're going to tire you out for good, and themselves with you. They wait whole days in the sun for you to answer them.'

Aaron intervened: 'Who else but Moses can judge sins, separate good from evil, show the path each person must take? Only he can do it. Only he, through the voice of Yahweh.'

'Do you need the voice of Yahweh to find a stolen cushion or sweep away a goat's droppings? You're dealing with a multitude. Let Moses indicate the way and the rules, and let him appoint those who are capable of applying them. Is Moses the only one in this mass of people who has an upright heart and common sense?'

'Could you do better? Everyone knows the Midianites are sly. It was they who sold Joseph to Pharaoh.'

'And by doing that kept him alive, whereas his brothers would have preferred him to die in the hole where they'd put him. Come now, Aaron, let's not argue about the past. We'd both be old and toothless before we reached agreement. Aaron, sage of the people of Yahweh, what matters is today and tomorrow. Lighten Moses' burden — appoint men to help him. Leaders of tens, leaders of hundreds, leaders of thousands. The petty thefts, the jealous quarrels and the arguments about goats' dung they can settle for themselves. Moses will decide about the things

283

that concern everyone. That's my suggestion.'

But the next day Joshua came to Zipporah. 'The camp is angry with Jethro. Aaron and his followers are saying that Moses pays too much attention to your father, that the Midianites are thieves by nature. The truth is, they're afraid of losing control.'

'Let them complain! Isn't that why you came for us?'

'Yes, of course. And Moses will follow your father's advice. But if Jethro wants to help Moses now, it's better that he doesn't stay here.'

Before they said farewell, my father and Moses spent some time together in my tent, away from prying eyes and ears.

'Did you feel the earth shake yesterday?' Jethro asked Moses.

'No. I'm so tired, these days, that all I can feel shaking now are my knees. But I heard about it.'

'Remember the wrath of Horeb, my son. The wrath you experienced when you were in my domain. That is what is going to happen. Tomorrow the mountain of Horeb will rumble. In three days, four at the most, it will be covered with clouds and spitting fire.'

Moses' anxiety was plain to see.

Jethro smiled. 'Have no fear. Yahweh will come to your rescue. You must compel those ears outside to listen. Tomorrow, or some time soon, at the first rumble from Yahweh, order fasting, purification and sacrifices. Order them to strike their tents and walk to the foot of Horeb. When they are there, leave them and climb the mountain, as you did once before, when we

284

thought we had lost you.'

'Climb for what reason?'

'To make yourself heard when you return. Today if you sit outside your tent and say, 'This is our law,' you will set a hundred tongues wagging, asking for it to be less strict, while a thousand others want it to be more strict! Such confusion! How do you plan to establish the justice of free men among these people if all they understand is fear and the whip? Don't forget, Moses, they were born and grew up in slavery, and in their hearts they are still as much slaves as children of Israel.'

'But the clouds, the ash, the fire! They will die.'

'Trust in the Lord Yahweh. No one will perish in the ash. It is time for this people to receive its laws and open its ears to hear them. Your voice alone will not suffice. But the terror of ashes and darkness should make them more receptive.'

★   ★   ★

My father was right, and Moses was wrong to fear for his people. It was I who had to fear.

Moses said, 'The Lord Yahweh will come down to the summit of the mountain. He wants me to go up there and hear His commandments. Anyone who tries to follow me will die. Wait for me, and when I return, we shall have our laws, which will make us a free people for all eternity.'

Like everyone else, I saw him disappear into the clouds amid the rumblings of Horeb.

Like everyone else, I waited. My sons and I

285

were well used to waiting.

But Aaron, Miriam, the multitude could not bear to wait.

Moses was still on the mountain when Joshua came to see me. 'When will Moses come back? The camp is noisier than the mountain. The clouds may not be killing them but they're making them as drunk as if they were guzzling wine from morning to night.'

All it took was one person to say, 'Moses won't come back! He has died up there!' and everyone believed it.

I ran through the camp, begging, 'Wait! The mountain is high. Give him time and he'll return. My husband isn't dead, I know it. Moses can't die — he's with the Lord Yahweh.'

To which they laughed and replied, 'What do you know? You're a Cushite. How dare you speak about the Lord Yahweh? Since when has He been the God of strangers?'

Miriam took my arm and led me back to my tent. 'Your voice is a blemish to our ears and your presence a blemish on our land. Know your place once and for all.'

When Moses still did not come down, they went to Aaron, first in hundreds, then in their thousands. 'Moses has gone! We have no one to lead us. Make us gods that we can see and touch.'

Then I saw them, the thousands of women and girls, the husbands and lovers, the fathers. I saw them bring out their gold, although they had said they had nothing, and melt it in a clay mould Aaron had made. I saw them laugh and rejoice as the golden calf took shape. I saw Miriam's brow stream with sweat and joy. I saw her scar throb with happiness when Aaron said to the multitude, 'Here are your gods, O Israel!'

Oh, yes, I saw them dance, rejoicing at Moses' death. I saw them, their faces and bodies gleaming like the gold they had melted, dancing naked in the night, singing and kissing each other, giving in to the fire in their bellies and the promptings of their fear, prostrating themselves before Aaron and his golden calf as they had prostrated themselves in terror before Pharaoh.

My voice was too weak to cry out, my hands incapable of holding back my sons, who were laughing to see such a great fire, such a great celebration and desperate to join in.

'Let Moses come down!' I begged the Lord Yahweh. 'Let Moses come down!'

Joshua was as appalled as I was. 'I'll go up and find him. I don't care what happens to me.'

He did not have to go far. Moses had smelt the stench of sin and was coming down. I saw him emerge from the cloud and walk down the path that none had trodden for many moons. I saw him stop at the sight of his people's madness, the golden calf on the altar. I heard the roar of his voice — or was it the rumbling of Horeb? I called Gershom and Eliezer and pointed. 'Moses is here! Your father is here!'

The children leaped up and down. 'Our father Moses has come back!' They ran to the path to join him, and plunged into the crowd. 'Our father Moses has come down from the mountain!'

The people heard them and they were swallowed into the throng. They did not part as the sea had parted before Moses' staff. They swallowed them. They did not part as the waters had parted before the stem of the canoe in my dream. They formed a dense, dark, raging swell. They heard Moses roar in anger and took fright, crushing my little children. They heard the wrath of Yahweh and panicked, trampling my sons. I ran to them, calling, 'Gershom! Eliezer!'

Up on the mountain, Moses broke in pieces the very thing he had gone to his God to find. Down here, the earth opened and caught fire. The people ran over my sons' bodies, fleeing in terror as the earth opened and swallowed the golden calf. They ran, trampling on the sons of Moses.

Nothing was left but two little bloodstained bodies. I clutched them to my chest and screamed.

Gershom and Eliezer.

★ ★ ★

Now Moses wept and raged, wanting to slaughter his people for the death of his sons.

He put the armourers' weapons in the hands of Aaron's descendants, the sons of Levi, and ordered, 'Kill them, your brothers, your companions, your neighbours, kill!'

The camp was wet with blood, as if my sons' blood were covering it with one huge wound.

Moses wept in my arms, he wept against my chest, which was still bloody from holding the bodies of Gershom and Eliezer. It was the second time my husband had wept over me, the second time I had marked him with his sons' blood.

'Go back up the mountain,' I said. 'Go back to your God and don't come back empty-handed. Your wife is the weakest of the weak. She could not even defend her sons. She is weaker than the slaves you led. She needs the laws of your God in order to breathe and give birth in peace. I need the laws of your God to stop Miriam shouting me down. The stranger needs laws to be considered more than a stranger. Go back, Moses. Go back for your sons' sakes. Go back for my sake. Go back, O my husband, to ensure that the weak man is not naked before the strong.'

'If I go back, what new madness will they perpetrate?'

'None. There's enough blood in the camp to turn their stomachs for generations to come.'

★   ★   ★

Moses took up his staff, and again disappeared into the clouds.

'I'm leaving,' I said to Joshua. 'I can't stay here any longer.'

'Where will you go?'

'To Midian, to my father's domain. There is no other place for me. When I'm there, I'll ask for food, grain and animals for you. At least your people will have enough to eat and won't have to nourish themselves with violence.'

'I'll go with you to bring everything back. Ewi-Tsour and his armourers will go with us. Hobab will stay here to help Moses when he returns.'

★ ★ ★

I was wrong. There was no place for me now in Midian, or in Jethro's domain.

When we reached the well of Irmna, a group of men were waiting for us.

'Look!' Ewi-Tsour cried. 'It's Elchem. He's come to meet us.'

He was smiling. I recognized Elchem's burned, disfigured face, which reminded me of Miriam's. I, too, had a scar now, but it was invisible.

But Elchem did not smile at Ewi-Tsour. From among the group of armourers he was leading I heard a voice I recognized. 'Where are you going? Who gave you permission to approach this well?'

'Orma!'

My sister had stepped forward. She was as beautiful as ever — perhaps even more so — her eyes as black, her mouth as scornful.

'I'm on my way to our father's house,' I said. 'I'm also looking for food for Moses' people. They're dying of hunger in the desert.'

'Jethro is dead. It is I, the wife of Reba and Queen of Sheba, who give the orders here now. It is out of the question for the multitude led by your Moses to descend like locusts on what belongs to us.'

290

'Orma, my sister!'

'I'm not your sister and my father Jethro was not your father!'

'Orma, they're hungry! My sons died because hunger drove the people mad!'

'Who wanted at all costs to be Moses' wife?'

She smiled, while Elchem and his men unsheathed their swords and threw themselves upon us.

When Elchem plunged his blade into my belly, I saw his scar throb, as Miriam's had throbbed at the sight of the golden calf.

But what did it matter? I was already dead. I had left my life in my sons' bodies.

Epilogue

Joshua returned to the tents of Israel.

Moses came down from the mountain. His face was so radiant that none dared approach him. None except Joshua, who told him of Zipporah's death.

Moses did not fly into a rage, did not curse Orma and the people of Midian. But, for the first time, those who had followed him out of Egypt saw tears in his eyes.

He whispered Zipporah's name. He called to her, as if she were lost in the darkness: 'Zipporah! Zipporah! Zipporah!' Softly, not wanting the syllables to be lost on the wind.

Then he uttered the names of his sons, Gershom and Eliezer. 'May they not be forgotten, they who were trampled by the madness of the crowd!'

Moses showed Joshua the tablets of the Law. 'Look,' he said, 'I have not come down empty-handed from the mountain. From this day on, Zipporah is here.' He touched some of the words with the tips of his fingers. 'Yahweh heard my wife, the woman of Midian. He heard her, Joshua!'

Joshua saw that it was true. On the stone, these words were engraved:

*If a stranger lives with you in your land, do
    not ill-treat him.*
*Treat him as you would your native-born,
    and love him as you love yourselves,*
For you were strangers in the land of Egypt.
*I am Yahweh, your God, and no injustice
    shall be done in my name.*

The next day, the breath of Yahweh descended
on the camp. He showed his wrath by punishing
Miriam with seven days of leprosy for her harsh
treatment of Zipporah, Moses' black wife.

But, as time has shown, men are fools, and
slow to learn.

Aaron's son came to see Moses. 'We must
march on Midian,' he declared, waving his arms.
'We must avenge the murder of your wife.'

'I want no part of your vengeance,' Moses
replied. 'Nor was vengeance ever in Zipporah's
heart. My wife would not have wanted her
memory tarnished with the blood of Midian. She
would not have wanted blood or wars. She loved
trust, respect and peace. She said that all men
were equal before the Everlasting, and that no
man should lift his hand against another.

'Zipporah,' he went on, 'wanted my caresses.
But how long was it since I'd caressed her? If
you want vengeance, kill me, for I, too, killed
her.'

Men are fools, and slow to learn.

Aaron's son did not heed Moses' words. He
persuaded those who would listen to him, and
they set off to wage war on Midian.

Moses had more deaths to mourn. Deaths

293

Zipporah had wanted to avoid.

'We are not worthy of milk and honey,' he said to the people. 'I freed you from slavery, thanks to the strong hand of the Everlasting, but in your hearts you are still slaves. In your hearts, you are in the desert. And in the desert you will die.'

'What do you mean?' the people answered, in surprise. 'How have we done wrong?'

'The word of the Almighty is addressed to free men,' Moses explained. 'Freedom is like water at the bottom of a well. We must learn to bring it out into the light of day, and then we must learn to drink it. You are not yet capable of that. Your children and grandchildren, who have never known slavery, will enter Canaan and discover the Promised Land, not you.'

★　★　★

And so it came to pass that the people whom Moses had led out of Egypt wandered in the desert for forty years, until all Pharaoh's former slaves had died and their bodies had become dust in the dust of the desert.

It was a new people who reached the banks of the Jordan. Old and worn by now, Moses still mourned his wife Zipporah the Cushite. He missed her voice, he missed her eyes, he missed her wise counsel. Not a day went by that he did not miss Zipporah.

When he reached the borders of Canaan, he climbed Mount Nebo to gaze upon the land of which the Everlasting had spoken.

At the sight of this land of milk and honey, his

heart was filled with doubt. Was he not, like all the others, unworthy of setting foot in the Promised Land? Hadn't he hesitated to accept the will of the Almighty? Without Zipporah, would he have had the courage to confront Pharaoh or even to listen to Yahweh? Without Zipporah, would he have known the beauty of a black woman, a stranger? Would he have known the breath that unites all hearts?

But Zipporah was no longer there to teach him what he still did not know.

So Moses gave the stones of the Law to Joshua. 'It is you and not I who will enter Canaan,' he said. 'It is you who will lead the people. I shall stay here. Mount Nebo will be my tomb.'

And he died, it is said, with a kiss from the Everlasting.

In accordance with his wishes, there was no stone monument, no sacred cave for his bones. Yahweh did not want idolatry. Moses was not a god, merely a man of flesh and blood who had died with his dream before his eyes. A man who will remain for ever in the vast mausoleum of words and memories.

Who, though, will remember Zipporah the Black, the Cushite? Who will remember what she accomplished? Who will still speak her name?

May this book serve as her humble tomb.

SARAH

Marek Halter

Book One of the Canaan Trilogy. Four thousand years ago, Sarah was born into a wealthy and powerful family in the Sumerian city of Ur. She was meant at twelve to marry a man chosen by her father. Instead, she fled to the banks of the Euphrates river, where she was destined to meet a stranger. His name was Abraham and, although he was a member of a poor nomadic tribe, their encounter was enough to convince Sarah that their future lay together. And so she abandoned everything to follow Abraham and his alien God; a God of whom no one had ever heard; a God who was invisible and who appeared to communicate solely through her husband; a God who, one day, would command Abraham to kill their beloved son in his name, and before whom Sarah would beg for mercy . . .

THE QUEEN OF SUBTLETIES

Suzannah Dunn

Lucy Cornwallis, King Henry VIII's confectioner, sculpts valuable sugar into 'subtleties', the centrepieces for royal celebrations. One day, she has an unusual visitor, someone curious to meet the creator of the famed sculptures: gorgeous Mark Smeaton, singer and musician. During a troubled year at court — the final year of Anne Boleyn's brief reign — Lucy and Mark become close. Anne Boleyn's rise has changed the history of England. Politically astute, intensely ambitious and uncompromising, she had easily caught King Henry's heart. But powerful forces are now gathering to make her pay for her prize — and Lucy Cornwallis is unwittingly in danger of giving them the means to do so . . .

BENEATH A SILENT MOON

Tracy Grant

London 1817. In the aftermath of the Napoleonic Wars, Melanie and Charles Fraser have traded the dangers of the war-ravaged Continent for the glittering world of the British ton. But Melanie soon realises how vital that spark of danger is to their partnership. She watches her husband transform into an aloof stranger as he steps back into his old life. Then, an assassination and a trail of clues plunge Charles and Melanie once more into danger. As they search for the truth in a labyrinth of lies, they discover that the answers cut shockingly close to their friends and family — and that beneath the shimmering veneer of London society, there lies an establishment that is rotten to its core . . .

LORD JOHN AND THE PRIVATE MATTER

Diana Gabaldon

London, 1757. On a bright June day, Lord John Grey emerges from his club, his mind in turmoil. A nobleman and a high-ranking officer in His Majesty's Army, Grey has just witnessed something shocking. But his efforts to avoid a scandal that might destroy his family are interrupted by something still more urgent: the Crown appoints him to investigate the brutal murder of a comrade-in-arms, who might well have been a traitor. Obliged to pursue two inquiries at once, Major Grey finds himself ensnared in a web of treachery and betrayal that touches every level of society — and threatens all he holds dear . . .

THE COLOUR

Rose Tremain

Mid-nineteenth century: Joseph and Harriet Blackstone, along with Joseph's mother Lilian, emigrate from Norfolk to New Zealand, in search of new beginnings and prosperity. But the harsh land near Christchurch where they settle threatens to destroy them almost before they begin. When Joseph finds gold in the creek, he guiltily hides the discovery from his wife and mother and is seized by a rapturous obsession with the voluptuous riches awaiting him deep in the earth. Abandoning his farm and family, he sets off alone for the new gold-fields over the Southern Alps, a moral wilderness where many others are violently rushing to their destinies.

EMMA BROWN

Clare Boylan

When Charlotte Bronte died in 1855, she left
behind the start of a new novel. The
twenty-page fragment introduced a lost girl
and signalled the author's most compelling
work since JANE EYRE. Now, Clare Boylan
has turned this intriguing beginning into a
story of mystery and page-turning suspense
. . . The arrival of Conway Fitzgibbon at
Fuchsia Lodge with his daughter Matilda is a
source of delight to the headmistress, Miss
Wilcox. The unsuccessful ladies' school is
eager for new pupils, particularly one so
finely dressed and boasting a father who is
'quite the gentleman'. But as Miss Wilcox
inquires about arrangements for the Christ-
mas holidays, she is in for a shock. Conway
Fitzgibbon, like the address he left behind,
does not exist . . .